A Knight for a Queen

MITTELAN
AND SURROUNDING TERRITORIES
NORRFALT
Kastöhm
Skåge River
Cliffs of Chainé
MITTELAN
Port Strabo
THE GREAT WESTERN SEA
Beacon of Merah
Basile Bay
N
W
E
S

Chartley River
REMAINS OF THE ROLESTOV EMPIRE
e Range
Swanstone
Lake Vertrois
nell
Beauhaven
Woodland Games
ening Tournament
Chartley River
farmland
farmland
KATYŌ
RAITS
Isles of Ionia
KATYŌ GULF
ALMORA

A Knight for a Queen

Hannah B. Olsen

Wise Valley Press
Nashville • Unicoi

WISE VALLEY PRESS

Published by Wise Valley Press,
an imprint of Big Small Town Books.

www.wisevalleypress.com

LIBRARY OF CONGRESS CONTROL NUMBER: 2020942476

Olsen, Hannah B.
A knight for a queen / Hannah B. Olsen
p. cm.
Summary: Chara, princess of Mittelan, is being used as a political pawn in her country's war against Norrfalt. To prevent her forced marriage to an enemy nation's prince, Chara competes in the Highland Games, where she convinces another champion-Elliot-to accompany her to the borderlands, where she hopes to reveal the conspiracy forcing her down the aisle. Elliot, meanwhile, is a peasant boy, whose stepfather has taken everything from him. Elliot competes in the Highland Games to earn back what is rightfully his. In their intertwined quests, Chara and Elliot must work together to rise above deception and danger. The fate of Chara's country-and of Elliot's birthright-depend on it.

Cataloging-in-Publication data is available upon request.

ISBN 978-1-7341660-4-0 [trade] • Available soon in eBook and audiobook.

Cover art by Sierra Palmer. Cover designed by Dustin Street.

This text of this book is set in 11-point Baskerville.

Printed in the United States of America. • First Edition: March 2021

10 9 8 7 6 5 4 3 2 1   21 22 23 24 25 26 27

To my husband.

For being my hero,

but never treating me

like I need one.

CHAPTER ONE

CHARA

I dug my heels into the mud and stopped my blow short, the tip of my blade hovering just above his heart. If this were a battlefield, he would be dead at the foot of his princess.

The cheering crowd faded to a buzz, their colored garments and flags blurring into a graying tapestry in the distance. The world slowed as I waited, my breathing still ragged.

His chin fell to his chest. Defeat.

The thrill of victory sparked through me, dancing like fire-crackers into every crevice of my being. Despite the biting cold of the early spring day, nothing could touch the fire that now pulsed through my veins.

The iron slats of my helmet distorted my view but I could clearly see the frustration etched into the wrinkle of my opponent's forehead. He had made it through four rounds of fighting before facing me in the finale. And this was the first tournament of the spring season: the highest bets, the biggest prize.

But I couldn't stay to collect my winnings and risk anyone questioning who I claimed to be. It's not like I needed the coins anyway. That's not what I came for.

His emerald eyes glistened with disappointment, the depth of which struck me. I hadn't expected to find such motivation in the forbidden tournament arena. He was only a peasant, after all, and one who chose to spend his few hours of freedom pissing away any coins he could get his hands on. Still, his ardor, paired with his exquisite bladesmanship, brought a smile to my lips. Perhaps he would fit my needs.

A few stray snowflakes appeared in the air around us, clinging to our still recovering bodies.

"I've traveled from the northern ice melts to the Almoran straits," he said, his disappointment cut with awe, "and I've never seen a man fight like you." My smile grew wider as I reached down and offered him a hand. I pulled him to standing, his rough fingertips brushing my tender palms: calluses from a bow.

A hunter. Well-traveled. Knowledgeable of the land. *And* an accomplished fighter? This was it. He was the one I'd been looking for.

His face now inches from my helmet, he dropped to a whisper. "Who are you?"

His voice thrust me back into reality, my shock dissipating into the deafening roar of the crowd. When I didn't respond, my opponent turned to face the audience, lifted my hand high into the air, and bellowed, "Show them the face of their victor!" His cry dripped with bright enthusiasm, but I could feel the anger simmering just below it.

I pulled my hand from his rough grip, knowing that the longer he held it, the more likely he was to realize that I was not the man I claimed to be. Or a man at all, for that matter. I smiled at him through my helmet, anticipation, fear, and excitement swirling together in my stomach. "I'll be in touch," I murmured under my breath, words that I knew would go unheard over the roar of the crowd, before turning and splashing my way across the arena. The mud had formed a thin sheet of ice over its surface which crunched under my boots.

I leapt over the fence. My high-quality armor—a lightweight chest plate with matching arm and shin guards—did not slow me down. Risking a glance back, I saw the fallen fighter being clapped on the shoulder by a familiar one-legged man, but I didn't have time to stare. I darted through the crowds, ignoring their shouted requests for me to show them my face.

My heart hammered as the crowd closed in on me, but I was just fast enough. Breaking into a full sprint, I made it to my grey mare. Stell was outfitted with a plain brown saddle, a change from the regal attire she usually bore. I untied her from a tree just beyond where the crowd gathered.

We galloped away from the Woodland Games, heading towards the forest edge and the country road that would lead us home. I leaned forward and squeezed my legs together until Stell was at full speed.

I hurried, not to escape the peasants but to escape my mother's suspicion. Now that I had found *him* and my plan was finally in motion, I couldn't do anything to tip her off to my disappearance. The last thing I needed was the Queen's Guard breathing down my neck. Skipping high church was one thing, but not showing up for Sunday dinner was another thing entirely.

The woods gave way to the gravel road which led to the bridge spanning Walter Ravine. On the far side of the deep granite canyon, I rode through the city walls and onto the cobblestone streets of Swanstone. The capitol city was abuzz with people just getting out of high church and making their way home for dinner. I salivated at the scent of fresh bread wafting through the streets, enticing nobles to grab a loaf on their return.

I pressed on faster, I could not be late.

I passed by the red watchtowers and the golden arched gates that led to the palace courtyard, navigating instead towards the town stables. The stables held one of Swanstone's best-kept secrets: it housed the only entrance to the castle grounds besides the front. The town stables and the royal stables were connected, just on opposite sides of the palace wall. Those who had a key to the gate within the stables could pass from one side to the other. It was a narrow, but very heavy, gate made of wood and iron. It was just wide enough for a carriage to pass through. Most probably assumed it led to grain and hay storage; very few knew the truth.

I navigated Stell into the stables at a full gallop, and down the aisle between where horses neighed and stamped their hooves at the disturbance. We wound around a bend in the brick cavern and I jerked the reins. Stell lurched to a stop in front of the unassuming gate where Grimm sat waiting impatiently on a bale of hay, his fingers tangled in his bright red hair.

"Your Highness, you're back. Thank heavens," he thrust the thick iron key in the matching lock hurriedly, "Master Marchale is expected back any minute and I have to return the key before he finds it missing." The gangly stable boy took Stell by the reins and led us across the threshold onto the castle grounds before turning to lock the gate behind us. He offered a hand to me, but

I was already swinging my leg over the horse's back and hopping down. With a sigh of relief, I lifted the helmet off my head, allowing the snarls of my thick, rebellious auburn hair to topple off my head and past my shoulders. I lifted the mess of waves off my neck as I shoved my helmet towards Grimm.

"*Oof*," he blurted as my helmet caught him unexpectedly in the gut. I followed the line of his sight to find a young woman with golden hair running across the courtyard with one arm flailing and the other clinging yards of fabric that I recognized as my dinner gown.

"You said you'd be upstairs an hour ago!" Emily chided as she neared us. "Now there's no time!" When she reached the stable, she carefully laid the gown over a bale of hay, put her hands on her knees, and took a moment to catch her breath. One beat later, she began to undo the strips and straps of my armor. "You. Take care of the horse," she ordered Grimm about, as if he were *her* stable boy and, for some reason, that made me smile.

Maybe everything was going to make me smile today. I'd done it. I'd found *him*. I had finally found a way out of this mess that was my life.

Em shoved me back into an empty horse stall and forced the dress over my head as soon as I was free of the armor. Her voice dropped low, "I swear, m'lady, if this plan of yours makes you late for one more dinner, I'll kill you myself."

I laughed loudly and began to fasten the buttons that trailed up the front of my dress.

She tied the bow at my back nimbly, and I whipped around to give her a hug. "No time for that!" she yelled, shrugging me off in annoyance. "Go!"

I didn't bother to collect my armor or weapons, as I knew Grimm would take care of them.

Emily stayed right on my heels as we raced through the castle grounds. She was still fussing about with my hair as I stood in front of the ornately carved wooden doors that led to the dining hall. One was ajar.

Swanstone's clocktower tolled in the distance. Quarter after. I was still late, but not *unreasonably* so. I peeked into the hall.

"The Norrfalters have already compromised one of our borders," a small droplet of spittle collected in the center of the Grand Duke's white moustache. His fists were clenched so tightly, I chuckled thinking about how tight other parts of him may have been clenched. "They could invade any day," he went on, "we need more troops. Another round of conscriptions might not even be enough!"

My mother sat by his side at the end of a long wooden table, surrounded by empty tufted chairs. Her hands were folded neatly in her lap, her dinner plate already clean. A gold, diamond shaped pendant with our family crest on it hung from her neck, as it always had since my father had gifted it to her at their wedding. Her dark red-brown hair was neatly braided away from her face and twisted into a tight spiral. A perfect vision of the perfect queen.

My matching hair fell tangled and unbrushed down my back, still slick with sweat. I twiddled the brass ring on my finger. A simple band that my father had found on the hunting grounds. I wore it always.

"Grand Duke," my mother addressed him with her usual formality, "we are a small, peaceful kingdom. The peasants don't know how to handle these conscriptions, and I would prefer not to spark a rebellion." My mother had been leading the country on her own since the death of my father two and a half years prior. She had always had a heart for the commoners and trying to persuade the Grand Duke to have one as well was never an easy task.

"Has the Norrfalt king agreed to the terms of the alliance that we have proposed?" she asked begrudgingly. "Surely more conscriptions will not be necessary once the alliance is confirmed and the date is set."

My skin prickled with betrayal at the mention of the alliance on my mother's lips. I knew she only agreed as a last resort, but the thought of my own mother trading me like land or goods still burned like a brand.

At first, I had held onto hope that the enemy king would reject my mother's offer, opting to wed his son to one of their own nobles. But when that hope faltered, I hatched a plan that I knew I could not pull off by myself.

Together, Emily and I decided that I needed an ally; someone who could confirm my cover story and could hold their own in a fight. Someone *almost* as good as me who would enable me to do what needed to be done to change my destiny. All the years of swordsmanship training—initiated by my father when I was still toddling—all the sweating, all the sparring, all brought me to this day. To *him*.

"Not yet—" began the duke.

"Ahem," I interrupted before I had to endure any more details of my delivery, packaged in white, to an enemy state.

My mother swiveled her eyes towards where I stood, disheveled but at least dressed, in the doorway to the large dining room. I picked off a piece of hay that clung to my skirt. The table had seats for fifty, but only the queen and the Grand Duke were present. "Ah, Princess Charissa, better to arrive late than not at all, I suppose," my mother's eyes flashed, even while the rest of her face remained completely calm.

Mother had done her very best to raise a proper princess; yet somehow she had still ended up with me. If only my parents had been able to have the son they had desired, instead of leaving me to be the sole heir to the kingdom, bound to serve forever under one man or another. In Mittelan, a never-wed woman—even the sole, rightful heir—was obligated to serve under a regent upon her coronation until she was married, at which point she would rule under her husband.

When my father died, my mother named the Grand Duke of Swanstone as head of her cabinet and regent in the case of her untimely death should I be found unwed. I swallowed my revulsion at the thought of him leading Mittelan while I sat helpless under an ornamental crown.

But marrying an enemy prince and being forced to live in his ice palace of the north was an even less preferred option.

"Mother, Grand Duke," I curtsied to them each. "I apologize for my tardiness . . . I umm . . . lost track of time."

"You know, Princess," the duke waggled a large finger at me, "a *queen* would not be late to dine with her *king*."

"Well, then it's quite lucky for me that I don't have one of those yet." I flopped into a chair sideways, my feet over the armrest.

"Chara!" Mother admonished, using my childhood name in surprise.

I swung my legs around and sat rightly in the chair.

She composed herself quickly, "I mean . . . Princess Charissa, you shouldn't speak to the Grand Duke that way. Or anyone at all, for that matter."

"More apologies, Grand Duke," I said as I removed my elbows from the table so the servers could fill my plate. My stomach growled audibly, and I paid no mind to the reactions of my company as I stabbed a potato greedily.

"If you want the Norrfalt prince to even consider you as a bride, you are going to have to start acting like more of a lady." He eyed me as he spoke, but I refused to meet his gaze. Hearing the plump man drone on and on about *acting like a lady* nauseated me. I suppressed the feeling by cutting a bite of the braised beef and popping it into my mouth.

Ignoring him did not make the duke stop. "You need to start acting like a princess, or better, a queen! This war is costly and we no longer have the upper hand. Your marriage may be the only hope we have to unite our countries. Don't you understand that, *Princess*?"

"Grand Duke, must we really put all the pressure of maintaining a kingdom on the back of a seventeen-year-old girl?" my mother asked, eyes fixed on her plate.

I could feel her unease and knew she hated the thought of sacrificing her daughter to politics, but my mother had been a queen long before she was a mother. Her sense of duty to her country was unwavering.

"And yet, here we are. Each battle we lose brings us one step closer to either *her* wedding," the duke didn't take his eyes off Mother as he pointed the tines of his fork at me, "or seeing our government totally overthrown."

Her jaw hardened, but she said nothing.

A wave of heat washed over me at the thought of a white

dress hanging in my wardrobe, of actually having to live in the ice country of Norrfalt, away from my home, from Emily, from everything I knew and loved. The alliance, once finalized, would surely stop the war and the wedding planning would begin. I had months to carry out my plan but—a terrifying thought lingered in my mind—what if I ran out of time?

I replaced the thought with the memory of the man I'd triumphed over today. Although he didn't know it yet, *he* was my key out of here. I was sure of it.

After a long swig of wine, I returned the duke's narrowed stare. "I'd rather you send *me* to the battlefront than force me to marry anyone, let alone some dodgy prince whose country finds it acceptable to invade their peaceful neighbors just to increase their own borders."

With that, the Grand Duke was rendered momentarily speechless while my mother sat silent, a proud smile toying on her delicate lips.

CHAPTER TWO

ELLIOT

I hadn't seen my little sister in over eight years, yet tonight Millie's bruised face haunted the twilight. I chopped wood on the skirt of my family's estate, but instead of seeing the ax in my hands or the wood splitting in two, I saw only her face marked by my mistakes.

My loss in the arena that afternoon had sent my mind to its darkest place. The memories of the events leading up to my sister's death felt as fresh as though I'd cradled her feverish body only hours ago, as opposed to years.

Instinctually, I reached for the leather pouch at my waist, which housed a single white ringlet. As I stroked the suede, worn smooth from nearly a decade of absentminded touch, Millie's face was broken by the dying words of my mother: *You're strong, little Elliot. Take care of your family—your sister—and yourself. Promise me, Ellie.*

I failed.

I failed eight years ago, and I failed again today.

I dropped the pouch and returned to the task at hand. But the rise and fall of my ax reminded me only of the rise and fall of his fist towards her face on the night he beat her because of my disobedience. The night we fled. The night she got sick.

The memory flooded me: *The woods were thick and suffocating. Her voice was growing weak and her bruises more pronounced. Why hadn't I kept my mouth closed?* I'd thought, *Why couldn't I have just done what the viper asked?*

"Elliot! Get in here, boy! The fire is dying!" His voice peeled from the cottage window through the evening frost. I was almost nineteen, yet my stepfather still called me *boy*.

I gathered the wood into the fabric carrier and started towards the house.

"What does it even matter?" Raymond whined to his pacing father as I hauled the heavy load across the living room to the hearth. My irritating step-brother sat on the shopworn chaise beside his brother, Lucas, who stared absently at the fire. "We stand no chance of conscription. Let the commoners kill one another off. Our countries will only be stronger for it."

"You fool," Silas snipped as I added wood to the fire, "under Norrfalt rule, we have no guarantee we would retain our business, our exemptions, or even our title. Would you like a job emptying chamber pots, or to be conscripted and sent to the front lines like the other boys your age? A new era is coming, and I will not allow us to be left in the dust."

I wiped a tear from her dust stained cheek. I knew where we were, how to hunt, how to feed us. But that didn't ease the growing knot in my stomach. We had nowhere to go.

Cinders gathered under my nails like they had for years. I could almost see those same dirty fingers—belonging then to a boy, a boy who was pretending to be a man—wiping the tears from Millie's face. I shoved the memory away and let Silas and his sons' debate fade into the background as I stoked the coals.

My focus had to stay here. Not on the past, but on the future: the Woodland Games. And not on the silly borderwar or the politics that didn't affect me. My war was here. I had lost a battle today, but I could not give up. I had been saving my winnings from the arena for almost three years; I couldn't stop just because I'd lost one time, no matter how important a battle it had been. My goal remained the same: keep winning and keep saving until I could buy Beauhaven and with it, my freedom.

"It's our home, Ellie, we've got to go home . . . please, take me home." Her tearful plea still echoed in my memories. I wouldn't forget the promise I'd made to her as she begged to go home: *"Someday, Millie,"* I'd vowed, *"I'll make our home safe for us again. I promise. Someday."*

Silas continued lecturing his boys on the repercussions of losing the borderwar as they retired to their rooms upstairs. I grabbed an armful of wood and followed behind.

I couldn't bear to meet the eyes of my step-brothers knowing that if I had won today then I would have had the coins right now, the coins I needed to never have to see them again. *Someday* could have been today. They ignored me as I tended to their fire.

I went to Silas's chamber next. He glared at me from his perch on the bed where my mother had died. The white canopies surrounded him as they had my mother, but where she had been an angel in the candle glow, he was a devil framed in tattered cloth and wicked flame. His sharp cheekbones, pointy nose, and black eyes peered over the top of the pages at me, a vulture eyeing his prey.

I didn't cough, mumble, or even breathe while I stoked the dying flames and added wood.

The whip of his hand across my cheek caught me off guard as I stood. I stumbled back, reeling with the memory of Millie collapsing after such a blow. It flashed through my mind with visceral pain, worse than the slap itself. Usually I sensed Silas's attacks coming, but this time I staggered from the unexpected sting and had to fight to hide my surprise.

"You've seemed distracted this evening," he stated as if that were a valid excuse. "Ever since your brothers and I returned from Swanstone. Is there something you care to tell me?"

Yes, my temper hammered at my temples, *I'm a champion swordsman and you are nothing but a selfish, decrepit, failed businessman and I'm distracted today by my overwhelming desire to gut you.*

I swallowed the retort, "No, sir. Of course not, sir."

Silas straightened the lapels of his nightshirt, "Don't forget, boy, who spent all of these years providing for you, giving you food and shelter and work. Don't forget who tended to your sickly mother all those months. And don't you dare forget how I emptied my purse to pay the healers to try to save your sister."

After you had beat her senseless, I wanted to spit. But the truth was, even I didn't truly believe that's what killed her. My defiance, my selfish choice to run away, and that night in the forest, that is what killed her. I could still see him, returning from the healers with no body and only a lock of her hair. He had barely enough money to pay the healers, there was none left for an undertaker. At least, that's what he said.

I haven't tried to run away since.

I didn't talk back; I said only what I knew he wanted to hear, "As always, sir, I'm ever grateful."

His black eyes narrowed in our locked gaze until a smile split the thin line of his lips. "Stay on my good side, boy," he patted my shoulder menacingly. "Trust me. One day you'll be very happy you did."

I fought to keep the disdain from souring my expression. Instead, I nodded and shuffled silently from the room as the old man beamed in the glow of his own pride.

Making my way down the hallway, hand on my burning cheek, I reminded myself over and over again why I couldn't kill him. Why I had to stick to the plan. If I killed him, my family's estate would go to Raymond and I would never get Beauhaven back. The only way to regain my birthright and return the home and property to its former glory was to earn enough money to bribe Silas into walking away and leaving me be.

"Someday, Millie, I'll make our home safe for us again. I promise. Someday."

Beauhaven was all I had left of my parents. Their bones were in its dirt and their memories were in these walls. This home—now barren—was once full of laughter and play and song, and I would do everything I could to restore that joy. A safe home had been what Millie longed for most. Someday, this little estate would be a place of beauty and safety once more, a tribute to the life our parents had tried so hard to build for us. I owed them that at least.

That's why I fought in the Woodland Games, why I'd been

fighting for over three years. It was why I'd bet so much today on the hope—no, the expectation—that this would be the day that I would finally have enough.

And I knew exactly how much would be enough. I'd done my research rummaging about Silas's office over the years. I knew what Beauhaven was worth and what I was worth. I planned to give a sum of over one thousand slips greater for Silas to just walk away and leave me alone. Ten thousand slips. A small fortune.

My plan had crashed down around me as the armored stranger defeated me in a handful of moves. Who was this armored stranger? Was he a seasoned knight returning from the war? Knights—along with any other nobility—were not even supposed to know of the Woodland Games, let alone enter them. But I'd been posing as a peasant for years despite my noble blood, maybe he was too?

It was true what I'd said to him. I'd traveled often with my merchant father, and for Silas, and even some for the various tournaments. Yet I'd never seen someone with his level of skill.

However, my respect did not temper my anger. Regardless of who the stranger was, did he have any idea what he took from me? He didn't even stay to collect his prize. My bets were long gone, along with anyone else who had bet on me: Parren and Bruno at the very least. I had bet the largest sum I ever had on myself: over one thousand slips. I had bet large, knowing that when I won, I would have it all. Ten thousand slips. Enough to buy my life back.

My cheek still tingled, but the pain was nothing compared to the guilt and anger souring my stomach. I knew I should rest and that there would be other days to train, to prepare to face the armored stranger again, but I couldn't wait.

As soon as I heard the snores of three sleeping men, I slipped silently out of the window.

My horse knew the route by heart. He followed the country path until it veered east and gave way to the cobblestone road that led to the bridge over the ravine and into the city.

The castle town came into view, and soon we were trotting over the drawbridge and into Swanstone. Candles from the windows of the castle sent shadows dancing around the buildings encompassing it. Within Swanstone's protective walls, the castle was isolated with additional fortifications, watch towers, and a large golden gate with guard towers on each side. We passed the market where I sold my pelts, now just a plethora of dark alleys and empty stalls. Everyone had taken their goods home for the evening and would return at dawn.

The marketplace ended in the city center, where the most profitable businesses had permanent storefronts. Steeply pitched roofs connected the whitewashed buildings and lavishly painted business signs hung above their colorful front doors. The shop windows were all dark by this hour, but the pubs were in full swing.

At my destination, I slid off my horse's back and stroked his velvety nose. I nuzzled into him, "Be right back, boy," and he returned my affection until he realized that I was slipping his reins through the metal circle of a hitching post. He huffed and stamped a hoof on the snow-dusted ground.

I ran down the damp stairs. My long legs skipped every other step as I descended into the subterranean pub. I ducked to avoid the establishment's sign, a black cat with curvy letters scrolling through its legs: *Lucifer's Den.* The dingy bar reeked of piss and hops, but I found the smell oddly comforting. Crowded around the drink-filled tables that lined the room were tradesmen, artisans, soldiers, and barmaids.

Bruno, the bartender and my good friend, already had his hands full telling off a group of intoxicated soldiers. They must have been on leave from the war front and were more than happy to be drinking away their free time. So many peasant boys had been drafted for the borderwar. Yet I remained. My noble surname protected me from conscription and did absolutely nothing else.

I caught sight of the familiar ponytail, tipped back with the bottom of a pint high in the air. His cane was leaning against the stool beside him, his peg leg on the seat. Parren slammed the empty glass back on the bar in front of him, signaling Bruno to fetch him another. The bartender pursed his lips in disapproval but fetched Parren an ale anyway.

"I could handle one of those about now," I squeezed both of Parren's shoulders and he whipped around with dramatized surprise, pulling his wooden leg off the stool beside him.

"Elliot, my boy!" He tossed an arm over my shoulders, "Where have you been? I thought I'd find you here hours ago after today's—"

I held a palm up to stop him. "Please, I don't want to even think about it, let alone talk about it. Trust me, I would have spent the rest of the day here if I could have gotten away any earlier."

"You should really kick that old money counting crock in the crack if I do say. If you left it up to me, I'd spear the dear man for you, but—"

"Soon. I'll be free of him soon." I assured Parren, hoping I myself would trust in the confidence I feigned.

Bruno handed Parren another pint of amber liquid and laughed his hearty laugh, "You'll only need about a half dozen to catch up," Bruno joked in his gruff voice as he picked up a glass to pour me an ale.

I chuckled but waved him off.

"You sure? You need it way more than this guy," Bruno tilted his head in Parren's direction. "We all lost a fair share of coin today, but only you did so with a blade at your throat."

I forced a smile, trying not to think about how much my friend lost betting on me. "No, thanks," I said, "next time. I need my head in the game for training tonight. Maybe after my next tournament win you can join us again. It would be nice to take a break from my sword. I need to brush up on those knife tricks you taught me."

"Any day," Bruno's bushy black beard didn't hide his sympathetic smile before he left to tend to another patron.

His sympathy only fueled my anger and I suddenly wished I could skip the pleasantries and go right to training. The blade—training, fighting, winning—was my only way forward. It was the only way out of this life that left me with bruises and scars: Silas's brands, intentionally placed to make me look and feel weak.

"I'm trying to put the loss behind me," I rested an elbow against the bar beside Parren, "but I cannot afford to lose to this stranger again. Any idea who he was?"

Parren shook his head with a bitter laugh before picking up the beer and taking another long draw.

I'd lost many coins today, but I was sure that Parren had as well. He could afford it, but still.

Master Andre Parren was the head trainer of the Queen's Guard and the closest thing I had left to family. He knew all about Silas's cruelty and how I had lost my parents and then Millie. Although he struggled to understand why I tolerated Silas for all these years just to get back my family's estate, he understood that I had my reasons. He knew how much was riding on this tournament.

Although nearly thirty years my senior, I'd always felt connected to the village drunk. Parren had been wallowing in his own self-pity ever since he lost his leg in battle almost a decade ago, and his soldier stipend disappeared quickly when he took to drinking away his free time.

When his liquor fund ran dry, he began training swordsmen. At first he trained peasants for the Games, but he worked his way up to teaching swordsmanship to noble children. Eventually, he made enough of a name for himself that the king recruited him to train the royal guard. When the king passed, the queen made him head trainer for her personal guard.

Parren and I met while I was selling pelts in the marketplace several years after my sister's death. After a brief conversation where he managed to draw out some of the more pathetic aspects of my life, he seemed to take pity on me and offered to give me a lesson for free. When I showed actual promise, he bought me a practice rapier and began training me for the Games. That's when I hatched my plan. Every time I won a tournament, I gave Parren a cut and tucked away the rest to someday buy Beauhaven.

"Whoever he was," I muttered, Millie's broken face still intertwined with my memory of the armored stranger's sword, "this mysterious newcomer will not catch me off guard again."

Parren sloshed his drink up to his face and gulped it until it was gone. He put a heavy hand on my shoulder, his eyes not quite matching one another, "Then we have got some work to do."

❖❖❖

Sweat beaded down my back in heavy droplets but I did not rest. The memory of the armored stranger, standing over me as I signaled defeat, drove me forwards. The pouch at my waist beat against my side, reminding me ever of my broken promises, pushing me to strike harder, faster, more precisely than ever before.

Parren bellowed, pointing out my every slight misstep or hesitation with a jab of the sword that he was currently using as a cane. He hobbled about the courtyard of his small home on the edge of the city, barking out maneuvers and combinations for me to practice. We were well accustomed to our training sessions now, but tonight he pushed me further, was more meticulous, than I'd ever seen him before.

And I was more determined.

The night tipped past midnight, and I knew my sleep deprivation would be evident the following day. I didn't want to stop. I didn't want to give up.

But I had to get home, had to be there when Silas roused. I returned my practice blade to its sheath at my hip. "Again tomorrow," I declared, "but tonight, I have to go."

"I will kill him for you, Elliot, you need only ask," Parren's sneer was surprisingly comforting in all its wickedness. "It's what family is for."

"Well, I appreciate the sentiment," I said as I crossed the courtyard, heading towards the gate where I'd secured my horse, Gus. The clack of Parren's wooden leg on the stone path followed me. I turned to meet his gaze. "But if anyone is going to have that honor, it's going to be me."

CHAPTER THREE

CHARA

You're joking, Chara, right? You can't be serious. You simply can't be."

That had been my friend's reaction when, three days prior, I had finally decided that I could no longer delay the inevitable and I had to tell Emily about my plan. The Games were two short days away, and I knew that I would need her help to pull it off. The exchange had gone about as well as could be expected.

She'd sat quietly on my bed as I told her that I had recruited Grimm to buy me armor. She hadn't panicked when I told her that I had used the secret she'd shared with me in confidence to seek out the peasants' illicit games and enter myself into the competition. But when I told her *why* I'd done those things, her bright eyes bulged and I thought they might pop right out of her skull and roll along my chamber floor like a pea flying unexpectedly from its shell.

"You must be joking!"

"Of course I'm not joking, Ems," I kept my tone as straight and even as I could manage. If I showed any doubt in my escape plan, Emily would never agree to help me.

"That's a truly horrible plan!" she yelled, her fingers digging into her tight blonde braids. "You're not a knight, you're a princess! And someday you will be a queen!"

I stuck my chin out, "Why can't I be both?"

"Because who wants a knight for a queen?" she raged, face burning scarlet as she paced across my chamber. I could see the details of my plan spinning like cogs in her head. She picked up my laundry again, straightening items to fold or put away, even re-folding undergarments that didn't lay perfectly crisp. I knew she was thinking up all of the ways this new scheme could go terribly wrong.

I ignored her remark because to me, the solution was simple. As long as the war waged on, I would be a pawn in this political game. Therefore, the war needed to end. And the only way to change the course of a battle was to be in it. So that was exactly what I planned to do.

I would travel to the Norrfalt-Mittelan border and attempt to negotiate new terms of peace. If that failed, I felt confident I could rally our troops behind me once they saw what I was capable of. I was born with a sword in my hand, and I felt confident I was among the best swordsmen in the nation. Surely, fighting alongside their princess would give our troops the motivation needed to defeat the Norrfalters for good.

I would be like the clan war chiefs in the Rolestov territory. It's a broken place now, but at least the leaders there fight alongside their kinsmen.

We would be free of Norrfalt's influence, once and for all, or I would be dead. I meant what I had said to the duke: I would rather die in battle than succumb to the marriage alliance and be forced to live and rule under a Norrfalt king for the rest of my life.

However, even I knew that it would be impossible to make the six-day journey through unfamiliar terrain on my own. It wasn't safe for anyone, let alone a woman, to travel that far by themselves. So I decided I needed an accomplice: someone who knew the land well and could help me hunt for some food along the way. Since I could not safely travel under my true identity, I would have to travel in disguise—at least until I reached the border safely—and would need a companion to corroborate my story to anyone we met along the way. It would be helpful if that person were a proficient fighter as well, should the need arise.

I pondered for days over who to ask, but I knew that no one in the castle who was skilled enough for the journey and capable enough in battle would be willing to go behind the queen's back to help me. I needed an outsider. A peasant was much more likely to know the routes and have the basic survival skills necessary to ensure my safety anyway. My ally would also have to be someone far from court, who stood no chance of identifying me as the princess, which is why I entered myself into the Woodland Games.

"I've gotten you *out* of a lot of nasty situations, Chara, I'm not about to get you *in* to the worst one of all!" Emily bit her nails furiously as she realized the full scope of my plan. I imagined her as a beaver, shavings of wood flying to either side as she gnawed nervously. She paused only to hang or fold a piece of my laundry. "Not even the queen herself will be able to get you out of trouble if you are dead! What do you even think you will do once you get there? Surely, if one more soldier was enough to claim victory, the generals would have succeeded by now. I mean, they have well over half the men in the land conscripted already."

"Yes, Emily, but they don't have me."

She straightened out a lavender petticoat with a sharp whip of her arms, refusing to meet my eye. She was two years younger than me but had never acted like it. She had been the voice of reason in my life since I'd met her all those years ago. She was less like a handmaiden or friend, and more like a sister.

"Remember when you first came here? With that nasty lady who made those horrible dresses?" I knew bringing back memories of our first encounter was a selfish way of making her see things my way, but that didn't change the fact that it would prove my point.

Emily cringed at the mention, but I pressed on.

"I knew after watching her order you about while she pinned me into that pink catastrophe that I couldn't let you remain with her. I made that joke about the dress looking like . . . like a . . ." I couldn't remember the interchange exactly, "a—"

"I believe you said it ruffled like a piglet's back end, if I do remember correctly," her concern momentarily softened with the hint of a smile.

"Yes! And you laughed so hard you dropped the tin of straight pins!"

Her smile dropped, "And spent an hour picking them up.

The mistress made sure I paid dearly after that." Emily had told me before that her mistress made her wear a gag for three solid days following our first meeting, removing it once daily for a teacup of water. Guilt knotted in my stomach for bringing up the painful memory.

"I'm sorry, Ems. I shouldn't have brought it up," I put a hand on her shoulder, "but I just wanted you to remember. I—at only ten years old—persuaded my parents to forgo the legion of help they already employed to make you my handmaiden. I insisted that, even though you were younger than me, I needed you; that you would keep me in line," I poked at her ribs jokingly, "I told them to 'give that mean lady whatever she demanded and to not take "no" for an answer.'" I flashed her a sincere smile.

"You always were a bossy little shit, weren't you?" her intensity broke, and she almost smiled.

"Yes. I guess I was—"

"—you mean, *am*," she interjected.

I chuffed, "Yes, I *am*. But that's my point. I know I can convince the Norrfalt generals to come to a peaceful agreement that doesn't require nuptials. I have to at least try. And if I fail, I *want* to fight, Emily."

"I don't want you hurt, Char." A twist of her yellow hair had escaped her braids, curling from the sweat of her brow. "But I don't want you sent to Norrfalt either." She stopped biting her nails and even put down the laundry for a moment just to look at me. Her gaze was all concern and hesitancy, but beneath it, I could tell she was going to give in. Her brow wrinkled deeply then relaxed. "If I help you," she said slowly, as if she might change her mind before finishing her declaration, "then you have to promise not to die."

I laughed and threw my arms around her. She squeezed me back, however reluctantly it might have been.

❖❖❖

I now sat in front of Emily as a champion. With the excitement of the day still fresh in my veins, I couldn't wait to share my success with her. I had excused myself from dinner as quickly as I could and rushed off to my chamber to see her. Emily listened patiently as I recounted every detail of the battle while she gently worked all of the tangles from my snarled hair.

"He's perfect, Em, really!" I gushed, "If only you could have seen us fight together, I know you'd agree."

She smiled hesitantly, her eyes meeting mine through the mirror in front of me as she ran the comb through a particularly stubborn knot. "What's his name?"

I watched the look of surprise transfer from my features to hers in the reflection, as we both realized my crippling oversight.

"Char, please tell me you got his name. Or the house he works for. Something? Anything?"

I swallowed, my heart toppling down to my toes. I shook my head.

The peasants would long ago have dispersed about the region and no one would be willing to disclose anything about the Games to a noblewoman like me, since the betting tournaments had been forbidden decades ago. I racked my mind for someone I could go to for the fighter's name. The only person I could even think of that I recognized at the Games had been the one-legged man clapping my opponent on his shoulder. He was someone far too dangerous to let onto my plan, but unless I could think of another solution, he was my only hope. As the head trainer of the Queen's Guard and a man who knew my skills with a blade, he would no doubt be suspicious of my inquiry. But the potential reward far outweighed the risk.

We needed to speak with Master Parren.

❖❖❖

The next afternoon, I watched as Emily hung around the edge of the men who were training in the castle courtyard. Parren marched around his men, his peg leg only adding to his characteristic stagger. He barked orders at the newest members of the Queen's Guard and stamped his wooden appendage on the ground when they made mistakes. Of course, he'd seen me observing his lessons my entire life, especially after Father grew too ill to continue tutoring me. I tried to absorb his teachings as if they were a form of art, and I spent much of my free time perfecting them with the blade my father had given me for my thirteenth birthday.

Although Parren had certainly seen me spear a large number of dummies, and even present a challenge to him in our friendly spars, he would *never* have anticipated that I would enter myself in the Woodland Games. I wasn't even supposed to know they existed. But neither was he.

"I've never even met this . . . Master Parren . . ." Emily said, stuttering over his name. She twiddled with the fibers of the basket she was holding with one hand as she anxiously gnawed on the nail beds of the other. I put my hands on her shoulders and we breathed together to calm her nerves.

Parren seemed to enjoy an occasional break from the company of young men, which is why I always thought of myself as his favorite student since he began casually training me after Father died. I'd filled Emily's basket with small loaves of bread and four jars of water to offer him and his parched students. Although I knew that Parren would prefer a bottle of a much stronger drink, I'd been unable to acquire one in time. That was probably for the better.

"You'll be fine," I reassured her. She pulled her coat tighter around her middle as the cool breeze picked up. We were hiding behind a large, leafless tree by the wall of the castle where we could watch Parren train the guards. "You can do this," I said.

She grimaced.

I turned her around and sent her out from behind the tree towards the group of armored men.

At first, Parren didn't even notice Emily as she passed by him, swinging her basket in front of her. She glanced back at me, a small pout on her lips. I motioned for her to try again. She walked by him once more, this time lingering beside him. He raised an eyebrow but when he realized she was not leaving his side, he barked an order I couldn't hear. His students paired off, facing each other to spar. The wind whistled in my ears, cutting through the ruckus of the courtyard and masking their conversation. I had to get closer.

I took the book I had brought and pretended to read it as I walked across the courtyard towards the sets of dueling students. When I was close enough to hear, I found a spot of brown grass beneath another leafless tree and sat, my back against the bark, being sure to keep my nose buried in my book. The spring breeze cut easily through my dress, causing a shiver. I peeked over the top of the pages, trying to gauge how the conversation was going.

"Yes, miss . . . I'm sorry, I didn't catch your name," Parren extended his hand to her.

She shook it. "Emily."

"Well, yes, Miss Emily, it was quite the match," Parren said, resting his arm on his cane and shifting his weight to his good leg. "You were lucky to have seen it. Who knows if that armored stranger will be around again anytime soon. He left without even removing his helmet, and I hear he didn't even collect his winnings!"

"You don't say!" Emily clasped a hand over her mouth, feigning surprise. "And who . . ." she began but paused when Parren leaned in closer. She swallowed. "Who did you say it was that the newcomer triumphed over? In the end? This was my first time ever at the Woodland Games and I'm still trying to learn all the competitors' names . . . so I know who to bet on next time." She smiled and even I was surprised at its natural glow of innocence.

"Oh! Yes!" Parren stood straighter, knocking his cane against the ground a couple of times with excitement, "That's one of my own students and a long-time friend. He hadn't lost me a match in nearly three years," Parren puffed his chest proudly. I shook my head. He hadn't even answered her question. He deflated, "Well, until yesterday of course."

Emily recovered quite nicely, swinging her basket gently and continuing, "Well, yes, but still you must be very proud. He's an excellent swordsman. And what did you say his name was again?"

"Elliot. I've been training Elliot for almost four years now; he must have been about your age when we started, maybe a bit younger. Elliot Cendrilon."

Got it. I grinned devilishly behind the empty words in front of me before coughing loudly, relieving Emily of her duties. She hurriedly handed over the basket to Parren with a mumbled excuse about why she had to leave.

She scurried away towards our prearranged meeting place. Her face grew as pale as if she'd just seen a ghost.

Elliot Cendrilon. Elliot Cendrilon. Elliot Cendrilon. I repeated the name in my head to keep from forgetting it.

Elliot Cendrilon. The name felt dark and mysterious in my head, but also bright and shining; like a gift from a stranger waiting to be opened.

He was my ticket away from this life. He had to be.

I faked a yawn before standing and brushing the dirt and dead grass from the skirt of my dress. Tucking the book under my arm, I had to refrain from skipping my way back into the castle.

"No time for a spar?" Parren's voice pulled me from my reverie. "I think this is the first time I've seen you choose a book over a blade. I'll face you myself," he smiled knowingly and pointed his blade in my direction.

"Umm . . . No thank you, Master Parren, not today," I stumbled, "I've actually got to be going."

"As you wish, Princess," he hobbled back toward his students, and I sent up a silent prayer that he thought nothing of the interaction. No matter what, I had to keep my distance from him or else this training yard would be the closest to war I'd ever get.

CHAPTER FOUR
ELLIOT

The hours of chores the following day made my bones ache, and the lack of sleep wasn't helping. Every time I felt the twinge of my bruised eye or the pang of a sore muscle, I touched the pouch at my waist and chose to replace my simmering anger with Parren's voice barking out a combination. Training was my only way out. The arena was my only way out. I focused my thoughts on nothing else.

Despite my exhaustion and aching soreness, I left for Swanstone once more as soon as Silas and the boys were asleep. I met Parren in his courtyard and we trained until the threat of dawn forced me to return home.

I rode through Beauhaven's wrought iron fence later than I'd intended. Lifting the hidden board in the barn floor, I returned my sword to its home beside my winnings. I gave in to temptation and took out one of the bags of winnings. Opening it, I stared upon the golds and glass glimmering in the lamplight. I dumped a few coins into my hand, a slip falling with it. These were my future, the only hope I had for regaining a fraction of the life I once lived.

I would not lose another silver nor glass nor slip. I could not. Not to the armored soldier, not to anyone.

"Someday, Millie, I'll make our home safe for us again. I promise. Someday."

Someday was too close for me to fail again.

I dropped the money back into the sack and closed it tightly. I replaced the board firmly and covered it with the bale of hay.

Jack, my barn pup, was snoring softly now, after perking up at my arrival to see that it was only me. I put Gus back in his stall before extinguishing the lantern and quickly making my way back to the cottage.

Something caught my eye on the second floor, but upon closer look, the house still stood quietly, windows dark. My exhaustion was making me see things.

The very early morning held the weighty hush of twilight as I slid the barn door closed behind me.

I walked up to the house, skipping the first—and loudest—of the front porch steps and slipped through the window I'd snuck in and out of more times than I could count. I never used the door due to the heavy whine of the hinges and loud click of the deadbolt. My practiced fingers latched the window shut without so much as a click.

Crawling onto my cot, limbs weighted with exhaustion, I closed my eyes.

"Well, I'm happy to see that you've arrived home safely, boy."

My stomach flew to my throat. I sat, dread creeping all the way to my fingertips like poison, to find my step-father sunken into the worn cushions of the fainting couch, my cot by the fire directly in his line of vision. He'd been waiting.

I stood.

He mirrored my movement. "Come here."

I crossed the living room slowly, as a man towards the gallows. The only light came from the dying embers of the fire, steeping the room in a glow as wicked as death itself.

As if in defense, my mind began to replace the horrors in front of me with memories of the home as it had been in my childhood. Once upon a time, the wood floors had been freshly stained and were polished and well-kept. The walls had been decorated with art from all around the world, and a masterfully woven carpet Father had traded for on one of his merchant trips flowed down the stairs like a waterfall. The fainting couch usually held my father with his atlas or my mother with her pen and notebook.

But the carpet and tapestries had long been sold, and the dull floorboards moaned with each step, low and painful as a funeral dirge. And in my parents' place stood the devil himself.

In an attempt to buy myself more time to choose my words and craft my lie, I knelt in front of the hearth and began to empty the coals and ash.

I felt the weight of his presence behind me.

"Stand up, Elliot, and look at me."

I did as I was told but an excuse slipped unexpectedly from my lips, "I'm only trying to help, sir."

He whipped the back of his hand across my face.

I refused to reach a hand up to my cheek. I refused to give

him the satisfaction.

"Don't talk back to me, boy." He gently placed his hand back in his nightshirt pocket. "Now. I saw you leave over four hours ago. Where did you go?"

I had been sneaking out to train for over three years and never once been caught. Of course, I had a hundred excuses formulated for just this occurrence—I'd only been out for more wood, I'd been checking on Jack, I'd heard the gate open—but each one grew cold in my mouth. He knew I'd been gone for hours. He'd seen me leave, and he had been waiting.

My eyes flicked out the window to the barn, where my sword was hidden along with all the money I'd been saving, almost six thousand slips. Any excuse I might make would not be good enough, would give too much away. So I said nothing.

He allowed the silence to swelter between us, while his glare grew more and more cruel. "Say something, boy, and don't you dare lie to me."

It was as if I had not aged a day since I was twelve. It was as if nothing had changed since the day I had decided to stand up to him, the day I'd told him *no* for the first time. The only time. Instead of punishing me for my defiance, he took it out on Millie. I felt every blow to her innocent face a hundredfold more than had I been taking them myself.

My hands clenched to fists and I fought not to lash out now for what he had done to Millie all those years ago.

That beating had been the beginning of the end for her, and it was my disobedience that had caused it. I had been rash, and I had been paying for it ever since.

I couldn't afford to be rash again. I knew my aim: reclaim and restore the estate. For Millie. For my parents. To honor them and make Beauhaven into a home once more. *Someday.*

I couldn't risk that.

Silas clucked at the silence that ached between us. "Then I'll add three lashes for your silence to the ten I've elected to give you for your disappearance." His gaunt cheekbones stuck out almost as far as his nose, casting his mouth into shadow.

Thirteen lashes. I'd never taken more than six or seven at a time. "Sir! I'm sorry, but—"

"And I'll add two more for your impudence." He put his hands behind his back and raised his pointy chin to let me know the decision was final.

Fifteen. *Fifteen* lashes.

If I couldn't even beat the armored stranger under normal circumstances, how would I stand a chance injured?

And now that I had been discovered sneaking out, how would I train? How would I fight? How would I win?

"Do you have anything else to add?" he asked.

I swallowed, fighting the rising panic. I shook my head, eyes on my boots.

"Look at me, Elliot."

Reluctantly, I obeyed, my gaze locking with his dark, spiteful stare. The hollows beneath his eyes sent a shiver down my spine.

"Don't *ever* leave this estate again without my permission. Do you understand?"

I nodded.

"Now, would you like your lashings tonight or in the morning?"

What graciousness, allowing me to choose when I would receive my punishment. No one said Silas Tremaine was not a gentleman.

I said nothing. I walked upstairs to my step-father's bedroom and picked up the belt he kept on his vanity. I returned to his side and handed it to him, peeling the shirt from my back.

CHAPTER FIVE

CHARA

I'd read through the record books three times and there was not a single mention of anyone with the surname Cendrilon. He was a lower-class male. He had to be listed in the conscription records. The Grand Duke was meticulous in his search for troops; the boy's name had to be here somewhere.

My feet rested on the solid piece of walnut that formed the top of the duke's desk, held aloft with elaborately carved legs. Its surface displayed trinkets and keepsakes from the surrounding kingdoms: Norrfalt, Almora, and other distant kingdoms. I chewed on a section of my hair as I puzzled over this mystery fighter.

Elliot Cendrilon. I had hoped to find that the boy had not yet been conscripted. If so, I could just write up a little counterfeit conscription notice and my job would be half done.

If he had already been conscripted, I was going to have to

come up with some reason to force him to re-enlist. It would be trickier, but not impossible. However, I hadn't accounted for the chance of not finding him on the ledger at all. I slammed the book closed and let my head sag onto its cover. I groaned and banged my fist on the desk. The duke's figurines shuddered.

"Achoo!"

I sat up suddenly at Emily's signal. Jumping to my feet, I closed the ledger and stuffed the book back on the shelf hurriedly, praying it was the right spot. I took one step towards the door.

"Achoo!" she faked another sneeze. "Apologies, Grand Duke, sir. It's the dust." She wouldn't risk talking to him except to alert me that he was very close. Footsteps, heavy and fast. I didn't have time to get out.

I whipped my head around the office, searching for a place to hide. I spotted the oversized, flowing drapes that blocked the bright mountain sun. I ducked under the window closest to me, folding myself quickly into the extravagant drapes, thankful for their excessive length and grandeur.

The heavy door flew open, slamming against the mural behind it. The wood paneling on the walls trembled. I heard the Grand Duke as he huffed about the room, landing heavily on each step.

The curtains covered me like blankets, the sun beating at my back. Beads of sweat blossomed along my hairline and one slipped down to my corset.

"How could she . . . " the duke muttered loudly.

"Uncle, I don't—" an unfamiliar voice, a man's voice, attempted to calm the duke. *Uncle*? The Grand Duke had a nephew? The only family I'd ever heard the duke mention was his sister who was married off to some Norrfalt noble in a futile attempt at peace decades ago.

"You don't know anything, child!" The Grand Duke interrupted his guest. "Her word is law. She is the queen after all. I am not king, not regent. I have no power, no *real* power. We simply do not have the time she is insisting on. We need this done yesterday! If she discovers . . . if she knew of Norrfalt's . . ." his voice drifted off as he harrumphed into a chair with a loud *oof.* "She would certainly call it off immediately. This situation is tenuous, child, more so than you could possibly imagine."

If she discovers . . . discovers what? What situation is tenuous? What was he trying to keep from my mother?

"What I was saying, sir," his nephew spoke with an imperturbable air of confidence, despite sounding considerably younger than his uncle, "is that, once the princess has met her betrothed, I doubt there will be any more objections. From either party."

I held back a scoff, almost giving myself away. Whoever this man was, if he thought that I would bend like a willow reed at the sight of *my betrothed* then it was obvious he didn't know a thing about me. Who was this boy to be sticking his nose into the business of my future anyway?

"You can't know that," snipped the duke.

"You're right. I can't," he said gently. I slowed my breathing and listened closely as the young man dropped his voice. "But, I do know that once the princess and I are wed, then both sets of troops will, in essence, be Norrfalt subjects."

My heart began to thump wildly against my chest, each hard and loud beat threatening to give me away. *This* man was the prince? The Grand Duke's nephew? How did I not know that the duke's sister must have been married to the Norrfalt king himself? And here the prince had, in no uncertain terms, admitted to wanting to take over the country.

"And, at that point," the prince continued, his voice as warm and intoxicating as chocolate melting on the tongue, "I see no reason why we need to continue the bloodshed."

The heat behind the curtain was suddenly suffocating, stars pricked at the corner of my vision. It was all I could do to hold myself upright.

"Norrfalt will have all the fertile lands it needs," he went on, "and I can take the princess home with to Kalamar with me to produce heirs for our newly-expanded kingdom. And you—"

Blood rushed to my head, my foot moving to catch me before my brain could tell it not to. The castle floor groaned its response.

"Hush," the duke ordered, cutting him off.

My heart hammered. I kept my breathing as low and shallow as possible. I clung to the curtains, desperate not to topple into the office. I imagined myself laid splayed between these men who were planning my entire life without so much as a murmur of consent from me.

The duke was quiet for a long moment. My vision spun. I focused on breathing as deeply and quietly as I dared.

"Yes," the duke's frazzled voice finally slowed, "that is what will happen, what *must* happen. Now that the king has agreed, we must make the marriage final before the queen finds out. It's the only way. This war is not over. Norrfalt needs its new princess, before any more battles are won or lost."

"I will fix it," the prince said calmly, "trust me."

❖❖❖

Even after the duke and prince had left, it took longer than I cared to admit until I was able to move again. The conversation I'd heard was like a riddle that I was struggling to puzzle out. Two things were undeniable, the duke was hiding *something* from my mother, and the Norrfalt king had agreed to the terms of the marriage alliance.

Unless I took action soon, I was going to be wed. There was no *if* anymore.

After pushing the door to my chamber open with my hip, I found Emily exactly where I'd expected—nails bit down to their beds—organizing and reorganizing my wardrobe. We both breathed a huge sigh of relief at our narrow escape. It didn't take her long to assess the disappointment present on my face.

"No luck?" she asked as we sat side-by-side on the couch by the window overlooking the red crags of Walter Ravine.

"Less than no luck," I buried my face in my palms, not trying to keep the panic from my voice. "Not only did I not find out anything about Elliot, I found out that the prince of Norrfalt is *here* and his father has agreed to the terms of the marriage alliance. I knew this day was coming, but I didn't know it would be so soon." My voice was muffled and shaking, but I knew Emily understood anyway. She laid a hand on my knee comfortingly.

"And that's not even the worst of it," I said, wringing my hands and fiddling with my father's brass ring. Emily cocked her head. I took a deep breath as I tried to piece together the duke and his nephew's vague conversation, "I didn't understand all of it, but I caught enough. Something is going on at the warfront that the duke doesn't want my mother to know about."

"But he's the one person on the cabinet your mother trusts the most. What makes you think he would betray her confidence?"

"Well, he all but admitted to it."

"Then you have to go to your mother, immediately, you have to tell her—"

"Tell her what?" I demanded, standing up suddenly, "That her most trusted advisor is deceiving her, but I don't know how or about what? That I accidentally spied on him while digging through the ledgers trying to find someone to help me escape? And that, because of all this, she should let me out of the marriage alliance? You said it yourself, my mother trusts the duke. She will see this as a ploy on my part to get out of the wedding."

Emily shrugged, "But shouldn't we at least try?"

"It will never work, Ems. If Mother discovers that I am trying to escape, I will never get out of here. But it's more than just an escape plot now, Ems, now I *have* to go. I need to see for myself what is happening on the warfront," I looked out over the window into the deep crimson canyon just beyond the castle walls; then I looked up to the pristine, snow-capped mountains in the distance. I began to breathe quickly, too quickly. There was so much at stake. "I need to find Elliot as soon as possible, but how?"

"Shhhhh . . . " the low hush of Emily's voice centered me. "We'll figure it out. We're so close." She took my hand and breathed with me until I calmed. When she did speak, her voice was low, almost scared, "But I did ask every friend I have in the castle and no one recognized the name of your Woodland fighter."

She swallowed hard, "And, I just don't know what it is, but something is off. Something about that name just . . . just . . . I don't know. It gives me the willies. Every inquiry, every time I say his name, some inexplicable dread rises in me. I don't know how to explain it, Char, but maybe it's a sign. Maybe it's time to come up with a new plan, something a little more . . . a little more . . ."

I narrowed my eyes at her as the fierce afternoon sun finally dipped below the peaks.

She looked dazed and somewhat afraid in the now dim chamber light, as if recently woken and still shaking off a nightmare. She shrugged her shoulders and finally finished, "A little more . . . realistic?"

"No." I pulled away from her touch. I don't know why I reacted so violently, but I just knew that this was it. I had to get to the border; I needed someone to accompany me, and it had to be Elliot. I couldn't explain why; I just knew that it *had* to be him. I remembered the shine of his blade in the arena and the sparkle in his eyes.

He was determined, but gracious somehow. Trusting, but also trustworthy. I sat back down, "No, this will work. It has to work. There's just something we are missing, something we haven't thought of yet."

"Perhaps he has some secret of his own that he's hiding," Emily suggested as she turned me gently to undo my braid. "Maybe he's an outlaw or a pirate or . . . or . . . or maybe he's some banished prince from a faraway kingdom! Maybe you're destined to wed one another." After she finished with my hair, she stood, crossed the room, and returned with my dressing robe.

"No," I chewed on my lip as I thought, "I'm sure that's not it. Anyway, another prince is not the answer. Another wedding is *not* the answer." I began to change into my dressing gown and pictured Elliot once more, my blade—its silver length etched with curling whorls and swirls intermixed with Mittelan's signature swans—poised over his heart. There had been something comforting about him, something familiar, as if I'd known him for years. His eyes had been wide, shining, yet almost guilty, before they had dropped in the nod of concession.

Maybe Emily was right about one thing, maybe he was hiding something.

"Ems!" An idea came to me so fast it stopped me in my tracks, halfway into my robe, "That's exactly it! He *is* hiding something. And what do all the peasants hide from nobility?"

"A better question is what *don't* they hide," she quipped.

"No . . . be serious," I said. "You all share a secret. Something *I* only know because *you* can't keep secrets from me."

"Well maybe I should start," she muttered to herself before realizing exactly what I was talking about. Her hand flew to cover her open mouth. "The Woodland Games!" she exclaimed. "The Games . . ." she began piecing it together in her mind, "the Games are a secret from nobles, so what secret would a *peasant* fighter have to keep from those betting on him in the Games?"

I could tell she already knew the answer to her own question, but I answered anyway. "He's not a peasant at all!" My smile stretched wide across my face, so relieved to finally have figured out the mystery that was Elliot Cendrilon.

"He's a noble," Emily's words hung in the air for a moment, shock coursing through us both.

But I thought I knew every noble in the kingdom. How could I have missed one who was almost my age? Especially one who was not *entirely* unpleasant to look at.

"That's why he isn't in the conscription ledgers," I said. "He can't be conscripted at all. And that's why none of the peasants know his surname, he doesn't *want* them to know." It was such a simple answer but posed a much more difficult question. How could I make him help me if he couldn't be conscripted?

"Well, there is a ledger in the study of the nobility and the lands they control," Emily said, "I've seen it a hundred times while fetching books for your tutors. He should be listed there. But you can't just draft him, Char, not if he's noble."

"I know," I said, fear knotting in my stomach.

Emily crossed and uncrossed her legs as she thought, the whole time biting feverishly on the nail of her thumb.

I chewed my lip, going through a million possibilities in my mind. "What if we—" I began but Emily cut me off.

"No, Chara," she said, staring fixedly at me through wide green eyes, "I know what you should do."

CHAPTER SIX

ELLIOT

My sheets were soaked through with blood when I woke only hours later. I couldn't move—thought that perhaps I would never move again. The pain was more crippling than anything I'd ever faced in the arena, like strikes of lightning still crackling across my back.

But the pain wasn't what woke me.

"Where's my breakfast?" Raymond whined. Sunlight streamed in from the windows on either side of the fireplace. Not the gauzy colors of the sunrise as when I normally woke, but bright, incriminating sunbeams. I'd overslept.

I couldn't stifle the deep moan of agony as I rolled over on the small cot, the old, unraveling blanket still stuck to my bloody back. I put my bare toes on the freezing floor and forced myself to stand. I looked through the cased opening to the dining room to find a blurry Raymond, Lucas, and Silas, all watching me force myself out of bed. Raymond was, rather unsuccessfully, trying to hide a snicker and Lucas looked almost as if he were holding back tears of laughter, the smile not yet reaching his lips.

"Apologies," I bit back the pain and reached for my socks and boots sitting at the end of my cot and pulled them on. I grabbed a somewhat clean tunic from my small stack of belongings. I tied the leather pouch to my trousers, not able to forget Millie despite the rush. "I didn't hear you wake. I'll fetch the eggs," I mumbled, "be right back."

"Obviously," Raymond said. I threw a glance back at them to find Silas's glare steely and Lucas straight faced. Raymond had a gleeful sneer plastered between his cheeks, his eyes lit with joy. I ignored his snide remark as I stumbled through the foyer, out the open door, and headed towards the well.

I washed my wounds as quickly as I could and bandaged them with some scrap fabric I kept in the barn. It wasn't the first time I'd found myself in similar circumstances, although rarely this severe.

The trees around Beauhaven had light-green buds prickling their branches, and the sight brought me the smallest ounce of comfort. My ancestors had planted those trees, and still they bloomed for me each spring. My great-grandfather had built a border fence of rock and mortar beyond the small peach grove. Stone grave markers ran along the inside edge of the wall dating all the way back to Alexandre Cendrilon, to whom the estate was gifted.

Silas had at least had the decency to make a headstone for my mother, even if he had insisted on burying her on the other end of the property from my father. After Millie died, I hand carved a stone and placed it over an empty grave beside Mother.

Tending this land, and eventually being laid to rest on it, was the only peace I saw in my future. Beauhaven was my nest egg, my only hope in this hopeless world.

Scars. Bruises. Blood. Loss. All the hurt was like a current, pulling me under and out to sea. And so I clung even tighter to my lifeline: the day in my future when this place would be mine again, when it would be safe once more. *Someday.*

Soon, Millie, I touched her tiny leather grave secured to my waist. *'Someday' will be here soon.*

The dozen chickens clucked loudly in their modest lean-to henhouse off the side of the barn. I lifted the hatch above their nests to find seven eggs, two still warm. Barely enough for breakfast, but enough. "Who's slacking, girls?" I muttered under my breath and the largest of the red chickens squawked loudly her response. I collected a handful of eggs before I realized that I'd been in such a hurry that I had forgotten to bring a bowl or a basket. I grabbed the edge of my tunic and stowed the eggs gently in the make-shift pouch. I secured the hatch closed again and rushed back towards the house.

"Well you're certainly off somewhere in a hurry," said an unfamiliar voice. I turned suddenly, startled.

Three eggs slipped out of my tunic and fell, shells shattering and insides oozing into the pebbled pathway. "Dammit!" I yelled, seeing my hopes at a breakfast smashed onto the stones. One of the broken eggs even had two yolks. I muttered a string of curses.

"Oh, I'm sorry. The gate…" the voice came again, "…the

gate was open."

"Ah, yes, my mistake," I mumbled bitterly, clutching the remaining eggs tightly—but gently—up against me. I looked up to the stranger and was surprised to find a young woman.

"Oh, here, let me help."

We both spotted a fourth egg I hadn't seen fall laying unbroken in the grass. The stranger bent over and grabbed it for me. She had on a simple handmaiden's dress and apron. The tattered wool coat she wore was unbuttoned down the front. Her face was speckled with dirt and ash, much like mine, but that didn't disguise the fact that she was quite intriguing.

She placed the egg back in the pouch of my shirt. I could feel heat rise in my cheeks. I bent my shoulders down awkwardly, trying to keep my tunic covering the whole of my abdomen.

"Thank you," I said. The sun was nearing overhead, far past breakfast time. Silas didn't like to be kept waiting, and I didn't want to do anything to raise his suspicions. "Are you here to see Monsieur Tremaine?"

"No, I—"

"Well, then. You said the gate was left open, so I expect you can see yourself out of it." There wasn't any more time for questions or answers or pleasantries.

I cradled the precious few remaining eggs and turned back to the house. A pang stormed through my back at the sudden action and I fought to mask my pain.

"Elliot?" the woman asked, but I didn't stop. If she was a peasant here to bemoan my loss in the arena—I knew many people had lost their wages in the last match—I didn't have time for this, and her presence would only raise Silas's suspicions. I couldn't afford that right now, so I kept walking. "Sir Elliot Cendrilon?"

My surname stopped me in my tracks. And hearing the title in front of it, all the color drained from my face. She knew my full name; and what was worse—she undoubtedly knew my station.

"Who's asking?" I responded cryptically. I was born a noble, into a knighted family, but I didn't deserve such a title. I had not earned my knighthood and she had no right to call me *Sir.*

I hesitated but slowly turned back to face the woman. She didn't look like she was here to accuse me of fighting in a tournament I didn't belong in. Her eyes glimmered, and I could tell she believed me to be the man she asked for. And she was happy about it.

"I am," she responded simply, vaguely. For the moment, it seemed she wished to retain her anonymity as well.

"Ah. Well, *miss,* I haven't time to poke around names with you. I have a master whose breakfast is late and I don't want to be at the end of his belt if I make it any later. Please, see yourself out." Her face fell, but I ignored it, instead picking up my pace back to the cottage.

Upon crossing the threshold, I hardly had a moment to think about the girl who'd wandered onto my family's estate. I opened the door and Raymond snapped, "What took you so long? Did our chickens escape to Katyō and you had to go hunt them down? Did you have to battle the hens for their eggs?" He chuckled at his supposed wit.

I said nothing and took straight to the kitchen and began cracking the eggs. I knew immediately there was not enough for us all to have some. Regardless, I whisked them, fried them, and divided them evenly onto three plates.

"That's it?" Raymond poked the small helping of eggs with his fork. Lucas looked up at me quizzically and then began picking at his eggs slowly. He took a few small bites and then sat back, twiddling his thumbs under the table.

"We may have to slaughter these chickens if they don't start producing more." Silas unfolded his napkin and placed it on his lap.

"Maybe they just had an off day," I suggested, remembering the four yolks laid to waste on the pebble pathway. I immediately regretted speaking. All three pairs of eyes were on me.

"You couldn't get up in time to dress yourself properly before making us breakfast?" Silas's eyes came to rest on blood seeping through my bandages and onto my tunic. He pulled out his pocket watch and clicked it open. "Although, it's so late, you may as well start on lunch."

"Yes, *brother*, you look exhausted," Raymond sneered, "perhaps you should start trying to get to bed at a more reasonable hour." His lips turned up with a maniacal twitch. I shifted in apprehension. What did he know? What had Silas told him? "And what's all over your clothes?" he went on, "Soot? Manure? Have you taken to actually sleeping in the fire nowadays? Or perhaps out in the *barn*?" He narrowed his eyes.

I swallowed a retort and forced myself to say calmly, "Well, there is more jerky and some vegetables left for lunch, but if you would like fresh meat for dinner, I need to hunt today."

How would I hunt with fresh wounds on my back? At least it was the season for small game, and—despite my aching pains, the biting cold of the early spring day, and the fever that

I felt rising at my temples—it was far superior to staying here with them. Stuffing quills under my fingernails sounded more appealing than a day at my step-family's beck and call.

"But Father," Raymond put the hilt of his fork on the table and beat it there as he complained. "I wanted Elliot to shine my boots today and repair my suit coat. I can't go to Swanstone with you tomorrow looking like country scum."

"Elliot will do it when he is home from hunting," Silas turned his attention to me, "And Elliot, good boy, I am quite tired of rabbit. But I do have a particular taste for venison right now, so let's do that for dinner."

No problem, master. I'll just walk right out to our private hunting grounds, shoot you a prized stag, and carry it home strapped to my butchered back in time for dinner. It would be my honor.

"I'll do my best, sir." I turned on my heel, but I wasn't fast enough.

"And, Elliot," Silas cut his eggs with a knife and popped a bite into his mouth, "Let's do dinner at seven hours past noon. Promptly," he smiled cordially.

It was all I could do not to grab the knife from his hand and use it to remove his eyes from their sockets.

"Yes, sir."

Once they had finished eating, they stood to leave when Raymond noticed two or three bites of egg left on Lucas's plate. "A pathetic helping like the one we got this morning and you're not even going to finish them?" Raymond asked his brother incredulously, bending to finish them.

"I found some shell in them," Lucas shrugged.

Raymond dropped the plate back to the table. "Wow, the oaf can't even crack an egg right," he said as he walked over to the fainting couch and plopped down. He looked at me from under arched brows, "Don't worry, oaf, soon eggs will be the least of your worries."

I ignored his goading and instead set the plate of eggs on the kitchen table. I dug through the small remainder of the helping with a fork, unable to find a single piece of shell. I shoved them into my mouth in one bite.

CHAPTER SEVEN

CHARA

It had been Emily's idea for me to wear her clothes and to put the ashes on my face, and together we had formulated the perfect cover story. But our perfect plan was falling apart. How could I persuade Elliot to help me if he wouldn't give me more than a minute to speak with him?

I huffed in annoyance as I exited through the gate, scrunching the dirty skirt in my hands. The iron gave a high-pitched squeal as I forced the gate closed, ending with the click of the latch as it fell into place, shut tight, just as it had been when I'd arrived.

I glanced back at the small estate as I made my way back to where I had tied Stell to a tree in the woods nearby.

There were no fields to toil on the Cendrilon estate. No mill or herd of cows to milk. There was nothing to generate income for the small household. It was just a small home on a wooded lot, with a barn, a carriage house, and some wire fencing for the chickens.

I'd read in the ledger that the land had been gifted to the Cendrilon family by my great-great grandfather when Elliot's ancestor turned the tides of the Battle at Beaufort against Almora, our neighbors across the sea. It mentioned that his ingenuity as a naval commander took down three key ships.

Many knighted families received much less, some lived in even worse conditions than their peasant counterparts. But it was still not much more than a place to live. Was this why the man pretended to be a peasant to fight in the Games? To feed his family? Would he not rather volunteer to fight for Mittelan and earn a stipend for his family as a soldier? Perhaps then he could afford a clean tunic rather than one covered in dirt and who knows what else.

The reason for Elliot and his family's poverty didn't matter to me; it would make him even easier for me to manipulate. He had no reason to stay and would certainly be motivated by the prize I was to offer for his services.

Only a few hours ago, I had left the castle under a sweet peach sunrise with one goal in my mind: convince Elliot to join me.

I'd already failed once.

The failure weighed me down like lead in my boots. I wanted to turn around, march back through that gate, and bang on his door. Could I force him to hear me out, or would the repeated disruptions only anger him? What other choice did I have?

I reached Stell, petting a hand down her long dappled grey hair. *Did I really come all this way—risk my mother's wrath, enter the*

Woodland Games, and escape the castle in my maid's dress—all for nothing?

No. I turned to head back to the Cendrilon estate when the wrought iron gate swung open with a fierce clatter as it banged against the stone wall from which it hung. Intuitively, I ducked behind Stell, but the maneuver was unnecessary. Elliot slammed the gate behind him, swung onto his steed, and rode in the opposite direction from where I hid. His gaze remained fixed on the forest ahead of him, bow tucked dutifully at his side.

CHAPTER EIGHT

ELLIOT

The weapon, a simple arch of wood and tightly wound cord, ached for a kill. I sympathized. How easy it would be to pull back that bowstring and release an arrow straight through Silas's black heart. Every spasm of pain that sparked across my back brought more and more hatred. I dug my heels into Gus and drove him on, deeper into the woods.

The shade and hum of the woods left plenty of room for my mind to run wild. *I shouldn't be here,* I thought repeatedly, *I should be training.* I flashed back to the moment I ceded to the armored stranger, then to my mother on her deathbed, to Millie in the woods, and then back to the arena. The pouch at my hip reminded me constantly of all that my shortcomings had cost. I couldn't lose again. I grit my teeth, wondering how or when I would train again.

But I would take the berating silence of the woods over waiting on my step-family any day, even if I were only here to hunt a prized stag for my *master.*

Fresh leaves burst from empty branches as the air finally felt crisp rather than bitter. Spring was here. Gus slowed as the trees grew closer together, and I pushed training from my mind. I needed to let my body begin to heal from the lashing before I could even consider a way to resume my training.

"Whoa," I pulled gently on Gus's reins to bring him to a stop. I tied him to a narrow pine tree whose branches were high and I could easily thread the reins around the trunk. I caught a whiff of butterscotch from the tree's sap on my hands.

I continued on foot. The evergreens blocked out most of the sun with their dense, emerald needles. A rabbit darted in front of my path and I ignored him, even though the thought of roasting him on a spit made my mouth water. It was too early in the day to give in to small game, even as my stomach rumbled at the thought of it.

As the world beyond the forest fell away my ears pricked to attention, noticing every robin's chirp or rustle of a squirrel. The slop of each footstep. The crunch on a patch of ice. The low cracks of thirsty branches threatened by the wind above me.

The snow had not entirely melted in the deep woods yet and my threadbare boots sunk in the slush. I shouldn't be hunting a deer in the spring, when they were skeletal from winter. But I had noticed scarce patches of grass had already fought their way through the cold and ice. Perhaps the deer had at least some food. If Silas wanted the tough meat of a skinny deer on his table tonight, so be it.

I walked deeper into the forest, the cool dampness swaddling me in its embrace. The forest sounds faded into the background of my consciousness as I scoured the area for signs of activity. I noticed rubbings on some tree trunks and, though they were obviously old, they reminded me that deer frequented this area.

I wandered towards the rippling brook, its icy snowmelt the deer's main water source, as it was mine. I bent down on its shore and cupped a handful of the glacial water and sucked it out of my hand quickly before it could disappear through the cracks between my fingers.

Shaking my hands dry, I returned to my hunt. I was far enough into the forest now that if Gus stamped or neighed, I wouldn't know, yet still I traveled farther. After over an hour of searching, I found a narrow path of stamped down ferns. The deer run was muddy and small, probably only traveled by a lone buck. I followed the path as it wound through groves and meadows, further and further away from civilization.

Away from Silas, his sons, and his belt.

Away from Parren and the constant desire to be training that barraged my thoughts.

I nearly lost the run three times, and each time it took a good while to find it once more. Finally, the run increased in width, now a large path used by multiple deer and probably other animals as well. I quieted my sigh of relief. My toes were freezing in my sopping socks. The sun had made its way past high noon and was on its retreat. I had already been in the woods for hours, but the deer had to be close now. Maybe with a stroke of luck, I could actually meet Silas's deadline for supper.

I followed the widened path, my eyes searching for more tracks, any more signs of the animals.

There. A dropped antler. It protruded from a patch of slushy snow, melting in a rogue patch of sunlight streaming through a leafless oak. The rodents hadn't begun to gnaw on the antler yet, so it was probably from this winter. I walked by it, picking it up and stashing it in my pack. It may be worth a gold or two at market.

I looked back up at the game trail and found a set of tracks. Fresh. Although I could not guarantee they were deer, as they did not hold their shape in the muddy snow, it seemed likely.

I followed the tracks between the trees, ducking to avoid low branches and climbing over fallen ones that I imagined the deer leaping over with ease. The tracks ended in an abandoned section of brush that had been bedded down. The crushed vegetation was covered in brownish gray hair. He was molting. His pelt would be worth more now, if he'd finished growing in the red-brown spring coat.

I was so close.

A branch snapped. I didn't move.

I looked around for signs of movement. Nothing. Slowly and quietly I turned my back towards one of the trees surrounding the animal's bed. My back made contact with the bark and the rough scratch brought my injuries back in full force. I breathed in sharply and pressed my lips together to quiet the groan of pain. I shifted, leaning into the tree as gently as I could. It creaked softly.

I waited.

Dead silence hummed in my ears and I squinted into the black between the trees, searching, begging, for movement.

There. Something brown passed between low-hanging branches, and I prayed it was the fat rump of a doe. Or a malnourished buck—at this point, I didn't care. I could already see the roast on the table with the carrots, potatoes, and onions I had canned in the fall. I drew an arrow and fitted it to my bow.

I waited, craning to see the ribcage under which its heart beat, about to be ceased by my arrow. The figure moved again, and I pulled the arrow back.

"Don't shoot."

The girl stepped out from her hiding place behind the tree and held her hands up in front of her in surrender. As if it'd been her that I was hunting. Her doe eyes pleaded with me not to kill her.

"Dammit, woman! What are you doing out here?" My voice raised, eliminating any chance of finding food within a mile's radius of where I stood, but I couldn't help it. I stood facing the same curious girl who'd been at the estate that morning.

She dropped her hands to her hips. "What are *you* doing pointing your weapon at me?"

My bow was still drawn. I let the string fall slack and dropped the bow to my side. "You're lucky I didn't kill you! I thought you were a buck. I almost shot you!" I stamped my foot, realizing my chances of avoiding another lashing this evening were slipping away by the minute. My temper boiled, even as an ounce of relief bubbled among it that I hadn't accidentally killed the woman. But still, I glared at her. "And thank you very much for that," I snapped, "now there is no way I will be having any dinner tonight, which is just what I like after a wonderful day of enjoying next to nothing to eat."

"I'm sorry," she spat back, her tone indicating that she was anything but sorry, "but I needed to talk to you, and you were quite rude this morning and didn't give me the chance."

"Oh!" I feigned surprise, "*I* was rude! My apologies, *m'lady*, that I didn't roll out the carpet and invite you in for breakfast when you intruded on my family's lands!" I was shouting at her now, and she stepped back in surprise. All the frustration I had about my unfeasible task, about Silas and Raymond, and even about my recent defeat, came pouring out of me like a broken dam and I was powerless to stop it. "I've been tracking all day and now what do I have to show for it? Nothing! Thanks to you. What are you even doing here? Did you follow me?"

"Are you Sir Elliot Cendrilon?" she asked, seemingly unfazed by my temper. So yes, I could assume she'd followed me.

"Who are you?" I countered.

"Sir Cendrilon, I—"

"Stop calling me that!" I stepped towards her aggressively but she didn't budge. I felt my lip quiver. Until today, I'd only ever heard that name and title in reference to my father. It hurt more than I could have expected, this time worse than this morning. Not just because I missed him and I wished he was here, but because I wasn't the man he was. Not by half.

Perhaps I never would be. Perhaps I'd never be knighted but would go on in life just like Silas, hiding out in my own safety and thinking myself better than others because one of my ancestors had done something heroic. I was not yet worthy of the title, *Sir Cendrilon.* It was my father's, not mine. The comparison of myself to Silas made me nearly ill.

Maybe the young woman had felt my anger shift to pain because she stopped talking. I backed up to the tree and leaned my shoulder into the bark. Soon enough I fell to a knee, then sat down in the cold slush.

After a pause, she continued, but more hesitantly, "I'm sorry I surprised you this morning. And I'm sorry I followed you here and that I disrupted your hunt. I—I mean, my mistress—will get food for your family—"

"They're not my family," I corrected her, spite sharpening my tongue, even as the cold snow soaked my pants.

She ignored the steel in my voice and reached out a calming hand while closing the distance between us. Her hands were small and free of calluses. Her hips were round and full. She must be a very well-treated handmaiden.

"My mistress can get you whatever you need. As soon as you need it. But she…" the woman tapered off. She was close to me now, and when she knelt, she was so close I could have reached out a hand and touched the pale pink of her cheek. And yet, she was the one who reached for me.

I ignored her outstretched hand and pushed myself to standing. Who was this woman and what gave her such a right to ruin my day two times over?

Her hand fell to her side. "I . . . I've come to ask . . . Sir Cendrilon, I've come to ask for your help," she stuttered at first but now she was picking up speed. She set her chin and asked confidently, "I've come to ask you to go to war."

CHAPTER NINE

CHARA

He didn't say anything. He just stood there, stupefied by my request. I knew he needed more explanation, but I wanted him to speak first. I waited, not letting my eyes fall away from his gem-like gaze, where specks of gold reflected against the green like the sunrise in drops of dew on the morning leaf.

After a long moment, he reached his hand up to his hard jaw, rubbing along it and then burying his face briefly in his palm. "You called me 'Sir,'" he said at last.

I nodded.

"Then you must know that, regardless of how it may look, I am nobility. I cannot be conscripted."

"And I am not the queen. I am not *telling* you to go to war. I am *asking* for your help."

He stepped even closer to me and I suddenly realized how

tall he was. Probably at least a foot taller than me. He was different here than he was in the arena. Unpredictable. Dangerous.

I didn't have my sword, and he didn't have his, but he was armed: a bow in his hand and a hunting knife dangling from the belt around his tunic.

"Who are you that you would follow me into these distant, silent woods, woefully unafraid, and ask me to put my life on the line, and for what? For you? A perfect stranger?" He hardened his jaw. "And don't bother with the cryptic responses like when we first met. The last thing I will do is agree to help you if I don't know who you are or what you are asking of me."

He leaned down, and I could feel his breath on my cheeks, warm and damp compared to the cold darkness rolling off the trees. Patches of light infiltrated the small clearing where we stood, sending his face into a chilling array of shadows and light. Unease slithered up my spine. His silky blond hair was trimmed just past his brows, face shaven except for a shadow of fair scruff along a firm, sharp jaw.

I swallowed my nerves and began, "My name is Kiera and I work for a very powerful family in Swanstone. We um, well we need your help. We . . . " I tried to go on but rising panic began to blur my thoughts, afraid that he would see right through my facade. "See, I . . ." I was mumbling now, about to ruin my only shot.

And then a vision of a white gown hanging in my wardrobe beside all of my packed trunks flashed in my mind. I would not get another chance. I summoned the confidence that had brought me my win in the arena, and I began again. "You see, my mistress' brother volunteered—very nobly, I might add—

to fight in the borderwar on behalf of Mittelan. Well, three months ago, his messages just stopped, out of nowhere. Before that, he had never missed a response. Monsieur Roberto Pentamerone is a very consistent man. An honest, *consistent* man. So when my mistress's letters began to go unrequited, she decided to take action." The well-constructed tale sizzled with the pain and ache of truth, just as I had hoped it would. "My mistress cannot begin to believe he is dead."

The deep wrinkle of his eyebrows returned, Elliot was just as perplexed as he had been at his loss in the arena. "And now you want me to travel to the front lines to . . . what? Rescue a stranger among leagues of soldiers?" He tilted his head subconsciously as he attempted to puzzle out my lies.

I lifted my shoulders, "Well, sort of—"

"No." He turned sharply and began to walk away.

"Well, let me finish!" I yelled after him, but he continued to stalk away from me, into the cover of the forest.

"It's a good cause," I went on as I followed him, "you can help reunite my mistress's family."

He kept walking.

"She can pay you."

He climbed deftly over the trunk of a fallen tree.

"Eight thousand slips."

He stopped. He didn't turn and face me, but I knew why he stopped. I knew full-well what eight thousand slips could mean to a man who worked for a living. Even if the tiara my mother made me wear was worth double that, eight thousand slips could buy a decade's worth of food from the market in Swanstone. It could buy pounds of fresh meat and barrels of dried vegetables, even in the winter. It could buy spices imported from Almora. A peasant could eat like a nobleman for years. Eight thousand slips was no small prize.

I finally caught up with him, tripping as the hem of my dress caught on a briar. It ripped and I stumbled, but righted myself quickly as I hurried in front of him and whirled to face him.

He immediately began questioning me, "So you're telling me that your 'mistress' will pay me eight thousand slips to go to the war front and look for her brother?"

I cringed a bit at the lie on his lips—*my* lie—but attempted to hide it.

He went on, "Not even to be a soldier? Just to *look* for this man?"

"Yes." I knew that answer was riddled with deceit, but I was desperate. I needed someone to protect me on the journey to the border. And someone to stay at my right hand in battle, if it came to it, would be preferable. Certainly he would be willing to fight when the time came, once he learned who I was. Together we could end this war and the foolish alliance with it. We had to.

I had to. Or I had to die trying.

"Why me?" he asked, "With that sum at her disposal, certainly your mistress could hire one of the Queen's Guards to go."

"No!" I answered too quickly, "I mean, my mistress has tried. They cannot spare a soul. But I . . . I saw you fight at the Woodland Games, and I told my mistress about you."

He shook his head. "Your mistress shouldn't even know about the Games, miss. You could get us all in a lot of trouble. She has the wrong guy. *You* have the wrong guy," he turned from me and began to walk away once more. But then he stopped and looked back over his shoulder at me, "If you saw me there, then you should know—I didn't even win."

"I know," I fought to keep the pride swelling within me from taking the shape of a smile on my lips, but I felt them turn despite myself as I confessed, "I know that you lost. I know because I was there. *I* was the one who fought you, and . . ."

All the depths of the black forest settled into the weight of my words, "I won. *I* was the armored victor of the peasant's forbidden Woodland Games. And that is why you will feel confident in having me at your side on your journey to the borderwar."

He laughed. The sound rang up through the trees causing the birds to flee from their nests. He wrapped his arm across his stomach and threw his head back. He slapped himself across a knee, laughing the whole while.

Then he stopped laughing and his tone grew dark. "It's not kind to tease me, madam."

My cheeks grew hot at the insult, my eyes narrowed to slits. In a split second, I closed the gap between us, pulled his hunting knife from his belt, did three quarters of a turn, and positioned the blade against the small of his back. His arm was pinned firmly between us, held steady with my free hand. He hadn't had time to move, and now he didn't dare. I let the knife's point pierce his tunic and prick the skin behind it so he knew I was there. So he knew what I was capable of.

"Whoa, whoa, whoa," he choked, "I believe you, I believe you."

I held him there, trapped. I had now bested him twice. His breathing quickened, beads of sweat rising on his nape.

I pushed him away with my forearm, and he turned to look at me, eyes wide with surprise and smoldering resentment. They came to rest on the ring on my finger, still wound tightly around the knife's handle. Any trace of doubt left his gaze.

I threw his knife into the air, and he caught it by the handle. "Together we'd be unstoppable." My voice was steady now, sharpened by my desperation and focus. I saw only forward, my way to battle, my way out of a marriage that would forever relegate me to a position of constant subjugation. Everything had led me here, to him, to my new life.

He lifted the knife in his hand, pointing it at me. "*You*," he glared from under the shadow of his long eyelashes, as his gaze ran up and down my form, still in disbelief that *I* had bested *him*. *Twice.* The wonder from only a moment before melted into something that looked a close kin to hatred, his features shifting to steel. "*You* were the man who beat Emmerich Thayer in fifteen seconds in full armor?"

I nodded.

I held up a finger of correction, "*Wo*-man, actually." His eyes narrowed further. "*Woman*, not man," I clarified, pointing to myself in an obvious, jesting manner. But apparently the issue was still too fresh for jokes because the thin line of his lips did not betray any hint of a smile.

"You used your first three fights to look like you barely knew what you were doing," he accused, "and then you practically slayed Thayer? And then me?"

This time I didn't nod. He wasn't asking, he already knew.

"You tricked us. You tricked me! You don't show your face—you don't even claim the prize? Do you have any idea what that kind of money means for some of us? It's the difference between life and death, feast and famine, slavery and freedom . . ." He clenched his teeth and his cheeks flamed as scarlet as a hot coal in the black of ash. "I practically kill myself training for these Games and then you come along, when I was finally so close, so damn close, and then you . . . hiding behind your fancy armor . . . you ruin it all. And now you show up—"

"I didn't trick you," I interrupted him, matter of fact, "I won fair and square."

He let out an angry huff, chin rigid, teeth clenched. For a moment I thought he might charge at me.

"Don't do anything you will regret, Sir Cendrilon," I kept my voice calm even as my heart raced. I had no idea people felt this strongly about the Games. Or that he would harbor so much resentment for my having beaten him at his hobby. I could feel my face grow hot as well, even in the cold forest that was quickly slipping towards evening, "Are you angry because you lost, or angry because you lost to a woman?"

He rolled his eyes like the tempestuous child that Mother always accused me of having been. It almost made me smile, but his raised voice kept me from it. "I'm angry because I *needed* that money, and if you left your winnings behind, you obviously did not. So why come ruin everything for those of us to whom it actually matters?" A vein rose in his forehead, and his voice dropped to a pained and desperate whisper. His lips trembled with barely concealed fury.

I refused to pull away from him, to show any sign of weakness. I refused to feel guilty for beating him in a stupid betting match. Fair and square. "If it's money you need, accept my mistress's offer. You will make more in one journey, one quest, than you ever would have in the arena."

I had no idea if he would accept, no idea if my statement was even true. He paced side to side, between a naked poplar and a pine with snow still clinging to its needles. He walked the same line, over and over, occasionally sending me another boiling scowl. I watched him deliberate my offer and then baffle at his loss with renewed perplexity, again and again.

"I want nothing to do with you," he spat eventually, "but . . . but I will consider your offer. But first, you must answer me one question. You're doing all of this for the brother of your mistress. *One* man. Why? Why risk so much for the life of *one* man?"

"He is one *good* man." I kept my chin high, eyes open and honest, even as the lie threatened to pull my gaze down.

He stopped pacing and faced me. "I need a deer. Immediately."

I nodded, "My mistress will get you one." I put a hand on his forearm, "Please do consider our offer."

He pulled away from me sharply and looked up between the branches at the slowly disappearing light. "The deer, miss. Just get me the deer."

❖❖❖

I probably would have gotten lost trying to find my way back to Stell had I not followed Elliot back out of the woods. He didn't say another word to me. And although he didn't speak, I could feel the anger coming off of him in waves as I followed behind him through the slushy, icy brush. I'd tied Stell close to where I'd seen Elliot's horse tied outside the forest. It had taken me all day to find him again in the maze of the woods. I'd braced myself to hear him reject my offer and I'd been prepared to persuade him.

But I had not anticipated the sheer loathing that would come from him finding out he'd lost to me. He'd seemed surprised that day in the arena, dazed even, but he had taken the loss with grace. It didn't even occur to me that the prize money meant more to anyone than simply a victory prize.

When I returned to Stell, I rode her as fast as I could back into Swanstone. Elliot agreed to meet me at sunset with the venison, giving him less than an hour to have it on the table. I would do anything to convince him to accept my offer, and that meant making up for ruining his hunt. I found what I needed in town and rode hurriedly back to our designated meeting place.

The sun was already perched on the horizon when I arrived at the mill, but he was not there. My memory was still haunted by his cold voice, *they're not my family*. And yet, he certainly worked very hard to feed them and feed them well, whoever they were. The warm spices of the fresh roast I'd purchased in town tempted even me. I could not imagine how it would smell to someone who had not had a proper meal in days.

I hadn't had time or an excuse to request the roast from the castle kitchen, so I'd bought it from a small pub on the outside of town. It was all the food they had made for the evening, but I offered double what it was worth and eventually they agreed to give me the whole thing.

I looked over the crest of the hill, down the road that led

to his family's estate, silently praying that this roast would be enough to convince him of my trustworthiness and agree to help me. Finally, his large brown horse trotted over the hill, and I released a sigh of relief. I hadn't realized I was so nervous that he wouldn't come, that his answer would be *no*, and that I would never see him again.

The large waterwheel turned in Chartley River, which flowed down the mountain range surrounding Swanstone and then southwest towards the ocean. The huge wheel was off a small country road, west of the city, between the capitol and Elliot's family's estate. It was the easiest landmark near to his home and town for us to meet and still give me time to ride back into Swanstone before Mother sent out the guard for me.

Elliot stopped his horse in front of me and jumped down. "I don't have time for pleasantries, Miss . . . Kiera, wasn't it?" He didn't wait for me to answer. He pointed to the wooden crate I was holding, "Is that it?"

I nodded, "Yes, and tomorrow I will bring you the meat of an entire deer. Cured, made into jerky, or raw, however you want. And gold, double the worth of a pelt. I will bring it all to your estate and you can give me your final answer then. When should I come?"

"Late," he answered shortly, "midnight. Tomorrow night." He took the box from my arms and nodded curtly. "Your mistress must be very powerful indeed. To get you a whole venison at the drop of a hat."

His words rolled with skepticism, and I feared I'd heard his answer already. I felt him declining my request in his harshness, but I ignored it. I held onto the glimmer of hope as if it were a rope from which I was dangling above a pit of dark despair. He had not yet said no. He could still say yes. He had to say yes.

"Yes, sir," I said, "my mistress is very powerful indeed. But oftentimes the most powerful find themselves powerless. She needs you." It was the most honest thing I'd said to him all day.

The powerful are powerless. Like me, if this marriage alliance were to take place as planned.

He balanced the roast in one arm and used the other to swing back up onto his horse. "Tomorrow," he confirmed, "I will expect the rest of the deer tomorrow." He whipped the horse's reins with his free hand and disappeared over the crest of the hill along with the final shred of the sun.

I walked back to Stell, glancing back at the empty sunset. "Tomorrow."

CHAPTER TEN

ELLIOT

The sweet juices of the roast dripped down my face, and I let them. Its salty aroma surrounded me with fresh rosemary and garlic, ingredients I hadn't been bothered with for years. It fell apart in my hands as I stuffed each delicious and gamey bite into my mouth, swirling my tongue and chewing the meat as long as possible. The carrots and potatoes were soft and saturated in the deer's juices, and I couldn't shovel them into my mouth quickly enough.

Less than an hour ago, I'd pulled the roast from the roaring fire in one of our own pans at the toll of seven o'clock, right as Silas walked down the staircase from his study. Luckily, no one had seen me put it there only ten minutes before.

Raymond complained that it was not hot enough and Lucas looked skeptical that I had somehow managed to meet Silas's unreasonable request; but, thankfully, he said nothing. Silas ate quietly, as I waited in the corner of the dining room, saliva rising off my tongue. I fetched them water as they needed it, and salt. When they asked where I had gotten the deer, I told them all about my hunt, replacing Kiera with a broad buck that I'd shot straight through the heart. I'd told them the rest of the deer was still at the butcher.

"You could have done the skinning and the gutting yourself," Silas admonished, "and saved the expense."

"Yes, sir, but there wasn't time if I was to have it on the table by dinner," I lied. "But I will remember that for next time."

"Good," he said as he buttered a piece of bread to sop up the gravy.

My stomach rumbled.

"We must be diligent with both our time and our money," Silas said with raised eyebrows and a stern jaw, "we ought not waste either. We are family, and our actions should benefit the whole of us."

Raymond smiled wide, as if anticipating something.

The pair of them were acting awfully strange, but I did not dare ask Silas what he was talking about. So I simply nodded and continued to feel grateful that at least none of them had seen me ride onto the grounds less than a half hour before their roast was in front of them on the dining room table.

After they'd eaten and I had packaged up three bowls of the roast for the icebox, I put the unsettling dinner conversation out of my mind to enjoy the first proper meal I'd had in a very long time. I served myself the largest portion I dared. We'd have to eat the leftovers before all the snow melted or there would be nothing to keep them from spoiling, but dinner would be taken care of for the entire week to come. When my food was gone,

I licked the juices off of my fingers and slurped from the bowl, letting the last of the gravy drip into my mouth.

That blasted girl may have cost me a real breakfast, but she had certainly made up for it with dinner. I stood up from the table and added my dish to the rest. If only she'd live up to her promise and bring the rest of a deer tomorrow. I took the large bucket we stowed under the sink and headed to the well for wash water. She had been honest about delivering the roast, why not the rest?

Of course, then I would have to refuse her offer, which I wasn't exactly looking forward to. There was simply no way I was going to come to her aid after she'd hustled me in the arena, stolen my victory, and risked my entire future by showing up at my home. I couldn't even look at her without boiling. I didn't trust her. How could I go all the way to the northern border with her? Why would I put myself in danger for her and her mistress? And what if they didn't even pay up at the end of it all?

Plus, I didn't need her money. She wouldn't dare show up at the Woodland Games again, not now that I knew who she was. I could win my money back in a handful of matches and be done with Silas soon enough.

The only light on the estate streamed from the candles in the manor's windowsills. The moon hid behind thick, dark clouds, flirting on the edge of storms, coating the world in black. But I didn't need light to know my way to the well and back; I'd made the trek hundreds of times.

I hooked the bucket to the suspended rope and turned the crank to lower it further into darkness. It plopped onto the water's surface, and I heard the whoosh as the water replaced the bucket's void. My muscles rippled and the lashings on my back screamed as I cranked the bucket back up from the depths of the well and unhooked it from its tether.

Tomorrow, I would meet the girl to retrieve the rest of the venison and then I would give her my answer. I was going to stay here, with my parent's estate, and continue to fight like hell for it. *Someday* was just around the corner. This home would be safe again. And maybe, just maybe, it would be a place of joy once more.

A high-pitched squeal severed me from the new training regimen that had already started running through my mind. I looked around for the source of the sound but there was nothing but darkness. I heard a familiar low growl. It was the barn dog, Jack. Someone was there. My head snapped to the east side of the estate where blades of light slashed through the night in razored slices.

The water sloshed out as I dropped the bucket of water and ran.

I rounded the side of the barn, my heart pounding from the sprint, to see the door wide open. Another squeal and I realized what the sound was. It was wood, being splintered and broken as it was torn from its nails. The bales of hay were broken, shafts of gold spread around the rickety floor like a shattered crown.

In the light of the flickering lantern was a familiar hooked nose and heartless glare, a steel bar in his hands. He'd already torn up four floorboards and was setting to work on another. *Did he know what he was looking for? How had he known to search here?* My throat closed as Silas reached beneath the fractured wood and pulled out my rapier, followed by both sacks of my winnings.

CHAPTER ELEVEN

CHARA

"He has to say yes," I said to Emily, now that we were back in my chamber after enduring another painful dinner and lecture on my lack of timeliness. Hoping to keep my own doubt at bay, I repeated, "He has to say yes. Doesn't he?"

We were sprawled out, deep in the fresh sheets of my massive four poster bed. I had just recounted the day's adventure to her, ending with Elliot's less than encouraging departure from the mill.

"No, he doesn't have to," Emily stated simply, "he's nobility and can't be conscripted. He's more free than you or I will ever be." Although her comment rang with jest, it stung like a blade. But she was right. I wasn't free. I was bound by the monarchy, by duty, and by the arranged marriage barreling towards me. It reminded me why I had to go through with my plan, even if it somehow seemed more impossible today than ever before.

I didn't respond.

She rolled over to her side, propping her head on her hand and asked, "Are you certain that you shouldn't . . . ummm . . . re-evaluate?" Her nail beds were bleeding and I felt her anxiety at the thought of me actually leaving. I knew she was probably regretting ever agreeing to help me in the first place. "I know you're wary of the duke and what he may be hiding, but perhaps the marriage might not be *all* bad. At least you know now that the prince is young and not some creepy, daft, old dimwit—"

I scoffed, as if anyone related to the Grand Duke stood even the slightest chance of not being a dimwit, but Emily went on.

"—and now you know that he is here, in your castle, perhaps you should just . . ." she shrugged, "meet him. Maybe he's lovely."

"Ems, you're missing the whole point. How would him being 'lovely' change anything?" I sat up straight and looked down at my best friend with what I hoped were daggers. "I may not have met the prince yet, but it's easy enough to see where his allegiances lie. Do you really want me to be sent off to live with him in Norrfalt? Is that what you want, Emily, to see me gone?" I knew it wasn't, but my tongue was loosed, releasing all of my pent-up anger and fear at the one person who I knew would love me the same despite it.

"Even if I am destined to be a figurehead, must the hands of my puppeteer be those of my enemy?" I felt the edge to my tone, but my frustration continued boiling out of my control.

"No matter how 'lovely' he is, Emily, do not forget that he will always be the *Norrfalt* prince, not a *Mittelan* king. If I'm duty bound to be captive to the throne my whole life—since Mittelan law has determined that I am not deserving of the crown of my own volition—is it also necessary that I be shackled in a foreign land? Enslaved by a foreign king? Unless, by some miracle, I'm given the chance to find a loyal king who sees me as a partner and not just a producer of heirs, I will forever be a prisoner. Is that really what you want?"

Tears budded in the corners of Emily's eyes and the depth of pain present there transported me back to Elliot's poignant gaze, his face churning with frustration, his breath casting warm waves on my cheeks in the depths of the forest. His jaw was set hard against me, but his lips were soft. Well, they looked soft at least.

And then the tears escaped like those of wounded children down Emily's cheeks, falling onto my silken bedspread, and I saw that I'd gone too far. I'd truly let my desperation, my obsession, get the best of me if I was causing pain to Emily—the one person who had never doubted me or my worthiness.

She choked back her tears to form a stuttered response, "Of course not, Char, you know that. You speak of being shackled, and I know better than most what that feels like. I wouldn't wish that on anyone." A haunted look fell over her face and I knew her well enough to know exactly where her mind had gone. I immediately regretted the callousness of my words.

I pulled her into an embrace, cradling her for a long moment until her head relaxed down into my lap. Rarely did I feel like an older sibling—ironically, despite her youth and station, Emily somehow always seemed to play the role of *my* guardian—but whenever she let her mind drift back to the time before we met, I stepped into the role instantaneously.

I ran my fingers up and down the side of her face as I soothed, "Shhhh . . . Ems . . . you don't have to go back there. I'm sorry, I shouldn't have—"

She interrupted me with a trembling lip, "The mistress bound my hands and feet from dusk until she returned to the boutique in the morning so that I wouldn't run away from the cellar where she kept me—"

"I know, it's alright, Emily," I wiped a tear from her cheek, "you don't have to live it again. I—"

"No, Chara, let me finish," she snapped as she sat straight up.

I shut my mouth.

"—but what the mistress didn't understand was that I wasn't going to run away. I had nowhere to go, no family to go to. However beastly she was, she was all I knew. Any childhood I may have had before her had been drowned in her torments. So what I am saying, Chara, is that *you* are all I have," her sadness was gone, replaced with rough cut anger. "Perhaps your mother would let me travel with you to Norrfalt if it comes to that, but I will have no one left if you are dead."

"Ems . . ." I reached out to stroke her two golden braids, neat and tidy and meticulously perfect as always. I let my hands fall from her head, to her shoulders, to her knees. She was shaking, whether from reliving her trauma or from her anger towards me, I couldn't be sure. Either way, I hated that I was causing her pain. "That's why I cannot fail, Ems. I won't. Whatever the duke is keeping from mother about the war, it's directly related to his constant efforts to push through the marriage alliance. And the only way I'm going to find out what *it* is, is to get to the border as soon as possible."

She harrumphed loudly, but did not counter.

"The duke is desperate to seal this alliance, and I have to find out why. And, besides, even the duke cannot make me marry the prince if I am not here."

I knew what it looked like to Emily. It looked like I was a child throwing a tantrum and my solution to the problem was to run away. But she hadn't been there to hear the duke and his nephew talk; she couldn't truly understand how high the stakes were. "If the prince and I wed, Mittelan will forever come second to Norrfalt. I can't let that happen. I have to get away from this marriage, even if . . ." *If it kills me,* I almost said, but I didn't want to cause my friend any more pain. So I said instead, ". . . even if it fails. But, Ems, I have to try. I—"

A rap on the door cut me off. Emily shot out of the bed and took to smoothing out the crumpled duvet. "Come in," she called, pausing to wipe some lingering tears from her cheeks. The door opened, and my mother's lady-in-waiting entered my chambers.

"Princess," she curtsied, "her highness requests your presence in the throne room. And she requests of you, Miss Emily, that you make her look 'halfway decent.' Apologies, Princess, the queen's words not mine."

I gazed down at the disguise I had not yet taken off since my tromp through the woods. My face was covered in the soot I'd smeared on it, and the torn and muddy dress had already ruined the sheets.

"Thank you, Madame Colombe," I dismissed her with a nod. The door latched behind her as she left.

"Oops," I regarded the mussed bed with regret; I knew how it frustrated Emily to see things out of shape. "I'll remake it, I swear, and I'll replace the dress too." I held out the filthy skirt of the dress I'd borrowed for the day.

"A dress is the least of my concerns right now, Char." Her eyes were still puffy from crying, but she composed herself so quickly that it would otherwise be hard to tell, "Let's just get you cleaned up before your mother sees you like this and puts me in the stocks."

I peeled off the filthy dress and bathed myself as Emily selected a yellow gown with floral appliqués on the sleeves. I scrubbed the soot off my face and the mud from my legs. After I was dry and dressed, Emily twisted and braided my unruly waves into an ornate bun, even tucking in flowers for good measure.

Once Emily had finished grooming me, I left my chambers, winding through the hallways, away from the royal apartments and up the large interior staircase that led to the throne room. Guards stood in each of the arches surrounding the large room, divided by gold columns. A massive, golden chandelier hung from the high ceiling, illuminating the walls which were painted, every square inch, in colorful murals. For my mother, I did my loveliest princess walk across the mosaic tiled floor. The tiles told a story from the holy text of a small man defeating a great beast with just a stone. At the front of the room were three white marble steps leading up to an exquisitely painted apse which housed two golden thrones with red velvet cushions, only one of which was occupied.

The empty throne of my father usually caused a lump to rise in my throat, and this time was no exception. The Grand

Duke sat, as he normally did, in his chair at the bottom of the stairs. However, unlike any time prior, on the arm of his chair perched a young man. I swallowed as I took in the young man's features, more perfect than any I'd ever seen. His sleek black hair was neatly combed and matched his strong eyebrows and dense brown eyes. His chin came to a prominent taper, as did his nose, but on him they didn't look harsh, just confident and undeniably handsome. He was taller than me, but not by much, and svelte. He wore a crisp white uniform with gold epaulets fringing his shoulders.

A sash the color of a clear winter sky lay against his torso: ice blue, the color of Norrfalt and its frozen tundra.

I gulped, knowing undoubtedly this was my betrothed and that this meeting was to alert me to that which I already knew: the Norrfalt king had accepted my mother's demands. I was to be wed.

When I reached the thrones, a guard stationed at the base of the marble steps announced me to the room. "Charissa Henrietta Cordelia Basile-Perrault, Princess of Mittelan."

The Grand Duke stood and bowed to me, "Princess, allow me to introduce my nephew—son of my only sister, a native to the great country of Mittelan and now reigning queen of Norrfalt—I present to you, Margueritte Marie Katherine Monmouth-Ludwig's only son, Christopher Everett Charles Ludwig the Third, Prince of Norrfalt."

The prince's eyebrows rose at the sight of me, and the look made me shift in my slippers. He bowed and I reached a hand out to him, which he kissed politely. He stood but did not release my hand cradled in his. "My friends call me Chris," he said with a smile that I'm sure he was quite used to women swooning over. Well, not me.

"My friends call me Chara," I returned in my most dignified voice, "however, as we are *not* friends, Princess Charissa Henrietta Cordelia Basile-Perrault will do just fine." I jerked my hand back.

"Charissa, like . . . charisma, yes?"

I ignored his futile attempt at flattery, even as a blush rose to my cheeks at the prickle of his lingering touch. "More like *careful*," I lowered my voice, "which is what I would be if I were you." All I saw in this boy's charming smile and good looks was my life crumbling apart in his greedy hands.

My mother cleared her throat. I turned to face her, curtsying. The Grand Duke and the prince bowed their heads slightly in respect, but she didn't address them or even spare a glance in their direction. She kept her regal stare fixed on me.

"Charissa," she paused—brows raised—waiting for my acknowledgement.

"Yes, Mother?"

"The Grand Duke and I have long weighed the costs and benefits of forming a lasting marriage alliance between the thrones of Mittelan and Norrfalt. While I have been . . . reluctant . . ." a pit formed in my stomach at the waver in my mother's voice, "the duke's informants report that the border-war has taken a turn for the worse."

I clenched my jaw but focused on keeping the rest of my features straight. *I'm sure the duke's informants are nothing but trustworthy.*

"You must understand," she continued, "that Mittelan cannot afford to lose our most productive fields on our northern border. So it is with my greatest relief, that the Norrfalt king has accepted the terms we proposed in the marriage alliance." Mother's smile stretched razor-thin as she announced, "In fact, the king has agreed to pull all troops out of Mittelan on the day of your wedding to his son, Prince Christopher, in two weeks' time."

The air in the room thinned. *Two weeks?* My head spun as I thought of having only days to escape my fate, to discover the truth of the war and bring it to an end before my life was overturned. *Fourteen days*. I pleaded with my mother through wide, desperate eyes to reconsider. To consider me, her daughter. For once, to consider being a mother rather than a queen. She returned my look with soft eyes but responded with resolution, "Princess Charissa, meet your betrothed."

CHAPTER TWELVE

ELLIOT

Silas pulled the first of the two heavy sacks of my winnings out of their hiding place, opening it and peeking in. My sword lay across his lap. His face lit with a maniacal smile which fell as quickly as it had appeared. He reached in for the second sack and held one in each fist.

Jack's growl grew to a full bark, but he did not attack. "Shut up, you damned mutt," Silas spat without taking his eyes off the winnings.

Jack spotted me, glued to the cold ground between the well and the barn, and darted past Silas to me. He whipped around to face my stepfather with a snarl. *No, no, no*, the word played in my mind on repeat as if it could stop my world from unraveling before my very eyes, but it was too late.

The dog growled at the old man and internally I begged him to stop, to keep Silas's anger from lashing out at the poor pup.

Silas looked up at me over his hooked nose, jaw suddenly slack.

My plan—three years' worth of work and training and combat—crumbled in my fingers like old bones, leaving only the dust of my dreams behind. He had the money now, my leverage was gone. He had the rapier. Without my sword, I could not practice. All of my efforts had been for nothing and every plan I'd made for my future was suddenly devastated; and yet, what infuriated me the most was the triumph in his gray eyes, lit by the single flickering flame.

"I knew you'd purchased the roast," Silas said calmly, pushing himself from his knees to standing. "I haven't had food like that since Elizabeth died, leaving me in this shithole with you and your needy, little sis—"

"Don't!" My chin trembled as I tried to hold my anger at bay, "Don't you dare finish that sentence. And do not speak my mother's name as if she meant a damn thing to you." I couldn't stand hearing my mother's name on the viper's venomous lips, but I refused to let him talk about Millie. My hand held onto the ringlet at my waist as if I were still protecting her.

Silas had stolen my life when he married my mother, he had stolen my future when she died, and then he somehow still managed to find more of me to destroy. The viper took everything I had left on the day he lashed out against Millie, and I thought all hope had died along with her. It wasn't until Parren entered my life, handed me a sword, and my savings started to grow that I saw any light. But now, even that flicker of hope—of a future worth living—had been snuffed.

My curling fingers ached with the desire for his flesh.

"Elizabeth," he drew out her name, taunting me with it. "Dear, Eliza," the nickname stung like a blow, exactly as Silas had intended it to, as only her closest friends and my father had called her that, "she wasn't just your mother, boy." He leaned against my sword, taking his time choosing the words that would cut me deepest. "She was my wife. My source of riches. My lover."

My blood grew hot, veins throbbing with the need to see his blood on this barn floor. Jack's snarling mounted but he waited for my command to attack.

Silas took a step closer, kicking Jack out of his way. The pup dodged the blow, and I risked a snap of my fingers to signal him to return to my side. He growled but obeyed. Silas continued to close the distance between us, daring to come within range of my clenched fist. "She loved you, undoubtedly, but she loved me too, in her own way. She wanted us to be a family, for you to take care of us."

"No. She wanted me to take care of *Millie*. She didn't love you, couldn't have loved a snake like you. You're *not* my family!" My temper raged, but Silas went on as if I hadn't said a word.

"And now you dare keep your loot to yourself when we are so poor we can't even afford proper help?" he sneered, still clenching my winnings tightly in his grip. "And on top of that, you shirk your hunting responsibilities and buy a roast with your dirty money? I thought I raised you better than to be a devious little thief." He spat at my feet. "You should thank your brother, for spotting you sneaking in and out of the barn and asking me to check in on you."

Raymond.

Silas edged closer still, "Now I don't know exactly how you got your nasty hands on this much money, boy, and I shudder to think what you've done with this sword, but I *do* know that your mother would be ashamed of you for being so damned selfish."

I didn't bother to tell him the truth or any version of a lie. I took the single pace between us, my fist already wound.

But my mother's voice stopped me, her voice trembling, dying. *You're strong, little Elliot. Take care of your family—your sister—and yourself. Promise me, Ellie.* I remembered the blossoming bruise on Millie's face when I'd acted rashly and she had paid the price. She was the only family I had left and I let her die. My mother's final request, and I failed her.

If I struck Silas—a weak, aging, defenseless man—how would I be any better than him? No, Silas wasn't innocent and he wasn't a child, but he was unarmed and untrained. In the end, he had paid the healers to care for mother and Millie. It didn't make up for what he'd done to my sister, but it had been my decision to run away with her.

Guilt made me take pause, but in that moment, reason spoke: if I killed Silas right here, right now, Beauhaven would go to Raymond. I couldn't let that happen. If I maimed the viper, he could take me to the courts and I would never stand a chance of inheriting that which was rightfully mine.

My fist fell to my side. I knew that I *could* kill Silas, and tonight, that was enough. I took satisfaction in picturing myself burying my knuckles in his wrinkled, hooked nose. Nearly a decade ago, he had tried to save Millie and so tonight, I would spare him. But I couldn't live any longer in this den of snakes.

I could control my anger, but I wouldn't let Silas abuse that for a moment longer.

"I didn't steal the money," I stretched my fingers free of their fists at my side. I wanted to tell him that I won it, that I was one of the most skilled swordsmen in all of Mittelan. But I couldn't risk exposing the Games and all the peasants who entertained themselves there, so I just said, "I earned it, fair and square. And I've spent years practicing with that blade you found, and trust me, you do not want to find yourself at the other end of it."

Silas cackled, the cruel and dark reverberations of his laughter echoing through the hollow night. "You are no hero, boy! And if you keep making up lies, I will add five more lashes to the thirty you are already getting for your thievery!"

"Keep the money and let your weak arms rest," the words dripped from my tongue, sweeter than honeysuckle and sharper than steel. I enunciated each word clearly, my feet set in the ground like pillars of stone. "Enjoy the roast, sir, because I don't know who will cook you your next hot meal."

Someday I would return to my parents' estate, knighted, outranking the bastard who wrenched it from me, and I would reclaim my rightful ownership. And I prayed that when I returned, I would find Silas's rotting corpse.

He swung the bags of slips and coins like a pendulum, clanking them against his palm, a wicked curve tugging up one side of his lips. He sneered at me as I walked past him, into the barn, throwing the saddle blanket onto Gus's back. "Run away, boy, just like last time." His voice cracked the raven night, bouncing off the stone walls of the courtyard. Raymond and Lucas came running out of the house, watching from beneath the awning.

His malicious voice kept taunting me as I prepared Gus. "You'll be back."

I put the saddle on.

"You're weak."

I cinched the girth around Gus's middle.

"You're useless."

I grabbed the bridle from its hook on the barn wall, slipping it onto the horse's face.

"You'll die out there on your own. Just like your worthless sister."

It took every ounce of my self-control not to beat him senseless.

I wedged my foot into the stirrup and hoisted myself up. My heart broke as Jack yipped around Gus's shoes. I put all of the pain and anger into a final loathing glare at my stepfather.

"You'll be back," Silas all but whispered.

"You'd better pray, old man, that you are wrong. Because if I come back, it will be to show you what I *can* do with a sword. To show you how easy it would be for me to gut you. Buy yourself a new horse with my money." I dug my heels into Gus's sides, and he took off.

I pulled the horse's bit towards the front of the house, where my step-brothers stood frozen on the porch. I halted, studying their wrinkled brows and parted lips. Lucas's chin quivered, and I thought for a moment that he might start crying, that he might beg me not to leave.

It hit me. He'd left the small bite of eggs—completely shell free—for me. He'd lied to his brother so Raymond wouldn't snatch them off his plate. Lucas hadn't been talking in his sleep when he thanked me for stoking his fire, and he didn't like it when his brother taunted me or his father beat me. He may have been afraid to intervene but he'd never participated in their cruelty.

"Take care of the dog, Lucas. Please. Don't let him starve."

I held Lucas's gaze. He nodded his head in a silent promise. Guilt and sadness crept over his empty eyes, and I suddenly felt very sorry for leaving him with these two devils. Sympathy radiated through me that he had to share the blood of these monsters.

Raymond's face fell slack, shocked at what his sneaking had accomplished. I ignored him entirely.

I pushed my guilt and sadness aside, ignoring Jack's bark that had morphed into a pathetic, crying howl. I let my anger engulf me. After one last glance at my childhood home, I turned my back on it and rode off into the empty, heartless night.

CHAPTER THIRTEEN

CHARA

I couldn't even stand to look at my mother, my rage burned so hot.

Two weeks to end a war or else my life as I know it is over.

The Grand Duke's eyes, and the handsome prince's, remained fixed on mine after the word *betrothed* rolled off mother's tongue. I set my gaze on the dandelion-hued hem of my dress where it swept against the colorful floor. The small mosaic tiles directly in front of me illustrated the small weapon the little boy used in battle, a slingshot. I followed the curve of his arm to find the collage of his face. His gaze betrayed no weakness, his brows straight, jaw hard. It was a look of sheer determination, relentless willpower, to triumph over the giant whom no one believed he could slay.

The image gave me the strength to look up at my mother, to where she sat beside my father's empty throne. Her expression was a well-practiced concoction of sympathy and strength, altered for today by only a hint of guilt.

"Mother, I—" I started but she put her hand up to stop me.

"No, Charissa," she snapped, the softness fading away and leaving only hard perseverance. She massaged her temples with her forefingers, not even looking at me. "The decision is final. I don't want to hear anything else from you. Except, perhaps, a note of gratitude to his highness for being so willing to negotiate."

Even as my rage burned like wildfire, her tone gave resolution to my plot. Whatever the duke had said or done to manipulate my mother into agreement would not be shaken by my words alone. She knew how much I opposed this marriage, so any reason I gave her to call it off would be instantly dismissed. I had to get out. I had to get to the border. I had to discover the truth of the battle and end this war. And to successfully accomplish any of that, my mother could have no indication that I was planning to escape.

I dropped my head back to the floor and found the tile rendition of the giant, lying on the ground with a hole in its head, vanquished by someone that no one expected to succeed. That vanquisher could be me, *would* be me. I would slay the giant and end this marriage once and for all. It no longer mattered that every odd was stacked against me. I would succeed because I had to.

My mother cleared her throat.

Smiling the royal smile that Mother had long forced me to practice, I clasped my hands behind my back, feeling for my father's brass ring. "Thank you, your highness." I dipped into my deepest, most polished curtsy, "I look forward to all that our countries can accomplish when working hand-in-hand." I rose and acknowledged my mother's curt nod of dismissal, before turning on my heel and princess-walking the hell away from those thrones of betrayal.

The massive carved wooden doors slammed behind me as I marched out of the throne room, away from my mother, the duke, and that pompous prince. My fury roared within me, face burning as I recalled the prince's arrogant smile and shameless flirtations. And then the betrayal coming from my own mother? How could she do this to me? Giving me only two weeks to prepare for a wedding that I didn't even want? Even if I was willing to accept, that wouldn't be anywhere near enough time to acclimate and prepare and—

The quick click of heels on the stone behind me interrupted my thoughts. I whipped around and found myself face to face with that same arrogant smile.

"I do believe we got off on the wrong foot." The prince smiled broadly and bowed, never taking his eyes off mine. I refused to acknowledge how downright charming his smile actually was, despite its pretension. His teeth were perfect, even, and as white as the snowy tundras from which he hailed, a fact that only amplified my instinct to knock them right out of his head.

My brain told me to stay quiet, but my mouth had other ideas. "Wrong foot?" I seethed, cutting him off before he could respond. "Wrong foot? You act as if you stepped on my toes while waltzing or brought me goose when I'd asked for duck. Whereas, in all reality, you lead a nation that invaded its peaceful neighbors and is now solely responsible for a wedding that will effectually deny Mittelan its independence." I could feel my cheeks blaze rich scarlet.

The prince took a step back. "Actually my—"

"And not only are you the leader of a terrorist nation," I closed the gap and dug my finger into his chest between the rows of gold buttons, "but you . . . you are a vile and despicable human being. You come into my castle," I gestured to the tapestry covered walls, "my *home*, plotting with your malicious uncle and brainwashing my mother to steal my only chance at happiness! I *know* there is something you both are lying about and I am going to figure it out. So don't act like you can flash a handsome smile and wink one of those charming, thickly-lashed eyes at me and that I will just fall into your arms.

"I will not be forced to play the part of your complacent queen. You are not the hero you think you are, and I'm not a damned doll for you to stage. I don't expect you to act like the former and you had better not expect me to act like the latter. Because you and your country will regret it."

He hung his head for a moment, but when he looked up—instead of the hurt or anger I expected—the smug bastard was grinning. "You think I'm handsome?"

My anger mounted and, without considering any possible consequences, I drew back my fist and punched him square in the gut.

He buckled over, reaching out an arm to me pathetically. "Wait," he groaned.

But I didn't wait. I wouldn't wait another minute before doing what I had to do. Though I doubted the prince would be eager to admit that Mittelan's gentle princess had knocked him to the ground in one blow, I dared him to tell the duke or Mother what I'd done. I wouldn't be here to see disappointment in my mother's eyes one more time. The next time I faced her would be to deliver the truth of whatever was happening at the warfront, proof of the duke's betrayal, and a definitive end to any conversation regarding the marriage alliance.

I wouldn't waste another day. I would give Elliot one chance to join me and, if he refused, I would risk it all and go by myself.

Nothing could change my mind now.

Stomping through the familiar stone hallways towards my chamber, I said a brief goodbye to the elaborate rugs and ornate tapestries. I went to my room to change and pack my saddle bags with the things I had readily available. After a quick explanation and a long hug, Emily and I made arrangements for her to obtain and deliver the rest of my supplies at the stable threshold the following night. I buckled my sword and made my way out of the castle unseen.

I vowed that the next time I returned to these halls, either the marriage alliance would be obsolete or soldiers would be carrying me in a coffin.

CHAPTER FOURTEEN
ELLIOT

As we crossed over Beauhaven's threshold, I refused to look back. I didn't even stop to close the gate behind us. Gus galloped down the winding woodland lane, carrying me away—really away—for the first time since Millie died. The dense evergreens lining the route melded into nothing but inky sky. We came around the bend, to the fork where the rocky path yielded to the well-kept road to Swanstone.

A flurry of neighs and squeals shattered the rhythm of his trot as Gus reared up on his hind legs so forcefully I nearly fell off backwards. Another horse—with a speckled, shadowy grey coat—bucked ferociously, startled by us riding full speed in the opposite direction. The horse's rider shrieked and plummeted from the saddle, landing hard on the dirt road.

"Whoa there, boy!" I pulled Gus's reins sharply to regain

control. "Shhh, calm down," I stroked his neck and repeated, "shhh, it's alright boy, shhh." Soon, he slowed his erratic movements enough for me to slip from his saddle and run to the fallen rider's side. "Are you okay?"

"Arghh," the hooded figure yelled from the ground, clutching a leg and cursing. Head thrown back in pain, the hood fell away revealing woven auburn braids, pastel flowers, and a look of sheer astonishment.

My breathing hitched as I recognized the face.

"Kiera?" She looked so different that I thought perhaps I was mistaken. I stooped beside her. "Is that you? Are you okay?"

"Well I was just fine until about ten seconds ago!" she screeched.

I put a finger into my now ringing ear. It was definitely her. "What are you doing here?" I asked.

"I was coming to see you." Her eyes were wide and frantic, only one of the dramatic changes from when last we'd met. She was no longer in a tattered dress with a filthy smock, but riding pants and a cloak. Her face was no longer smudged with dirt and cinders, but clean and smooth in the pale moonlight. By the shadows of night, she was almost unrecognizable as the girl I'd met earlier that day.

"Stop gawking, twit, and help get me out of the middle of the road." She threw a surprisingly firm punch at my shoulder.

"Ouch!" I rubbed it, and she responded with a dismissive wave of her hand before returning to rubbing her injured leg. I helped her up to standing, putting her arm around my neck and holding her firmly around her waist for support. "Can you put any weight on it?"

She put her hurt leg to the ground and slowly pushed, whimpering as she did.

"Oh, don't be such a girl," I muttered.

"A girl who could have killed you *twice* by now."

Her sharp reminder brought an angry rush of blood to my face.

"I can put some weight on it," she winced in pain, "but it hurts. Help me find a place to sit off the road. I need to talk to you."

"And I you."

She nodded and leaned her weight into me. We slowly and awkwardly hobbled off the road and into the woods. She breathed heavily, squeezing a word in between each gasp when her weight was on her strong leg. "Where . . . were . . . you . . . going?"

With the surprise of the encounter, I'd almost forgotten why I'd left home in the first place. Then I remembered, with a sick turn of my stomach, the squeal of breaking wood in the barn, and the jingle of my winnings against Silas' bony hands. "Ironically… to find you too," I admitted, to myself as much as to her.

I lowered Kiera down to sit on a stump near a small circle of pines. As I stood, she slapped me hard on the back of my head.

"Owww!" I yelled, more out of anger than pain, as I rubbed the bump. "What is wrong with you?" This girl was really starting to get under my skin. First with her aimless victory in the arena, then spoiling my hunt, and now this? I ground my teeth together and glared at her.

She massaged slowly from her knee to her calf, never taking her stormy eyes off me. She winced in pain when she pressed just below her knee.

"You're such an idiot," she shook her head in disgust, "what the hell were you thinking?"

What idiotic thing could she possibly be accusing me *of?*

I shrugged, "What?"

The maiden rolled her eyes. "And where exactly were you going to go to look for me? You don't know where I or my mistress lives. I was supposed to come for you tomorrow! With you gone I would never have been able to find you!"

"Then what are you doing here?" I snapped, "*You* were supposed to meet *me, tomorrow* night. Were you going to stake out my house for an entire day, or come around knocking hours early? You're lucky you didn't because then I would have had to explain your presence to Silas. Were my instructions not clear enough for you?"

She looked at the ground and mumbled, "Plans change."

"Yes, they do." The memory of Silas' greedy hands all over my winnings still burned, fresh and more painful even than the barely scabbed lesions littering my back. "I'll tie up the horses," I grumbled before stalking away. Any excuse for a moment of space from her before I had to face my fate.

Gus and Kiera's mare had both relaxed and were grazing the few weeds and blades of grass that were just beginning to show the hope of spring. I grabbed each of their reins and led them away from the road to an oak with some sturdy branches near Kiera.

After tying off Gus, I took an extra moment to nuzzle into his neck, taking comfort in the familiar smell of sap and sweat and hay. Aside from Millie's single ringlet at my side, he was the only remnant of home I had with me. "It's just you and me now, boy," I soothed before giving him a final pat and returning to the stump where I'd left the girl.

"You said you were coming to find me," Kiera continued to massage her injured leg, "well here I am. What did you have to say?"

Now that she was here in front of me, my words dried up. I was suddenly so unsure of what I wanted from her, what I even wanted from life anymore. Instead of responding, I knelt between us and began to clear a place for a fire, arranging some dry pine needles into a nest as tinder. I stood and collected some kindling, as well as a few logs for fuel. As I arranged the fire, I felt Kiera watching me as if I were a mildly entertaining spectacle, like a beggar playing a fiddle or a chicken who flew the coop. I went to light the fire and cursed, realizing my pockets were empty.

"In Stell's pack," she gestured to the dappled gray horse. "Front left pocket." I nodded and retrieved the flint and steel. The little handmaiden was surprisingly prepared, unlike myself who had nothing but my horse, saddle, and the clothes on my back. Kiera's mare carried two full packs and the girl had a small purse fastened around her chest. She had certainly packed some provisions, but not nearly enough for the week-long journey to the borderlands.

I struck the steel to the flint, showering the tinder in sparks. The fire struggled to catch due to the damp and muddy ground, but after more than a dozen strikes the needles finally ignited. I blew on the lit branches gently until they glowed white hot. Flames finally took hold of the bundle, setting the kindling ablaze.

Fires were warm and familiar, and building them was one

thing I was good for. But was it presumptuous to think maybe I was destined for more than a job stoking fires?

The silence between Kiera and I began to grow awkward as it stretched between us, broken only by the crackling flames. I began to notice even more stark changes to Kiera from the homely maidservant I'd previously met. Her dress and apron were gone, replaced with tight leather riding pants and a buttoned white blouse. Her riding coat was thick black suede and beautifully embroidered. And her mess of hair had since been impeccably groomed, braided, and adorned with petite spring blooms. I might not have noticed such things if they weren't so starkly contrasted to her previous self.

Eventually, Kiera spoke. "I can only assume you came to give me your answer."

Before Silas discovered my secret, I'd been sure that I was going to tell her no. Then I'd left home in such a rush, I felt lost as to what to say to her now. My money was gone, and the way Silas took it without question made me wonder: would I have ever been able to strike a deal with him, or were my years of fighting leading me to this all along? Would Silas have found a way to take the money and keep Beauhaven anyway? If I went on Kiera's mission, was there any way I could use the money to get Silas to leave?

I knew now in my heart that the answer was no. He had my fortune and although his greed was great, his pride was greater. Silas would never render Beauhaven to me now, no matter the sum. He ended up with the estate *and* the money, and would likely find a way to do so again and again.

Unless . . . I found a way to outrank him, some way to legally *prove* that Beauhaven was rightfully mine. Silas may have been a noble by birth, but if I were to become a knight by deed, I would outrank him and the property and its holdings would fall to me. Since only royalty could bestow knighthood, in order to receive the rank, I would also gain audience with the queen. Surely then she could personally direct that the Cendrilon assets would pass rightfully back to my hands.

I had to be knighted by the queen. It was the only sure way.

Furthermore, what sweet vengeance would it be to finally and truly claim my title as *Sir* Cendrilon and outrank the malicious viper? He was lucky to have been born into the ranks because Silas would never have put himself in a dangerous situation in order to prove his bravery and receive knighthood any other way.

I stood, taking my hunting knife from my waist. Could Kiera's quest somehow be enough to get me the knighthood I needed? Or would I be better off enlisting to go to the border-war?

As my thoughts churned, I began to absentmindedly throw my hunting knife at a tree near our camp site. My childhood friend Bruno—now the bartender at Lucifer's and really the only friend I had besides Parren—had taught me the basics of knife throwing throughout the years. We shared a booth in the Swanstone marketplace where I sold my pelts from hunting and he sold the clothing his sisters had made, but we really bonded over the mutual caretaking of Parren.

Sometimes Bruno would join me in my training sessions, which always gave me a welcome break from the sword. *Now, focus your mind and take a deep breath*, he would say in his gruff, serious voice. *Picture your target.*

Bruno had been saying the same thing to me for nearly a

decade, since we were barely more than children. And never had I pictured a target so clearly as I did right now: Silas. A fresh wave of anger urged me to throw the knife harder and harder each time. My knife landed dead center in the image I'd conjured of Silas's face. After about a dozen throws it was becoming difficult to remove from the wedge in the bark where I pictured Silas's right eye.

I glanced at Kiera, still massaging her injured leg and looking at me through narrowed, coal-lined eyes. This girl certainly was an enigma, as if she had three separate identities in one being. Was she a polished and well-dressed rider on a mission from her leader? Was she a simple handmaiden hell-bent on destroying my day? Perhaps the most befuddling of them all, was she a fierce competitor who could take on any man in combat? Whoever she was, she jiggled her good leg as she anxiously awaited my response, biting at her lip to keep from pressuring me.

I looked back to the tree. *Now, focus your mind and take a deep breath.* I released the knife again and it landed in the wedge once more. As I pulled the steel blade from the bark I was reminded of the clink of *my* golds, *my* silvers, *my* glass clanking together in Silas's grubby hands.

He took whatever he wanted, no matter what it cost those around him. From my mother, to Millie, to my years of servitude—he took and took and took and never gave anything. He ran my parents' business and estate into the ground. He destroyed my life. I couldn't let him take away what was probably my last chance at fulfilling my final promise to Millie.

"You said your mistress was very powerful, correct?" I broke the silence between Kiera and I at last.

The furrow of her eyebrows told me that was not the response she had been expecting. She answered slowly, "Yes, she is very powerful."

"Is she close to . . ." I swallowed hard, "to the queen?"

Kiera's eyes grew instantly wide as if I had struck a nerve. The log she sat on was covered in moss and it left green streaks on her black pants. They were finely made and obviously expensive—belonging to her mistress no doubt.

She nodded, "Very."

"Then I will agree to accompany you under *one* condition," I stopped throwing my knife and crossed the opening to kneel at Kiera's side, fixing my eyes on hers. The moon reflected as a dancing snowflake in her bright eyes.

"My mistress has already offered you a small fortune," a deep furrow wrinkled her forehead. As the night's ghostly light illuminated her hardened jaw, she transformed once more. This time into a warrior. "What more could you want?"

"I don't need her money, not anymore. All I need is a guarantee that, upon our return with her brother, she will see to it personally that I . . . um . . . that I receive an audience with the qu-queen," I cursed myself for stuttering, "to be knighted." It was risky. I knew there was no guarantee that I would find the man Kiera sought. I could end up caught up in battle or taken prisoner by the heartless invaders from Norrfalt. The monsieur Kiera spoke of could already be dead.

But right now none of that mattered. I had no life, no family, no home, no sword, and nothing to lose. I touched my leather pouch. This is what Millie would want me to do. For us. For our home. I no longer knew when *someday* would be, but this could be the only chance I had left for it to be on this side of eternity.

If the man we were fetching really was as influential as Kiera said, then the queen would gladly knight me upon his return. Then, for the first time since he married my mother, Silas wouldn't be able to touch me. I could use the money from the Games to restore Beauhaven to its former glory. And I would never have to look at Silas or Raymond ever again.

I could already picture it: me returning to the viper in armor gifted from the queen herself, with her guardsmen flanking me, bearing an edict evicting Silas and proclaiming my rank. He would regret what he did to Millie, what he took from us, and I would finally restore the life he stole from me and fulfill my promise to my sister. *Someday* would be here at last.

Kiera was quiet for a long moment.

"I need my knighthood. Without that, you will have to find someone else." The hesitation in my voice was gone, only determination remained.

Her lips curved and she laughed, "Oh, that's it?" She teased, "A small fortune is not enough, you think that you deserve one of the country's greatest military accolades. That's what you think your services are worth?"

I nodded slowly.

The memory of the laugh still lingered in her faint smile, but her expression grew serious as she considered my request.

For the first time in my life I felt the glimmer of an aspiration to become something more, more than the winner of a betting match, more than a servant, more than '*boy.*' The flicker was quickly overshadowed by the memory of Millie's pleas for home and my promise to make it safe for her again somehow, someday. So that's what I had to do. I would go with

Kiera, find the monsieur, receive my knighthood, and then use it to safeguard my family's legacy.

Someday was once more within my grasp. If only Kiera would agree.

She ran her tongue over her lips as she thought, and then pressed them together coyly. Something dangerous flashed in her midnight eyes and the light of the crackling fire only added to the fear that gripped me.

"I can assure you an audience with the queen upon our return," she responded, "but only the queen herself can decide who is deserving of knighthood. However—"

Kiera held up a hand as I began to interrupt.

"—with the Monsieur Roberto Pentamerone in tow, I have no doubt she will look on you quite favorably."

It was a far cry short of a guarantee, but it would have to be enough.

Kiera reached out her hand and I shook it. Her skin was smoother than it ought to be, and for some reason I found myself not wanting to let go.

"I guess that will have to do," I ceded as our hands fell away, and I felt myself smile—the first true smile in what felt like a very long time. I raised a hand and tipped my head as if toasting with an invisible pint, "We are coming for you, Monsieur."

She smiled back at me, the curve of her lips deliciously wicked in the tempting firelight.

CHAPTER FIFTEEN

CHARA

He held my hand moments longer than felt natural, something flashing across his features—relief, excitement, maybe even something a bit . . . giddy? I briefly wondered why a man who could have asked for anything from me—any prize, any sum of money—cared only about receiving his knighthood. He was already noble; why was getting knighted by the queen so important to him? But my own relief quickly eclipsed any lingering questions. My heart pitter-pattered. This was it. My plan was finally in action.

Two weeks to expose the duke's plot. Two weeks to stop a wedding. Fourteen days to escape my fate.

Elliot stood and began to throw dirt on the fire and stomp at the quickly disappearing flames.

"What are you doing?" I choked out, scared to face the cold night now that I'd become accustomed to the fire's warmth. "Stop that!"

He paused and looked up at me, eyebrows knit quizzically. "What? Why? I'm assuming your mistress resides in or near the city, doesn't she? I assume we need to finish gathering our supplies and get a good night's rest before beginning our journey. I have nothing to go home for, so it's only forward for me. I'm sure that your mistress would like to meet me, and I can't say I would mind a night in a real bed before weeks of sleeping on the ground. If we get there in time to make final preparations tonight, we could leave tomorrow at first light."

He continued going on and on with ideas that were quickly poking many holes in my carefully constructed cover story. I tried to swallow my rising panic.

"No!" The word slipped out so fervently, my mind raced for a way to temper my reaction. I hadn't thought through this part. Perhaps my cover story was not as carefully constructed as I had believed. I had no mistress, no place to take him. I hadn't expected to find and persuade him to join me so quickly. I knew Emily would need time as well to gather the remaining supplies, so I still had an entire day before our arranged meeting time. "I mean, yes," I forced myself to sound calm, "she has a large parcel of land just to the west of Swanstone and a residence within the walls, but I'm too injured to make that ride tonight. I'd like to give my leg the evening to rest."

His expression grew even more skeptical, "But we are not *that* far from the city and the journey to the border is not a short one. We really mustn't delay. If Monsieur Penta-Penta-whatever—"

"Pentamerone," I interjected.

"Yes, him. If he is in danger we really should depart with all due haste."

Of all people, I knew that we were on a pressing timeline but I had no way of getting the supplies we needed any earlier than tomorrow night, not without risking going back into the castle, and that was a risk I was not willing to take. And I definitely could not risk Elliot trying to meet my "mistress."

Elliot walked over to the horses and began untying them. My heart began to beat double time as I searched for any believable excuse to slow our progress and ensure I could retrieve the supplies on my own. What was I thinking would happen when I confronted Elliot prematurely? I felt so stupid at my obvious oversight.

"We will not delay long," I assured him, "but my mistress will still be gathering supplies, she is not yet expecting my return. I wasn't even supposed to meet you until tomorrow evening. All that said, I cannot afford to damage my leg any further before our journey, so we will camp here for the night."

Truthfully, my leg only ached. I knew I could ride if I needed to, but how else would I explain why we could not call on my mistress early?

He opened his mouth to speak but I spoke first, "If you are too soft to spend a night on the ground, then perhaps I found the wrong future-knight in the first place, and I will have to find another." I gave him a stern look and he stopped what he was doing.

He shrugged his shoulders and—despite his obvious lingering confusion—began to tie his horse back to the tree. "As you wish."

A heavy breath of relief escaped. I had dodged this unexpected hiccup, but what was coming next? I had to get to the border before Elliot discovered the truth of my identity.

I could not risk him turning me in or abandoning me. If this was only the beginning of his questions, how was I going to keep up?

Elliot sat on the ground across the clearing from me and began to stoke his fire back to life.

What other aspects of this plan had I completely overlooked? Fear clawed at me, but I pushed it aside, replacing it with feigned confidence. Something was amiss at the border, something the duke feared would ruin the marriage alliance. I had to find out what that was. This plan would work because *it had to*.

Tomorrow, I would stall long enough for me to fetch the supplies from Emily. It was only a day; I would figure it out. I had no other choice.

I laid my head in the dirt, an ache running down my leg as I shifted. I had never spent the night on the ground before, and truthfully, *I* felt a little soft. I tried laying on my riding cloak, but then the night wind cut right through the thin fabric of my blouse and the cloak was soon cold and soggy from the damp ground.

My injured leg ached in the frosty night and I longed for my bed at the castle. I remembered the pad beneath Stell's saddle and decided she probably wouldn't miss it. I limped across the clearing, avoiding branches as much as I could to keep from waking Elliot. Spiders of pain crawled up my shin and into my knee, not the worst pain I'd endured, but enough to be annoying.

I silently thanked the heavens for the mild injury. What other excuse could I have formulated to convince Elliot it wasn't an option to go to my mistress?

Stell's eyes flickered open when she felt my hand on the warm round of her face, stroking her soft charcoal hair. She nuzzled her nose into my free palm, and I rested my forehead against her cheek. "What are we getting ourselves into, girl?" She didn't whinny, but I felt as if she understood my apprehension and commiserated with me.

Elliot had unsaddled the horses before bed but had left their riding pads on their backs for warmth. I took her blanket—she didn't protest—and hobbled back to my place by the dying embers of the fire. Elliot looked completely at ease sleeping on the ground, his knees drawn up almost to his chest. His head rested on his folded arm, silky white blond hair spilling over it, the tips dragging in the mud.

I laid the saddle pad down on the driest spot of ground I could find, curled on top of it, and covered myself with my damp cloak. Pine needles protruded from my braids and stabbed at my hands and arms when I tried to use them as a pillow. I sat up, untying the braids and pulling out all the flowers, leaves, and pine needles, shaking my waves free.

How had I gotten here—a princess, picking pine needles from my hair and sleeping on the muddy ground in the woods? I let my mind wander over everything that had happened since I'd delivered Elliot that roast, what seemed like eons ago, even though it had only been a few hours.

So much had changed: meeting Prince Christopher, my mother's announcement of the engagement and its timeline, my sudden departure. Still, her words felt like a betrayal, like a poisoned blade to my heart. I couldn't risk speaking with her before I ran, but I longed to cry into her arms and ask her how she could do this to me.

The prince was handsome and charming, but how could he think that would change anything? I couldn't let Norrfalt win. I refused to be a political pawn any longer.

Perhaps someday I could convince my mother to let me marry a man of my choice—someone who would respect me as partner and equal—and we could ascend the throne together when the time came. But that would only be possible if I could discover the truth behind the duke's lies and stop the wedding. If I accomplished that, perhaps Mother would trust me enough to make my own choice.

I found a smooth rock and laid my head down.

Monsieur Pentamerone didn't exist, nor did his sister, my "mistress." Mother would have no reason to knight Elliot; in fact, she may hold it against him for helping me escape. But if Mother wouldn't knight Elliot, I would just do it myself. I was the future queen, wasn't I?

For now, I had to focus on staying anonymous and getting to the front lines. What if the truth I sought did not bring peace between Mittelan and Norrfalt after all? Would Elliot and I end up in the heat of battle ourselves? I wasn't afraid to fight, and I was more than willing to sacrifice my life, but had I volunteered Elliot to do the same? I imagined Elliot and I standing alone, facing leagues of Norrfalt soldiers. The sense of dread intensified as the image of us, surrounded by my dead countrymen on a frozen battlefield, threatened to consume me.

My wandering mind drifted into a fitful sleep.

❖❖❖

A jabbing pain in my shoulder woke me, surrounded by the citrus rainbow of dawn. My eyelids parted, squinting up to see what was poking me. Elliot stood above me, repeatedly prodding me with the end of a long stick. I swatted the branch away, moaning with exhaustion and squeezing my eyes shut tight.

"Wake up, princess," he cooed. I sat up sharply.

"What the hell did you just call me?" Terror raged through my veins so profound I felt like he should be able to see it exploding from the surface of my skin.

"Calm down," he tossed the branch aside and faced his palms towards me in what I presumed was supposed to be a calming motion. "I figured you must sleep on a fairly comfortable bed normally to have to steal the blanket off your horse."

He was joking, Chara, of course he was joking. Keep it together.

"If you can't make it through a night on the ground without your duvet, are you sure you're ready for war? I guess that's what you get for calling me soft."

I wiped the sleep from my eyes as my heart steadily retreated from a stampede to its normal trot.

Stretching out my leg, I was surprised how much better it felt today. I stood up, putting weight on it with no more than a twinge.

Leaves fell from the tangles of my hair. I ran my fingers through the waves to brush the rest of them away, suddenly self-conscious. Elliot, on the other hand, looked as if he had just woken from a fulfilling night's sleep. The mud must have dried and fallen right out of his glossy hair because today it shone vibrantly in the pink and orange of the sunrise. His eyes were a bright and familiar glittering hazel, wide and ready for the day. His tunic, filthy and untucked, billowed out from his muscular form. I was annoyed at how good he looked overall when I was in shambles.

I puffed my chest with faux assurance. "My leg feels much better today after my night on the ground, so the real question is, are *you* ready for war, Sir Cendrilon?"

His easy expression hardened. "Stop calling me that."

I pursed my lips, cursing myself for forgetting again. But his forcefulness was completely out of line. It was his name. It was his title. Why was he being so damn sensitive? I picked up Stell's riding blanket from the ground and tried to dust it off. "But why not? You are of noble blood, aren't you?"

"Is your mistress so high in the noble ranks that you know nothing of how knighthood works in this kingdom?" He looked truly baffled at my ignorance. The royal crest on my scabbard was hidden from his sight, but in that moment it throbbed against me. He had no idea how high in the hierarchy I really was.

I said nothing.

He shook his head. "Why do you think I want to be knighted? Why do you think I agreed to help you? Families and descendants of knights are the lowest rung in Mittelan nobility. Most have no special lands or fields to earn us money so we must earn our own money like any other peasant. A person can be born into a knighted family, but that really only makes them noble on paper. They do not deserve the title of *Sir* or *Knight* until they have earned the honor for themselves. Being a true knight is more than just a birthright. It's an honor that can only be bestowed by royalty after an intense act of bravery. Only then can a born knight be called a true knight. Only then would they earn the title *Sir.* After we are successful, Miss Kiera, once Monsieur Pentamerone is home safe and sound and the queen has knighted me, only then can you call me *Sir* Cendrilon."

I kicked myself for agreeing to his terms without fully understanding them. His request was about much more than an audience with the queen, and I had a feeling he wouldn't want his knighthood from the princess who lied and cheated him. He was seeking his own honor.

I put the blanket over Stell's back and put the saddle on top. "And you've not earned this title before?"

He laughed without humor. "Not even close. It is not something you earn more than once. A man is only knighted once in his life, and the honor is permanent."

Obviously, I admonished myself, *what a stupid question, Chara.* I had learned the ranks of nobility from my tutors, but they'd never explained this facet of the hierarchy to me, or perhaps I hadn't been listening. I thought that when a man was knighted, he was brought into the ranks of nobility and then simply passed that status to his kin. I knew nothing of the nuances to the title of which Elliot spoke.

He finished bridling his horse and then looked back to me. "I'm no soldier," he said, "having never seen a battle that didn't take place in an arena. But I do know this land well and I will see to it that you make it to the border safely. I'm also a decent tracker. I will help you find Monsieur Pentamerone and bring him home. Until then, please, just call me Elliot."

"My deepest apologies, *Elliot,*" I forced myself to respond, even as his words *I'm no soldier* turned over in my gut. "Yes, I know we are not soldiers but we should be prepared for anything."

Prepared. We were currently anything but prepared. We didn't have any armor and Elliot didn't even have a weapon. I looked at my riding coat, the embellishments now tarnished with mud and the fabric tattered from my fall. We needed supplies or we would never survive the journey through the trading city of Carnell, past the maize fields and through the Montane Range, to the borderlands that separated Mittelan from Norrfalt. There was no doubt that I had to retrieve the armor, weapons, and supplies from Emily. Once I had them in hand, I could easily play it off as if my "mistress" had provided them; however, Elliot could absolutely not accompany me when I went to collect them and my gut told me he would insist.

I had to come up with some excuse as to why Elliot could not meet his benefactor, and quickly.

"And prepared we shall be. You said your mistress is making the preparations at her residence in Swanstone, correct?" he asked as he finished buckling the saddle onto his horse.

"Yes," I lied, "but we do not need to go there yet as I previously explained," I stumbled over my words and hoped he didn't notice. "She's not expecting me until tomorrow." I mimicked the movements Elliot did to prepare his horse in order to ready Stell for our departure. I hoped he couldn't tell that I'd never saddled my own horse, but he must have noticed my trembling hands, or the way I fumbled to buckle the saddle around my mare's stomach, because he came to my side and helped me adjust the bridle over Stell's face.

"How about we take today to train together," I suggested. The idea seemed sound. We could make a training ground for ourselves here, far enough from the capitol city to avoid unnecessary attention and close enough for me to sneak in and back by myself tonight after he fell asleep. Then I could be back with the supplies before he had time to ask any questions. "We can make good use of the day until my mistress is ready for me first thing tomorrow. We will be underway in no more than a day's time, I promise."

He tilted his head, and for a moment I thought he would argue, but then a smile seized him, and genuine excitement wiped away the uncertainty. "Then you're in luck, Miss Kiera, because I know the best trainer in all of Mittelan."

My stomach knotted up as I realized what I had just done. I knew exactly what he was going to say before the name left his lips.

"Sir Andre Parren."

CHAPTER SIXTEEN

ELLIOT

We packed the campsite with anything but haste. Although there was almost nothing to pack away, Kiera was moving agonizingly slowly.

She packed and repacked her saddlebag three times. She took several long draws from a canteen and gnawed a piece of jerky at a tortuous pace before eventually offering me some as well. As I chewed, Kiera began meticulously burying the remnants of the evening's fire with fistfuls of mud and dirt.

"You really don't have to do that, you know?" I said for the third time. "Those embers have been burned out for hours now."

"Better to be safe," she said, somehow getting herself even muddier in the process of leaving the camp than she had while staying in it.

I watched from atop Gus as she washed her hands with her canteen and then began combing and braiding her hair as if it were the first time she'd ever done so. This girl was undoubtedly odd. Instead of spending her final day before our journey resting or saying farewell to her mistress, she'd rather muck about in the woods and practice her swordsmanship.

Based on her performance in the arena, though, she didn't seem to need any practice. However, I couldn't deny I was excited for the excuse to see Parren and tell him of my new plan before I left. It would certainly be disappointing to share that all these seasons of training and saving—almost three years of them—had been for nothing, now that Silas had confiscated my winnings, but I was looking forward to telling him of Kiera's offer. I knew he would understand that the reward was worth the risk.

The risk: a long journey, a dangerous warfront, the possibility that Pentamerone was not even alive.

The reward: knighthood, freedom, and—most importantly—Beauhaven. *Someday* would be here at long last, and finally it would feel like my family could come together once more to rest in peace.

Parren would definitely agree, the risk was well worth it.

Kiera painstakingly folded her riding coat and stuffed it into one of her horse's packs. The sun was quickly warming up the day, and it was finally beginning to feel like spring. Kiera, with a shake of her head, must have decided she was still cold, because she pulled out the cloak once more and put it on. I held back a chuckle.

A chuckle! An actual laugh. I couldn't remember the last time I had laughed so lightly, so genuinely. That's when I realized that I was away from Silas—truly, truly away—for the first time since he married my mother all those years ago; no meals to cook, no hunting or skinning or selling pelts, and no chores.

I couldn't help but smile.

Kiera may have been undeniably odd—denying my request to see her mistress, stuttering over answers to simple questions, and shaking like a leaf as she saddled her horse—but despite all of that, she had given me a second chance.

I still felt a hot pang of anger when I remembered that this woman was the same person who had ended my winning streak and left the Games without even claiming her prize, but now I felt a bit of respect along with the simmering frustration.

Kiera had entered a tournament full of skilled and trained men, and beat round after round of them, just to find me. She was talented and persistent, and probably dangerous as well, although she didn't seem like much of a threat now, hobbling around on her injured leg and splashing mud everywhere as she stomped through each icy puddle.

As odd as she was, she held my future in her hands. There was no going back.

Truthfully, I didn't want to go back. I didn't want to train for the Games and pray that when I had enough money, Silas would be willing to strike a bargain. I didn't want to be his servant boy for even a day longer. So I would do anything Kiera asked of me if it meant one day I would be able to stand before Silas as a true knight, like my father and grandfathers before me, and reclaim what was rightfully mine: Beauhaven.

CHAPTER SEVENTEEN

CHARA

My riding cloak was coated with mud from acting as my blanket overnight, and my hair was in a snarly, messy braid hanging down my equally mussed blouse. It had been only the third time in my life I had braided my own hair, and the first two times were when Emily was trying to teach me how. I'm sure I looked more like a stable hand than a princess, which occurred to me was probably a good thing as we traveled back into Swanstone.

I could hear Elliot stifling a laugh as he watched me 'accidentally' dirty myself even further as I packed my few remaining belongings. Mud and grime seemed like my best chance at an impromptu disguise.

It had been nine hours since I went missing from the castle, eight of which were sleeping hours. Mother would probably not have sent anyone out looking for me quite yet.

Now I was heading off to meet with the head trainer of her guard. While Parren had been training me on and off again for years, we were anything but friends. He was fiercely loyal to my mother. I would never make it out of Swanstone if he discovered my plot.

But I hadn't yet come up with a suitable reason as to why we should not spend our day of training with one of the most highly sought after swordsman mentors in all of Mittelan. What was I thinking when I suggested spending the day training? I knew Parren had trained Elliot, I should have known that this would be his suggestion. I felt mortifyingly foolish at my oversight. It seemed at each turn, I was making more and more of a mess of the plan that had seemed so perfect in my mind. I should have foreseen that Elliot would make such a suggestion at the mention of training.

Until I could figure out a logical reason to not see the Head Trainer of the Queen's Guard, I would play along.

I climbed into Stell's saddle, looking behind me to make sure I hadn't missed anything.

"You think you left something behind?" Elliot teased, "You didn't have anything out in the first place."

"Bugger off." I clipped the reins and tried to hide the fact that Elliot already seemed keenly attuned to my interesting behavior. I had to pull myself together if I stood even a sliver of a chance of getting out of the capitol without being discovered.

We rode in silence for a good while. Closer and closer to Swanstone. Closer to Parren. Closer to the duke and the prince. Closer to danger.

Still, not a single plausible excuse for changing our course came to my mind.

The country path ended, and we turned south onto the cobblestone thoroughfare that led to Swanstone. If I could explain my predicament to Parren, maybe he would let me go quietly? Or perhaps I could order his silence. I was his future queen, after all. Both options were dead ends, and I knew it, but what other options did I have?

Walter Ravine came into view, and the huge walled city loomed just past it. I was usually in a carriage when I traveled this stretch, but by my estimate, I had a matter of minutes—fifteen, maybe twenty at the most—to decide what to do about Parren.

A group of rowdy men in crumpled soldier uniforms lumbered solemnly down the road opposite us, heading away from town. It would have been easy to ignore them if waves of anger were not radiating from them. The gang spoke obvious dissent amongst themselves, occasionally raising their voices heatedly.

As we drew closer, their complaints rose to loud grumblings of protest. They were still too far away to understand. I tried to focus on the predicament with Parren that grew more pressing with every step, but for some reason I could not draw my attention away from the battered looking soldiers.

It wasn't long before the distance between us closed enough that I could start to hear their grievances.

"Another conscription notice not even two months after I get home," complained a man with pasty skin and greasy brown hair pulled into a long tail, "they've gone too far this time." He wasn't the largest man in the group, but had a presence that seemed to command the attention of his comrades. They huddled around him as they walked, clinging to his every word.

Another conscription notice? I tugged on Stell's reins to slow her and Elliot trotted on ahead. I wanted to hear more.

"And now I've got to go all the blasted way home, halfway across the country, after walking all the blasted way here just to have the damn queen dismiss me like I was a whiny git." The men all grunted their agreement. They passed by, hardly taking notice of me at all.

Except one. A brute of a man, large and hairy, exposed a mouth missing at least ten teeth when he smiled at me in a way that made me feel like charging him with my sword, like he was somehow seeing more of me than I had exposed. His eyes lingered on my legs, clothed in smooth leather and one to each side of the saddle, not both to one side like a 'proper' lady. The brute seemed to like it.

Then his gaze traveled up my body and over my cloak as if he was imagining what lay under it. A man had never dared to look at me like that before. Sure, I'd felt a sidewards glance or two from a guard throughout my life, but most of them knew I could likely kill them if they looked too long.

"I'll tell ya what, men," the leader spoke again, oblivious to my lingering presence, "the queen doesn't have a damn clue how to lead this country. Been getting worse and worse since the day the king up and died on us. But guess maybe we deserve what we get for letting a woman on the thro—"

"Excuse you, sir," I yanked up on Stell's reins and she stopped, stamping her feet in place. I hadn't intended to confront the disgruntled soldiers, but their open disapproval of my mother combined with the brute's hungry glare made my blood boil. I was the princess, in line for the throne, and no one had the right to look at me like that. And, sure as hell, no one was allowed to talk about my mother like that. Such talk was nothing short of treason.

"Who do you think you are that you can speak of your queen in such a manner?" I said, and the leader turned to me slowly, as if he'd misheard. I went on, "Are you an emperor that Mittelan does not know it bows to? A prophetic angel, maybe? Or, perhaps, the Creator himself? Because in my mind, those are the only ones with a legitimate excuse for disrespecting the queen."

The greasy man looked bewildered for a moment, apparently unused to being talked down to, let alone by a woman. He guffawed loudly and began to cross the road towards me. The brute followed closely behind him, licking his lips. For a moment, a spark traveled across the leader's gaze when he looked up at me.

I swallowed a breath. *Did he recognize me? What have I done?* I kicked myself for exposing myself so brazenly, but my anger was in full force now and I could not back down. It wouldn't make a difference if I did. The leader came up beside where I sat atop Stell and I refused to flinch away from him.

"I fight for the queen, ain't that enough?" He put his hand on Stell's mane and the horse huffed and pulled away from him. "Or do I have to kiss her ass too?"

I felt my jaw drop. "You have to show resp—"

"Beautiful horse," he cut me off, continuing to stroke Stell's neck.

The hairy brute, with his knotted beard and mangy hair that grew all the way down the back of his neck, stepped past his cohorts and stood beside the leader. He gave him a knowing glance and the leader said, "My friend likes you, and I like your horse. Could get me to Carnell in less than half the time,

I bet . . ." Before I even had the thought that perhaps my own subjects could present a danger to me, he'd slid his arm around my waist and yanked me to the ground from Stell's back.

"Let me go!" I shrieked, throwing punches every direction I could but none of them met flesh. The men all chuckled.

A horse stamped up to the ring of hungry soldiers and I realized it was Elliot. I struggled even harder against the man's grip, my fingers only a breath away from the hilt of my sword which hung hidden under my cloak. The leader manhandled me as if I were nothing more than a rag doll, but the more I struggled, the tighter he clung.

Elliot swung down from his horse. "Whoa, there, men. Please, that's my sister you have there," he flinched as he said it, which didn't entirely help to sell his story. "She's all I have in the world. Please, let her go. I . . . uh . . . I'll take her off your hands." He forced a smile.

"Ah! We've got a hero come to save the wench!" The leader whooped and his friends laughed while reaching for their weapons.

I stomped on the man's foot as hard as I could. He hollered in surprise and released me, nearly falling over himself. I pulled my blade from its scabbard and poised it between myself and them. His men drew their blades just as quickly. "I'm *not* a wench and I don't need a hero," I snapped at him. "The next time you touch me, I promise to maim something far more precious to you than your foot." He hopped around on one foot, face wrinkled with pain, as his friends began closing the circle around us.

Elliot held his palms out in front of him, "I'm sorry men, you must excuse my sister, she thinks herself quite brave and sometimes that gets her into a little trouble."

The leader put his injured foot down with a wince. Even though I'd just escaped his grasp and threatened to cripple his manhood, he seemed completely unafraid of the tip of my blade. "That's alright," the leader said to Elliot, faux enthusiasm barely masking his anger, "a bit of luck for me actually. I could use a couple horses." The leader gave his friends a knowing look before addressing me, "How about we make a little arrangement, mademoiselle, we won't kill you or your brother, but we get to keep your horses, eh? Sounds fair to me."

"You will do no such thing," I commanded. "These are our horses and you are all being quite disrespectful. Especially when talking to a lady."

The brute licked his lips again and smiled as if this was the most fun he'd had in a long time. He raised his eyebrows and grinned. "You sure don't *sound* like a lady," he hissed.

Elliot watched as my every muscle tensed. "Stand down, Kiera, we can't take them all," he whispered to me.

But I was already moving. I swung my blade in a deft arc, cutting the brute's sword-bearing shoulder deep and fast. His blade fell to the ground. The leader pulled his own blade and charged. I met blades with him once—his lack of swordsmanship obvious—but before I could strike a blow, his friends surrounded me like a flock.

I could easily take down the leader, but I didn't dare strike with the entire gangs' swords aimed at me. Where had Elliot gone? I spun around, but found only six sets of hungry eyes and five blades closing in on me.

Had Elliot taken their focus on me as an opportunity to escape? I cursed. Why would that surprise me? I'd known the man a grand total of one day; he'd sworn no allegiance to me.

My heart quickened as the leader's gaze turned even more spiteful. He snickered and lifted his shoulders in false concern. "What? Prince Charming run away?" He frowned in mock sympathy, only to continue sneering once more.

If Elliot had abandoned me, he'd left me with no other choice. I had to fight. I lifted my sword faster than any of the clumsy soldiers could react, stabbing the leader in the hip. His flesh resisted little more than the hay-stuffed dummy of my training. The thought barely slowed me as the man sunk to his knees. I dodged blows from either direction, narrowly missing a swipe that almost took my ear.

Then the blows started coming too quickly. I only had time to deflect, never attack. Suddenly a soldier ambushed me from behind, grabbing my arm and jerking so hard I thought it might pull from its socket.

I screamed out in both pain and surprise. Then something lifted me from my waist and I was on top of a horse, facing Elliot. He'd swept me up with such force, I'd assumed an attack. He had one arm leading Stell behind him and the other wrapped firmly around my waist. The horses galloped away, the men hollering at us as we fled.

Shock rolled over me as I processed what had just happened. I'd cut down two men and almost died in the process.

Elliot's arm held firm around my middle, his face mere inches from my own. My pulse raced and I couldn't be sure if it was from the close encounter with the soldiers or Elliot's breath on my cheeks and his hand on the small of my back. I'd never been this close to a man before in my whole life.

"What the hell were you thinking?" he fumed, not letting

the horses slow. Not yet.

Whatever I'd been feeling moments earlier quickly morphed to brazen anger. I blushed red hot and my teeth clenched too tight to snap back.

He shook his head with exasperation. "What came over you? Provoking a group of six armed soldiers?"

"I could have taken them. You should have let me!" I yelled, my chin quivering. "You have no idea what I'm capable of. *You* underestimate me just like everyone else."

"Better for someone to underestimate you and come to your aid than to do the opposite and find you sliced into ribbons," he said through a tight jaw, "and trust me, that's a better fate than what they had planned for you."

My mouth went dry.

When the men were far enough behind us, Elliot stopped his horse and lowered me to the ground. "You could try saying thank you," he said.

He was right, of course, and I knew it. Six on one—even with my training and their lack thereof—would have been extremely difficult, nearly impossible, odds. I couldn't have taken on all six men at once, but when I'd originally spoken to them, I hadn't expected to have to. It didn't even occur to me that I could find myself in danger facing my own citizens.

Their anger at the crown was foreign to me and I didn't understand it. This world was a darker and more violent place than I'd imagined. If this was what happened against six untrained, drafted soldiers on Mittelan's own streets, how did I expect to fare if I ended up fighting in a real war?

I knew I should thank him, but doing so felt like admitting defeat. I felt my chin wobble again with barely masked tears. I clenched my teeth.

Looking ahead I saw that we were close to the bridge that would take us into the city. It wasn't even mid-morning yet. We were heading to see Parren, and I hadn't a clue as to how I was going to stop it.

Still, I was alive. I'd escaped those men and their hungry hands, if only just barely. I took Stell's reins in my hand and wrapped an arm around her neck. I couldn't believe how close I'd come to losing her . . . or worse. Yes, I should thank Elliot, but somehow I just couldn't.

I brought him on this mission to help guide me through unfamiliar lands, to lend authenticity to my backstory, and to fight *together* if the need arose. I didn't bring him along to fight my battles for me, to sacrifice himself for me, or to come to my rescue as if I were some damsel in distress.

"I could thank you," I said, fanning the flames of my pride as I set my jaw and planted a fist on my hip, "but then you might start to think I needed you to save me, and that is something I simply cannot allow."

CHAPTER EIGHTEEN

ELLIOT

It was clear that Kiera wasn't ready to admit the danger that her lapse in judgement had put us in. Yes, she had raged like a fierce mountain cat against those ruffians—I didn't know of any other fighter who would have lasted as long as she had—but I still cringed imagining the ghastly fate she could have faced had the men overtaken her.

We needed to let the horses rest after our rapid retreat. I slid off of Gus and began to lead him towards Swanstone. Kiera copied me without a word. Perhaps she could sense my anger and annoyance at the fact that she barely acknowledged that I had just saved her from what could have been a huge mess. She may have been a better fighter than me, but no one could take those odds.

As my racing pulse finally began to slow, my brain spun with questions about my mysterious new companion. Why did she know how to fight so well? Who had trained her? Why was she so oblivious to the obvious danger of confronting six armed soldiers? Did I make a mistake agreeing to her plan when I knew next to nothing about her?

Kiera walked beside her mare, keeping a good distance from me. The scarlet flush finally started to drain from her cheeks as she calmed down. She had been honestly unafraid to speak to those men with such presumption and had genuinely thought she could take every one of them down.

She stroked her horse's neck as she walked, her eyes glazed over as if she were thinking intently about something exceedingly important. As she thought, she moved her jaw back and forth, rubbing her rosy lips together subconsciously. She kept her eyes on the dusty stone road, then on a budding tree, and then up into the cloudless sky. She looked anywhere except at me.

I wanted to let the situation go, to focus only ahead. Monsieur Pentamerone. Knighthood. Beauhaven.

But for some reason I couldn't leave it be.

"Why did you engage with them?" I asked, trying not to sound hotheaded, but probably failing. "I mean, they were quite obviously raging idiots, you could have just let them pass by. Why provoke them?"

The bright mid-morning sun was shining on my back and she looked at me through squinting eyes. "They disrespected the queen," she said plainly, as if I should have known without asking.

"Well aren't you the loyalist," I laughed, surprised by her genuineness. It was one thing to fight for the crown as a soldier in the face of enemies, but to put your life at risk completely unnecessarily for the honor of someone not even present was another thing entirely.

"Yes, of course," she said defensively. "Are you not? I mean . . . what I mean is, of course I am. Aren't we all? I mean, we all live under royal rule. They protect us, they lead us, why wouldn't we be loyalists?"

"Well, yes, to an extent," I answered, "but weren't you afraid for your own safety? As a woman? Talking down to six men?"

The woods hugging the road gave way to rocky terrain as the crags of Walter Ravine crept closer and closer. The drawbridge was in sight now, down for merchants and citizens to cross into the capitol city.

Kiera's pace slowed. A few farm carts and a merchant or two made their way around us without stopping. I turned to face her.

"Why should I have been scared?" Her lips were parted slightly, eyes wide. She looked truly baffled. "Am I just to assume that everyone I meet is hell-bent on doing me harm? Should I have been scared of you?"

She suddenly seemed so innocent, despite the fact that she could fillet a trained swordsman blindfolded. I laughed, this time in earnest, at this fighting handmaiden who saw herself as completely and totally invincible. She saw the world as a safe, padded place. She had obviously not seen the darkest sides of humanity as I had.

Suddenly I was jealous of her. "Well then, I take it you work in a very kind home," I said, trying to keep my bitterness at bay. Any trace of a smile that remained disintegrated from my face as I thought of Millie, as I habitually reached up to touch the pouch at my waist.

Had my sister lived to see today, she would never have had Kiera's innocent view of the world. She would have always been broken, as I was broken. We'd been taught, day by day, to expect the worst from people.

I was lucky to have had people in my life to remind me that it wasn't always true. My mother, namely, but also Parren and Bruno. The Pentamerones must be very good people after all, if Kiera remained so naïve. Perhaps the mistress's brother really was worth all this trouble.

We inched towards the bridge, Kiera ambling along with anything but haste. *Please let her not walk like this all the way to the border,* I thought. Perhaps she was still recovering from our recent trauma. I decided not to push her just yet, perhaps I could use the time to get some of my questions answered. "How did you come to be the Mistress Pentamerone's handmaiden?"

She looked closely at the marbled grey and white hair of her horse's neck, inspecting the way it bristled under her hand as she stroked her mare. "Well . . ." she paused, as if trying to remember the answer to a simple question. "I . . . ummm . . . well, I came to them as most servants come to the upper class."

"You were sold?"

"No! No, no. My parents just sent me to the Pentamerone's to work . . . you know, to make some coin for the family?"

Her answer sounded more like a question. She fiddled with the hilt of her blade atop the scabbard.

"So your parents are alive then?"

"Yes," she said, "Well, no. I mean . . . no." Her eyes darted to me and then back to the ground.

"You've forgotten if your parents are alive?" I scoffed at

the thought. I'd give anything to forget the pain of losing my parents.

"No, of course not, don't be silly. Your inquisition is just making me nervous," she said, stopping to stamp her foot on the ground like a child throwing a tantrum. "What I meant to say is that my father is dead, but my mother is alive."

"Oh. Sorry about your father then."

Kiera nodded to accept my sympathies, and I noticed her pink cheeks return as she began to spin the brass ring on her finger with her thumb. Why were my simple questions so discomfiting?

The traffic on the thoroughfare picked up as we neared town. Tradesmen, coaches, merchants, and livestock were all trying to get to and from the market. But the world around us seemed to go quiet as Kiera walked closer to me. I found myself unendingly puzzled by her, but also insatiably curious.

"Any siblings?" I asked as we walked between a farmer's cart loaded with sheep and a few men wearing the signature bright colors and patterns of Almoran dress.

"No," she answered without pause.

"How about friends?"

"Yes, one."

"What's her name?"

"Emmm—" she began but let the single syllable hang on her closed lips. The heat rose even further in her cheeks. I quite enjoyed watching the scarlet flush return to her face. I wasn't sure why my simple questions were causing it, but I did like watching Kiera squirm. It did not instill trust in her, but it was kind of fun.

"I assume it's a her . . ." I joked, tossing a loose elbow into her arm. She sputtered for an answer but ended up just biting down on her lip and shooting me a ruthless glare. "How interesting . . . a girl who doesn't hesitate to take on six rogue soldiers and doesn't flinch stepping into an arena with a man twice her size stutters over a few simple questions."

"I—I—I . . . uh . . . I just—" she stammered.

"Don't hurt yourself, m'lady, I'm not trying to make you uneasy," I flicked her tangled and messy braid over her shoulder and a half smile joined her deepening blush. "Miss Kiera, you do befuddle me. So how did a well-treated, working handmaiden such as yourself come to fight like such an expert?" A real question, one that would beg on every person's lips who would ever see Kiera fight.

"My father taught me," she answered without hesitation, her chin high and proud.

"Your father who died?" I asked, immediately regretting it when I noticed her cringe. "I'm sorry, that was rude."

She ran her hand along her blade's sheath subconsciously and then gripped the hilt possessively. "It's fine. Yes, my father did teach me most of what I know. Before he died."

"I'm sorry," I said as I watched ache blossom behind her shimmering brown eyes. It was so honest and deeply familiar that I felt somehow tied to the strange little handmaiden in that moment. "Mine too," I said, "my father and my mother are both gone."

She pressed her lips together and nodded, a silent commiseration. We shared a quiet moment of grief despite the hustle and bustle of the road. We stepped onto the drawbridge and Kiera looked up at the jagged crimson cliffs of Walter Ravine as if they were precious to her.

I wasn't sure why, but I briefly considered telling her about Millie. But I didn't, even *couldn't* somehow. The guilt of how my actions had cursed my sister was like a deadly wound that had been barely bandaged. If I spoke of her, it would be like ripping off the tourniquet. Then I would bleed out and there would be nothing left of me to remember her.

"He taught me from a very young age," Kiera said, pulling my attention back to her. "He wanted me to know how to defend myself. He showed me proper footwork, how to handle a blade, when to strike, when to block. He always needed . . . " She let out a quiet laugh, as if amused by a punchline she hadn't gotten to, "I mean, wanted, he always *wanted* a son. I think that's one of the reasons I trained so hard, with such determination. To show him that he didn't need a son. He had me, and I could be just as good." She shrugged her shoulders as if recalling a sweet and fleeting memory that left her happy and sad all at the same time.

Kiera stopped in the very center of the bridge to peer over the ledge, down into the rocky depths, where the Chartley River rapids raged far below. She then looked up, staring ahead at the white city walls and the castle's picturesque spires beyond it. The frenzied travelers surrounding us seemed to somehow exist beyond where we paused, suspended between the life I was leaving behind and the one I was heading towards.

Her hand rested on the old wood railing of the bridge and I found myself still in awe that those delicate hands could so easily bear a sword with far more skill than my own. "You're father would be very proud of your victory, then, eh?"

She cocked her head to the side.

"In the Games?" I clarified, "He was training you to fight in the Woodland Games, correct? Well, you're the newest champion."

"Oh! Yes, yes, of course. Obviously." She gazed off to the side, catching sight of an auburn strand that had fallen into her view. She blew it out of her face with a huff and began walking once more, leading her horse by the reins. "But, also, he saw swordfighting much like an art form: completing the correct steps, finding the exact maneuver to best your opponent. Father had absolutely no *need* to know how to fight, and yet, he was an expert. I don't think he ever imagined that his daughter would inherit his skill and seeing me spar always made him so proud."

I smiled at the honeyed look she bore, pride that swirled with joy and sadness. Her cheeks were full and her eyes bright as she remembered him. Despite the mess of mud and dirt she'd managed to somehow cover herself with, she still looked remarkably lovely. A fierce and passionate fighter, and also a handmaiden? Kiera was definitely hiding something, but somehow the mystery of it only made her more interesting to me.

I'd never met anyone like her. Yes, she was hiding something deep, something I didn't understand; but, for the first time, I didn't look at her and see that armored stranger who had destroyed my life and enraged me nearly every moment since we met. Instead, I saw someone brave to the point of foolish, someone loyal beyond comparison, and someone willing to throw herself into harm's way in an attempt to rescue her mistress's missing family member.

Because of her, I finally had a way to earn my knighthood and save Beauhaven. I was on a real and meaningful quest instead of answering to Silas's beck and call, or training for another cursed betting match, and it was all because she'd found me.

I didn't trust her exactly, but I was drawn to her in a way unlike any friend or acquaintance I'd ever had before. And, as we walked through the bustling city gates of Swanstone, I realized I wasn't likely to ever meet anyone quite like her again.

CHAPTER NINETEEN

CHARA

Walter Ravine's rugged walls had always been a sign that we were nearly home. Our diplomatic tours, holidays at our summer castle on the southern coast, and royal visits all ended with our carriage clattering back over this bridge. It was the only way in and out of the city, and—although it remained lowered nearly all the time—it was always a comfort knowing it could be lifted. The deep crimson ravine, with its sparkling blue river rushing far below, meant safety. It meant home.

But now, as we crossed the threshold into Swanstone, despite its immense fortifications, the city felt like the antithesis of safety. Returning here could mean the end of my plan, the end of my freedom. And yet I couldn't think of another way.

"This way," Elliot cocked his head in the opposite direction of the castle and market, before swinging up into his horse's saddle. I did likewise, thankful for the relief from walking. Although my leg felt much better, it still ached from spending much of the morning on foot and probably also from my brief battle with those conscripted soldiers. I knew I was lucky to have such a minimal injury after being thrown from a horse and facing off against that treasonous clan.

Being back in Stell's saddle turned out to be a relief in more ways than one. Finally, Elliot had ended his barrage of questions. All morning, however harmless they may have seemed, each question he posed felt like the makings of a trap: one wrong step and I would find the spring releasing to snap me in its steel teeth. He had not allowed me a moment of peace to come up with an excuse—any excuse—not to pay a visit to Parren.

I followed closely behind Elliot, not wanting to lose him on the frantic streets of the shopping district. Citizens from the surrounding countryside were in town shopping for their spring necessities: new clothes, flowers, seeds—anything and everything they had learned to live without all winter.

However, it was impossible not to notice that many of the people crowding the walkways were not shopping at all, but huddled into groups, as if sharing an immensely juicy piece of gossip. Perhaps I was seeing things, but it seemed to me they were all acting sort of . . . nervous.

Was news already spreading of my disappearance or was something else going on? I pulled the hood of my cloak over my head.

The crowds dwindled and the streets became dirtier tenfold as we left the shopping district behind and entered the pub district.

Elliot pulled his horse to a stop between two sketchy looking boarding houses, where a dingy stairwell descended beneath the rickety buildings. A sign hung from the building's side, out over the stairs. The words were so weathered and gray they were hardly legible, but I could make out the shape of a black cat.

We tied up our horses and descended the stairs, slick with mud and vomit. There was no banister to grasp, so I treaded carefully, not wanting to end up with my clothes covered in that particular mess.

I followed Elliot through a pock-marked wooden door at the base of the steps and immediately reached up to my face to pinch my nostrils closed. The bar reeked of hops and vomit and urine. The floors of the subterranean tavern were even dirtier than the treads of the stairs leading down to it. Elliot chortled when he saw me. I dropped my hands to my sides and fought back a gag. He seemed unfazed by the stench.

My eyes adjusted from the bright morning light to the windowless dark of the cellar-like establishment. Without the warm mountain sunshine, the air felt frigid. I suddenly felt an extra dose of sympathy for all those nights Emily spent locked in that heinous seamstress' cellar as a girl. Gooseflesh blossomed on my arms, despite having both my blouse and cloak for warmth. I pulled the cloak tighter around me.

The tables were all abandoned. In fact, the entire pub was empty save for us, the bartender—a burly man with a dense brown beard, diligently wiping table tops—and the oh-so familiar Parren, seated at the bar top in the corner.

He leaned against the wall and rested his peg leg on a bar stool in front of him. His pint was in his hand, three-quarters of the way gone, three empty glasses on the counter beside it. His silvery gray hair was neatly parted and combed into a low tail. The dull cast of his gaze disappeared when his head turned, eyes shining as they came to rest on Elliot.

Even though I doubted it would help at all, I pulled my hood further over my face. I clung to the mere seconds I had before Parren inevitably recognized me and sabotaged my last chance at freedom. My mind grappled for any way to halt the disaster that was about to befall my perfectly laid plan.

"My boy!" Parren slammed his pint down and the amber liquid sloshed up the sides, leaving foam clinging to the glass. "What are you doing here?" His thin lips nearly disappeared as they stretched wide in a smile.

"I've done it, Master Parren," Elliot's statement was wrapped in the hush of a whisper, but woven with glee. "I've left him, the lot of them." He was facing away from me but I could hear the intensity in his voice, a mixture of joy, relief, and fear.

Parren's features seemed to melt in response to Elliot's news. His smile loosened but traveled to the crow's feet surrounding his eyes and deep wrinkles crowded his forehead, smile lines emphasizing his high cheekbones. His gaze grew warm as he pushed his peg leg off of the seat, stood, and reached out his arms to Elliot, who buried himself in the embrace. I didn't know what Elliot left behind or the whole story of Parren's role in his life, but a lump grew in my throat anyway as I witnessed the intimate exchange.

After numerous pats on the back, Parren pushed Elliot to arms' length but kept his hands on his shoulders. He then moved a palm up to his cheek, almost as if he were looking for something or someone in Elliot's eyes.

"Bruno? Bruno'd you hear that?" Parren hollered at the bartender, who took a moment from his work to lay down his washcloth and cross the room to pat Elliot on the back as well.

"Proud of you, mate," Bruno said after a few more affectionate pats, "but why? After all this time, why now?"

"Silas found everything. All the winnings and . . . and my sword," Elliot choked out the last part, but if Parren was supposed to be upset, he didn't seem it. Stunned, but not angry, he opened his mouth to say something, then closed it again.

"You don't say . . . " Bruno looked sad for his friend, but not half as surprised as Parren. He gave Elliot another pat before returning to his post behind the bar to help a customer who had just entered.

"But I have found an alternative," Elliot said tentatively, focusing all his energy on Parren, "a way to end this, once and for all."

I swallowed my fear. This was it. *I* was the alternative. *This* was why Elliot agreed to my plan, why he requested his knighthood and the audience with the queen. He needed the queen to help him finish *this* . . . whatever *this* was. A chill splintered down my back.

"But I need your help," he said to his mentor.

"What? Anything Elliot, you know that." Worry tinged Parren's voice, the same type of worry I'd heard all my life: from my father, mother, Emily, even Grimm.

"Actually, *we* need your help," Elliot said and—before I even thought to stop him—he had turned around, slung his arm around me, and pushed me forward to "meet" Parren. My hood fell from my face and I fought to keep myself from ripping it back over my features. A hot flush burned my cheeks.

Instant recognition dawned on Parren's face. His jaw fell slack and his eyes grew wide, but then the surprise softened into understanding.

"And who is your *friend*?" he asked Elliot.

I focused to keep my own shock from showing. He knew who I was; he knew *exactly* who I was. He could have exposed me right here, right now. Why wasn't he?

"This is Kiera," Elliot gestured to me, "Kiera, this is Master Parren. He has been training me for the Woodland Games for the last four years."

Parren's lip twitched into a knowing, one-sided smile as he reached his hand out to mine. I gave it a curt shake.

"Pleasure to meet you, Miss . . . what was it again?"

"Kiera," I blurted, tossing his hand aside quickly. "Kiera."

"Ah yes, Miss *Kiera*. Happy to make your acquaintance. And how can I be of service?" he asked over a deliberate eyebrow raise. Elliot either didn't see the knowing glance or chose to ignore it.

I spoke before Elliot could, "We need your expertise. We have one day to polish our swordsmanship and to learn to work together as a team before we must leave for the borderlands."

"What? The borderlands?" His long eyebrows knit together with concern. He glanced at Bruno pouring ales for a pair of soldiers who had just entered the pub and dropped his voice, "Why would a nice *maiden* such as yourself go somewhere so dangerous?"

"We are going on behalf of Kiera's mistress," Elliot explained, "she wishes us to find the mistress' missing brother: Monsieur Roberto Pentamerone. He has been out of contact for months but has not yet been tallied with the dead."

"Ah, of course. Son of Lord *Pentamerone*, I would assume," Parren dragged out the fictitious name. He backed away from the pair of us, until he reached the bar stool and sat. He tapped his fingers along the bronze head of his cane.

My breathing grew ragged as I awaited his response.

He tapped his cane twice on the grungy wood floor before acting like he'd just remembered something, "Ah, yes, I do think I remember hearing that a Mittelan captain had been reported missing for quite some time."

I released a weighted breath. Parren had corroborated my story; Elliot would have no issue believing it now. But my real question was why would Parren do such a thing? What was in it for him?

"Kiera—it was Kiera wasn't it?" he looked at me with mock inquisitiveness. I nodded while trying not to roll my eyes. "Kiera, what makes you think you are well suited to war? Why would your mistress put you at such risk?"

"I—" I began a fabricated response but Elliot jumped in on my behalf.

"Kiera is an expert swordsman. In fact, she fights masterfully, even under a suit of armor." He lingered on the final word, raising his brows high.

Parren understood. And now he looked more shocked than he had all morning. I couldn't help but stand a little taller, proud of my win in the arena, proud to have Parren know that *I* was the armored man that had beaten his protégé.

Would this be the line that Parren would not allow me to cross? Perhaps he could handle me impersonating a maidservant to a fictitious family and training me alongside Elliot for a day, but would Parren approve of me entering myself in the Woodland Games when I wasn't even supposed to know the Games existed?

"Please, sir, our time is short," Elliot put a hand on Parren's shoulder, "and I have to track down a blade for practice."

The aging swordsman returned the young boy's gesture, throwing his arm around Elliot and winking at me as he did. "Of course, my boy. I think I can help you there. In fact, I have just the blade for you." He smiled broadly at me, and I returned a grimace.

For whatever unknown reason, it seemed that, at least for now, Parren was going to play along with my little rouse.

We left the pub immediately. Parren didn't even bother to pay his tab. I had a suspicion that the friend they called Bruno wasn't concerned. Parren would be back again soon and they'd add his debt to what I imagined was already quite the tab.

Sun drenched the village, now bursting with people, in stark midday light.

By now my mother must have known that I was gone when I hadn't shown up for breakfast or lunch, but if she sent out the royal guard every time I missed two meals in a row, she'd never have any guards left to protect her. Although it wasn't uncommon for me to briefly disappear from her sight, and I was fairly certain that no guards were out hunting me down just yet, I still needed to be on high alert. I pulled the hood back up and cast my eyes down onto Stell's clopping hooves. She and Gus trotted dutifully by our sides. I preferred that we weren't riding as it would draw undue attention to me, and that was one thing I could not afford.

Elliot strode beside Parren, who kept pace with the youth despite his handicap. The ease with which they fell into step told me that they had walked this same path together many times before. I followed closely, keeping my eyes locked on Elliot's fraying boots and Parren's wooden leg, not wanting to lose them in the crowded streets, but I didn't dare look up.

A cool breeze blew down the main thoroughfare, whipping my cloak around my legs. Clouds drifted over the sun, and the air cooled instantly. The crowd began to shift, parting ways off the busy street and collecting under the brightly colored awnings of the storefronts.

Fanfare trumpets sounded. In Swanstone, that meant only one thing: royalty. But something was different. The trumpets were not playing the tune of my family's dynasty as they usually did to clear the streets for the royal carriage. The trumpets were playing a different tune—something low and distinguished—something I'd never heard before.

Peasants bumped into me as they pushed themselves out of the way of the oncoming traffic. Stell neighed loudly, growing nervous as she became cornered.

I ducked behind Elliot, going down the alley just far enough to give Stell some space and to keep my eyes on what was coming. Elliot and Parren had frozen too, attention glued on the street. I racked my brain for a reason for the fanfare. Spring solstice had passed. Mittelan's Independence Celebration was still months away. There was no extended family in town that I could think of, and Mother would not leave the castle without warning.

Parren slipped me another knowing glance, accompanied by a half-smile that told me he was enjoying watching me squirm. The town crier was on the horse in front, followed by five trumpeters on foot. The men were clad in blue and white, the colors of Norrfalt.

Their straight, skinny horns fell silent as the crier drew a deep breath and projected, "Hear ye! Hear ye! Citizens of Mittelan, gather round to honor the magnanimous Christopher Everett Charles Ludwig the Third, Prince of Norrfalt, betrothed," the entire crowd gasped, "to the princess Charissa Henrietta Cordelia of the royal families Basile and Perrault. The wedding will commence in one fortnight. Long live the future king!"

My throat closed and my heart seemed to stop beating. I felt myself go pale, like a tree feels the colors drain from its leaves before fluttering, dead, to the ground. Parren and Elliot—along with all of my subjects on the crowded streets of Swanstone—repeated the crier's apocalyptic call, "Long live the future king!"

I should have turned. I should have run, but it was as if my feet had landed in pitch. *Leave! Go,* my mind screamed, *run while you still can!* But my body wouldn't listen.

The crowd split into two groups. One chanted, "Long live the future king! Long live the future king!" The other group muttered amongst themselves, stamping their feet and cursing the Norrfalters in hushed tones. Some even spit at the royal trumpeters.

I don't know when I had stopped breathing, but when my head began to spin and Parren put his arm on mine to steady me, I focused: *inhale, exhale, inhale, exhale, hold yourself together, Chara.*

Parren put his weight on his good leg. "Looks like you need

this more than I do," he held out his cane to me. It was made of a deep cherry wood, with a delicately carved handle of flowers and winged creatures, "you look a little pale, *Princess*." His voice was no louder than the sound of a sword pulled from its sheath, melting into the chants and groans of the crowd, but I heard it as clearly as the trumpets' fanfare.

Elliot's gaze stayed locked on the slowly passing parade.

Parren spoke again. "Is this what you are running from? Your engagement?"

Panic began to set in, and I forced myself to drop my chin in the slightest of nods.

Then I saw him. As the crier and the trumpet players passed us, they were followed by ten lines of blue and white guards with Prince Christopher right in the middle. The chanters intensified and those who cursed the prince loud enough to be heard were threatened by the lances and rapiers of the prince's guards.

The women—who were seeing the handsome prince for the first time—swooned, some even dared a whistle, and others offered themselves up for his hand in marriage in my stead. How easily they were willing to take the position that I was so desperately running from.

My feet finally listened, and I backed further down the alley, ducking behind Parren's shoulders. I prayed that Elliot wouldn't turn and find me cowering from the prince's view.

Christopher rode on a sleek horse with a sleek black coat and white socks. The pair of them dripped in royal blue regalia with gold medals and epaulettes. He held his chin parallel to the ground, a captivating smile plastered to plump lips. His steely eyes looked almost black in the harsh sun and made contact with nearly every female in the crowd. Was he looking for me, or was he just being his normal, charming self?

His horse cantered down the thoroughfare, stopping directly in front of us. Only a handful of peasants separated him from me. My fingertips trembled and I crossed my arms, turning away from the spectacle. I glanced over just enough to see Prince Christopher accept a rose from a voluptuous maiden and then continue down the parade route.

I relaxed, as Elliot turned from the street to where Parren and I stood, and released a heavy breath.

Elliot seemed to notice the relief in my composure and mistook it for something else. "Yuck," he crinkled his nose, "we don't have time for this." He wasn't so irritated only moments before. "Let's go."

Elliot set off towards the city's outer edge, where I believed Parren resided. We all walked in silence, and it took me two whole blocks before my breathing returned to normal. Bruno, the bartender from the pub, came out of the hubbub. He was out of breath, as if he had been trying to catch up with Elliot for quite a while. The two began to walk and joke; perhaps Elliot was telling his friend of his new mission, about how he was going to become a knight.

The thought made my insides knot. The fewer who knew about our plan, the better, but there was nothing I could do to stop his gabbing now.

Bruno's arrival gave Parren the perfect excuse to fall behind and walk by my side. He crossed his cane in front of my legs to stop me, putting even more distance between us and Elliot.

"That boy, that Norrfalter prince, cannot be our king," he said through impossibly tight lips. He returned to the rhythm of his walk. "You cannot trust the Norrfalt royal family. I know this firsthand."

"What?" I stopped walking for a moment, urging him to continue talking.

"I knew his father."

"You know the king of Norrfalt?" What excuse would Parren have to be in contact with the leader of our enemy? "But how?"

"If I tell you, Princess—"

"Don't call me that here," I interjected sharply.

"I'm sorry, it's habit. If I tell you, *Kiera*," his sideways glance sent a chill down my spine, "then you must promise to keep it from the boy." He tilted his head towards Elliot and Bruno. I knew he was referring to Elliot, but I doubted there was anyone with whom he would permit me to share whatever he was about to divulge.

"But—" I began but Parren didn't let me finish.

"You keep my secret, and I will keep yours."

I nodded.

"The king of Norrfalt is dangerous. He craves power and has always had a vested interest in Mittelan, as long as I've known him. I have no doubt this 'marriage alliance' is another attempt to seize power over the country that betrayed him. His life has left him distrusting and bloodthirsty. He has, and will, cross anyone—even a queen—who gets in his way."

"I already know that the alliance would forfeit much of Mittelan's power, which is exactly why I'm here," my guts tied themselves in endless knots, "but how do you know all of this?"

"Because I myself have been crossed by the king. I'm just lucky that I didn't lose more than my leg. Tell me what you are up to, maybe I can help."

My instinct was to trust the old drunk since he had been given every opportunity to expose me to Elliot and yet had remained silent. Still, revealing any more of my plan risked sharing something that could trigger him to change his mind and turn me in. However, it did sound like he understood the danger of the situation, and his expertise could be invaluable.

I twisted my ring nervously before deciding, "Fine, but you have to promise not to try and stop me."

"Stop you from what?"

I gritted my teeth. There was no turning back now. "I've been planning to run away for weeks, okay? That's why I entered the Games—to try to find a nobody and convince him to lead me to the border so I could help Mittelan fight. Then I overheard the Grand Duke talking to the Norrfalt Prince—who is his *nephew*, by the way—about convincing my mother to make the alliance final *before she finds out*." I quoted the duke.

"Finds out what?" Parren was clearly invested in my story now.

"Well, I don't know exactly," I admitted, "but he kept talking about the war and battles, so I am pretty convinced it has something to do with what's happening there. Then, out of nowhere, my mother announced that the wedding would be taking place in *two weeks*. I have no idea what suddenly convinced her to not only agree, but to move the timing up so drastically. So I decided it must have to do with whatever lies the duke is feeding her about the war. I have to get there and figure out the truth."

"Aye," Parren tapped his foot nervously as we both watched Bruno break away from Elliot who then turned towards us,

"I've never trusted that two-sided bastard further than I could throw him. Your union to the prince would leave the duke much to gain. His history with Norrfalt has always made me question his allegiance to your mother—"

"Mother? Do you—"

He ignored me, talking as if thinking out loud. "With Norrfalt at the helm, nobody is safe. Whatever happens, you cannot marry the prince."

"I agree. That's why—"

"Going to the border isn't much of a plan, and it's obviously dangerous for you, but it looks like we might not have another choice. We will come up with something, something that will ensure that you're—" Parren caught sight of Elliot, only a stride away, and changed topics instantly, "and that's how you make indigo dye!"

I thanked him for sharing with me the intricacies of making blue clothing, as my mind ran over everything Parren had actually said. It all brought me to one conclusion: my plan was even more important than I had previously thought. I didn't just need to expose the duke and escape the marriage alliance, I *had* to ensure that Mittelan win the war and crush Norrfalt's ever-present threat.

And, as unexpected as it was, Master Parren was turning out to be the best ally I had.

CHAPTER TWENTY

ELLIOT

I'd never before heard anyone converse so enthusiastically about the process of dyeing clothing. Well, at least Master Parren and Kiera were hitting it off. He was the closest thing I had to a father now, and it comforted me seeing him approve of my new course of action.

"Now that we have sufficiently wasted half our day," Kiera's eyes shifted between Parren and me once, and then again, "let's try to get some training in before we leave?" We all agreed and resumed in the direction of Parren's home.

Kiera, as dangerous and mysterious as she was, continued to fascinate me. I had to stop myself from lingering too long on her compelling eyes, the way they were nearly always fixed with determination, or her messy hair, which looked brunette until she moved into a blade of sunlight, and it almost seemed to catch fire. But I guess fixating on those features was far safer than letting my gaze rest on her figure. That was another battle entirely.

I'd never met a woman like her before, not just that she could best me in a sword fight any day, but also a woman whose tongue was not shackled, who was so unafraid. She'd proved that today, facing off against six angry soldiers. I still balked at the memory. And yet, hidden kindness permeated even her most sarcastic remarks. She had an unashamed fire within her, but also goodness. Kiera reminded me vaguely of Millie, of the type of person my sister could have grown into, should life have given her the chance. Maybe they'd have made great friends.

The thought brought me back to a time before Millie had gotten sick, maybe a year after Mother died. Millie and I had finished all of our chores early. It was the first time that had happened in a long time. Silas allowed us to leave the house to pick peaches from the grove at Beauhaven's far end. The only reason he allowed us such a freedom was because picking and preserving peaches saved him money.

It wasn't a long walk to the grove, but it somehow felt worlds away. The heat of summer had passed, and I hoped they'd be perfectly ripe. Of course, they weren't. They did not yet have their golden blush and were as hard as apples. Still, Millie climbed the trees deftly, with monkey-like swiftness, practically hopping from branch to branch, giggling the entire time.

"Ellie!" she called to me from the treetops. "I found some ripe ones." When I came to collect her fruit, she began to pelt the hard peaches at me like cannon fire, one after another. I climbed up into the tree after her, but she was smaller and faster than me. No matter how close it seemed I got to her head of curly white locks, she was always a step ahead.

I couldn't help but laugh when we dropped from the branches and she gave me her ridiculous puppy dog eyes, begging for forgiveness. "I'm sorry, Ellie," she puffed out her bottom lip. The gold in her hazel eyes was brighter than the leaves on the changing aspen. Like fire. Eyes like our mother's, like mine.

I pulled myself from my reverie as we reached Parren's house. The small cottage was against the west side of the city wall. It wasn't large or ornate. It had no bedrooms, just one large room with a small table, a sitting area, and a bed. The most important thing about Parren's cottage was the large courtyard behind it surrounded by a wall of whitewashed brick. The courtyard had been my practice arena since I was scarcely a teenager.

Kiera led Stell to a trough of water outside of Parren's home. As she fumbled to tie her horse, I recognized the slender fingers and the brass ring from the arena—a time when I'd known nothing about the armored stranger whose skill would have left me dead on the battlefield.

She took off her cloak and tossed it over Stell's saddle. My eyes traveled over her. Her filthy blouse and ruined riding pants did nothing to hide the grace of her shape. Even her laced up boots caused my eyes to linger. That day in the arena, I never would have believed that this woman was what was hiding beneath all that armor.

I peeled my gaze from her when I noticed Parren observing our interaction; I didn't want him to think I had been ogling her. She pulled her rapier from its scabbard hanging off her horse's back. Any doubt Parren may have had about Kiera being the steel-clad newcomer who'd beaten me at the Woodland Games disappeared when he saw the silver blade, with its expensive black and red stone hilt. I knew now that she must have gotten the sword from her mistress's family, and that likely, she'd been sent to the Games by them to fight, in search of a nameless peasant to help get her to the border.

I tied Gus beside Stell before we followed Parren onto the porch towards the splintering wooden door that led into his house. Kiera and I tried to walk through the narrow opening side-by-side, her hip grazing against me. I pulled away and put my hand forward to let her enter first. My cheeks burned.

I shut the squeaky door behind me and turned to find Parren hobbling about his home. He putzed around, looking under chair cushions and beneath the covers of his bed until eventually he found the bottle of brown liquor he'd been searching for in the bottom drawer of his nightstand. He took a swig before standing up, clenching the bottle in one hand, his cane in the other.

"Now that that's taken care of," he took another long pull from the bottle, "I have something for you, my boy." He slammed the bottle down on top of the dresser and opened the top drawer. He dug around in what appeared to be his undergarments—Kiera shot me a narrow-eyed look and I shrugged—until he finally found what he was looking for. "Ah, here she is."

I recognized it instantly. The soft, worn, black leather belt I'd worn in every arena fight, with a matching scabbard attached. The leather hugged the slender silver blade that I hadn't lost with in years—until I'd faced Kiera. The hilt was studded with tiger's eye and matched the small dagger that I'd occasionally seen Parren wear tucked into the waist of his pants. He ran his palm down the length of the sheathed blade, as if uncovering the memories enveloped there. He looked up at me, a trace of a smile pulling at his lips, and tossed the sword, scabbard, and belt as one unit to me. "It's yours now."

"No, no, no," I threw it back to him, "it's too much."

He caught it with ease in his cane-free hand.

"No, it's not." He crossed the room, picked up my hand from my side, and placed the gift there. "I can't explain, but I can assure you that this blade was always destined for you. Go with Kiera, protect her. Do what she asks. With her, you will find much more than just your freedom." He wrapped his fingers, deep with cavernous wrinkles, around my hand with the encased sword still clasped in my fist.

For some reason, Parren trusted Kiera almost implicitly. Somehow, that made me want to trust her, too, but that didn't explain why he was gifting me one of his most prized possessions.

I hadn't received a gift, aside from my cheap practice blade, since my mother had died. With Parren's hand still on mine, it felt almost as if the blade were a gift from her. I looked up to thank him and caught a glimmer of aspen-leaf gold there in his gray eyes that I'd never noticed before.

❖❖❖

Parren instructed Kiera and me as we sparred for hours. The bright sun drowned in the watercolor strokes of sunset and was then covered by the monochromatic palette of night, and still, we fought.

My stomach rumbled, the last energy from my insignificant breakfast fading until it was gone and I felt faint. Each movement was labored. Blisters bloomed down the pads of my palms and the insides of my knuckles from gripping the stone hilt. I longed for the familiar leather hilt of my practice rapier, but it was gone now, part of a life that was no longer mine.

A moment of distracted thought, and I lost all the headway I'd made that day. I'd learned many of Kiera's habits and styles, and was getting much better at predicting her movements, but not good enough. She thrust her rapier at the edge of my torso. Her perfectly controlled jab cut through my tunic, leaving a thin and shallow gash along my side. I pushed her away with my forearm, but she spun back around and kicked me hard in the chest. The pavers of the courtyard sent my tailbone into my spine as I landed hard on my rear before falling to my back, trapped with the frigid tip of Kiera's blade hovering a hair's width above my Adam's apple.

Her chest rose and fell with heavy breaths that steamed against the frosty night air. Her boot, firmly on my chest, pinned me to the ground. Wisps of hair surrounded her face, having escaped from her braid which was almost entirely undone by this point, cascading in muddy tangles and snarls down her shoulders and back. She looked victorious, as well as exhausted, but her blade did not waver.

I knew she could best me and, now that I knew better how to fight by her side, I hoped that meant together we could take on anyone who might give us trouble on our journey.

"Well, done, Kiera!" Parren slapped her on the back and the sharp point stung my neck. I batted it away. Add the two new scrapes to a long list of bruises and cuts from the hardest day of training I'd ever had. "You've reached near balance. Each spar a toss-up." He winked at her, a silent signal promising her that if the battle were real, she'd beat me every time. But I didn't need another reminder of that.

Kiera finally lowered her blade, stepped off of me, and reached out a hand to help me up. As bitter as I was about the loss, I was also completely drained, so I took her hand. The moment reflected like a mirror of the arena, right down to me noticing the slender brass ring on her finger. She pulled me roughly to my feet. I rubbed my hand along my bruised rump, then my bleeding side. She shook her head and laughed so contentedly that it almost made it worth losing.

"Don't worry, partner," Kiera said under high, teasing brows, "you have skills beside the sword to lean on. Your humor, your boyish charm, your . . ." she bit her lip in a way that made any offense I may have taken to her mockery melt into a relenting grin.

"Your . . . well, that's two things at least," she smiled brightly at her own humor.

"Well, I don't recall you mentioning your skills at throwing a knife," I said, grappling for anything that maybe I stood a chance of besting her at. I knew I wasn't incredibly skilled at that either—I was nothing compared to Bruno—but his assistance over the years had made me at least satisfactory.

Kiera sauntered towards the gate exiting the courtyard. "How would you know?"

I took my hunting knife from my waist and listened for Bruno's voice in my head, *Focus your mind and take a deep breath* . . . I breathed deeply and squared my feet. *Picture your target.* I set my mind on the gate where Kiera would soon reach for the handle to exit.

Don't miss or you'll hit her, I thought briefly before letting the blade fly. It hit the fence limply and toppled to the ground.

"Uh-oh," Kiera said sarcastically, "I surrender now! Please, teach me your ways."

I blushed and ran to pick up my blade. "Not fair! I'm injured," I said, pointing to my cut side.

"Oh, woe is me! I—"

"Now, now children," Parren interrupted our squabble, "quit bickering and get yourselves some rest." He grabbed a bottle that had been resting on a window ledge and took another long draw. The bottle was almost empty. "I don't have much, but you can probably scrounge some sort of food up from that kitchen," he said, his speech beginning to slosh together. "After you feed and water your horses, get your arses to bed."

Kiera shot me a cocky smile before disappearing out of the gate, and I rolled my eyes. She had quite the way with people, earning their affection—and their annoyance—so quickly. Parren had been awfully willing to help in our search for Monsieur Pentamerone. I hadn't questioned his generosity, as it was appreciated and much needed, but it did strike me as odd—especially the sword. Why part with something so valuable, and separate the rapier from its matching dagger, when I wasn't even leaving for battle? Not really, anyway.

Swanstone had quieted around the small home on the edge of the city grounds and the empty night air was chilly, but surprisingly peaceful. We dragged our tired feet from the courtyard into the small cottage.

Rummaging through his practically empty cupboards, I found a loaf of stale bread that was mostly free of mold and Kiera found a small satchel of turkey jerky. Parren must save his money for alcohol. We ate the scraps slowly, savoring every nourishing bite.

"I'll needa talk ta you some more in the morning m'lady," Parren gave her a slow wink, "but for now, can ya give me a moment with my boy?" He'd barely eaten any of the bread I'd given him, but had managed to find a new liquor bottle to sip from. The brown liquor he'd started with was gone and he was already almost a third of the way through this new bottle. This one was clear, in a pear shaped glass bottle, and its sharp smell took up the whole interior of the single room house.

Kiera shot him daggers but nodded politely. "I'll see to the horses." She left out the front door, and I forced myself not to watch.

"C'mere, son," Parren waved me over to his bed, patting his hand on the mattress beside him. I'd seen my mentor inebriated more times than I could count, but after a whole day spent away from his duties with the guard and a bottle in his hand pretty much the entire time, this was by far the worst.

I crossed the room from where Kiera and I had been eating at the table and sat beside him on his bed.

"There something I gotta tell ya before girl ges back," his words were slightly slurred, but surprisingly clear all things considered. He was well practiced in the art of functioning while intoxicated. "The sword," he nodded his head towards where my new blade was resting beside Kiera's satchels, "is yours."

"I know," I reminded him, setting my hand on his where it was grasped tightly around the neck of the bottle. I slowly peeled his fingers from it and removed it. "You gave the sword to me earlier."

He shook his head adamantly, but he didn't seem to notice as I set the bottle on his dresser. "No, it's yours," he insisted.

"See, was a gift to me one . . . once. Before I left for Norrfalt. It was from . . . " his eyelids grew heavy, fluttering closed and then open wide again. "From a love one. Is yours."

"A loved one?"

He nodded. "I shoulda gave it to you age . . . ages . . . ages ago." He was so drunk, his meaning was getting more and more buried in his slurred words. He fought to keep from passing out. I left him just long enough to grab a canteen from his kitchen. I tipped the bottle up, forcing water down his throat. He sputtered but eventually drank. "I fought, you know that?" he stared at me sincerely, his eyes glazing over. His face drifted heavily down.

"I know," I said. He'd told me many times of his battles at the Woodland Games but spoke very little of his time as a soldier.

"Not in the woods," he snapped his head up, "no arena. Norrfalt. This blade, save me life. But . . . " his chin trembled, "but I could not . . . did not . . . save her." Tears pooled in the pink crescents of his bloodshot eyes. "So I watched out for you, best I could, but I shoulda done more. Is too late." He was gone from me, his tales too intricately spun by the webs of alcohol to have any merit.

But he continued. "Take care of the girl," he said clearly, "promise me." I hadn't realized Kiera and him had made such a strong connection. He yanked me down towards him by my tunic. "Promise me!"

"Yes, yes, I promise," I stammered, pulling myself free. I stood beside his bed, taken aback by his forcefulness.

Parren's eyes glazed with concern and fear. I put my hands on the man's shoulders and wiped a bead of sweat from his brow with my thumb. "Get some sleep, sir. You'll feel right as rain in the morning." He nodded, eyes closed, and sunk into the pillow behind him.

I shook my head, puzzling at Parren's drunken soliloquy, as I walked out of the house to help Kiera with the horses. Outside, Kiera had a bucket of grain at her feet and was offering them to Gus who licked them greedily from her cupped hands. The scene was golden and shadowy from the candles burning in each of Parren's windows. Stell nosed Gus away, trying to get at the food in Kiera's palm, but Kiera pushed her mare away gently, scratching under her chin to keep her happy. She glanced up at me when she heard the door open. Gus licked the last crumbs from her hands and she wiped them on her blouse, leaving streaks of horse saliva behind.

"I was just about to fetch some water," she picked up an empty bucket that hung off the end of the water trough.

"No, I can do it," I took the bucket from her hands and she released it easily.

"It's fine, I can," she said, even as she grabbed another handful of grain, offering it to Stell who dug her velvety nose into it hungrily.

Amused, I left to fetch the water from the well, returning minutes later. Before I poured any into the horses' trough, I faced Kiera. "Give me your hands." She dropped the last few remaining morsels and looked at her palms with disinterest. She sat down on the stoop in front of Parren's home and held out her hands in front of her. Her calluses were ripped open, much like mine, blisters already come and popped and bled. Most of the blood was dry, but some of the wounds still seeped. I knelt in front of her and trickled some water onto her fingers and palms, wiping the blood away with the pads of my thumbs. I repeated until the water ran clear.

"I like your ring," I ran my thumb over the band, "it's the real reason that I believed you were . . . you."

"It was from my father. One of the few things I have from him." Her longing covered my heart with a deep shroud of sympathy. I knew her pain all too well. The pouch at my hip meant much the same to me, the only thing I had left to treasure of someone taken too soon.

I placed my hands on either side of hers and moved to dunk them in the remaining water for a final rinse, "We need the water for the horses," she breathed, our faces now close together over the bucket resting on the dusty ground between us. Her cheeks flushed crimson at our sudden proximity. I could feel her breath on my face and had to fight the impulse to move closer, to somehow lessen the hurt and longing that I identified with in every possible way.

"I'll get more," I whispered, gently dunking her small hands and rubbing away any last bits of dried blood. She inhaled sharply. "Does it hurt?" Perhaps I was too rough. She shook her head back and forth and curled her rosy lips in, biting down.

She pulled her hands from the bucket, retreating from our closeness. "Now yours," she wiped her hands on her pants then pointed to the bucket, "then I'll fetch more water." I dunked my hands and rubbed them together until the blood was gone, leaving the water a muddy ochre. I shook my hands out to get most of the water off of them and picked up the bucket.

"Let me," she took the bucket, "then we will see to that cut on your side."

I looked down, the blood from the gash that I'd gotten in our final spar had soaked through my tunic, leaving a blotchy line of scarlet. I nodded.

Sitting on the cottage's front stoop, I let myself watch her walk away until the pitchy dark of night consumed her. I ground down my teeth, frustrated with myself for being so easily caught up with the first girl I'd ever spent more than ten minutes with. I had only agreed to this quest to receive my knighthood and reclaim Beauhaven, not to find some embarrassing romance; but it was difficult to deny that I was eager to go on this adventure with her by my side. All the way to the borderlands and back . . . with her. The idea of it thrilled me more than I cared to admit, especially to her.

I forced my focus back to my wound. I pulled my tunic off to get a better look. It had bled a decent amount, but was clotting fine. The gash was not deep, but I couldn't help but think that maybe I'd gotten myself in deeper with Kiera than I'd bargained for. She was beautiful and curious, but she was also dangerous, and her secrets could be dangerous too. She had almost slit me open without so much as a second thought. My stomach dropped to my feet as I looked up and found her curvy silhouette swaying out of the darkness, the water bucket dangling at her side.

CHAPTER TWENTY-ONE

CHARA

He was staring at me when I returned, and it was hard not to gawk back. The candles burned low in the sills, but still, I could clearly see his shirtless form waiting for me on the front porch. I tried to look anywhere other than the lean, hard muscles of his arms and shoulders, his stomach. Such a form could only have developed from years of grueling manual labor, which explained why I had never seen anyone like him before.

"Let me fetch a rag and a bandage," I stammered as I stepped towards the cottage, feeling heat rising to my face. I needed a moment to compose myself. "I'll be right back." I crossed in front of him, barreling through the front door. I rummaged through Parren's home, not bothering to be quiet, as he was thoroughly passed out and snoring on his bed. I found a clean dishrag in the kitchen and grabbed an old tunic from one of the dresser drawers. "That'll do," I muttered to myself.

Outside, Elliot had disappeared into the darkness. Had I been too forward and scared him off? *Come on, Chara, get it together. You need him to get you to the war front, you can't go scaring him away. If you should go at all . . .* the nagging voice in my head caught me off guard. I stopped, ashamed at myself for the thought. I had to go, there was no other option. As soon as I could sneak away, I would go to Emily and retrieve the rest of our supplies, and Elliot and I would be off first thing in the morning.

Glancing out the window, I saw Elliot returning from the well with a large bucket of water in each hand. Relief flooded me. I realized I had not expected to feel this connected to him at all, let alone so quickly. I had not anticipated these feelings, especially not the crippling guilt. My deception felt wrong and that made me fear the plan as a whole. I had put my life, my hope, and my future in this plan. I could not second guess it. Too much was at stake.

The bucket I'd fetched still sat on the porch, untouched. His shoulders flexed as he dumped the water he'd retrieved into the horses' trough. My cheeks scorched pink as he had still not put his tunic back on despite the early spring chill. His side was dripping with fresh blood.

"Elliot!" I scolded as I came out of the house with the rag and tunic. His labor had reopened the wound my blade had accidentally caused. "You're making it worse." He looked down at the dribble of blood leaking from the cut and shrugged. I scowled and pointed to the stairs beside me, "Sit. It has to be cleaned and bandaged." He joined me on the front steps where the light was best. I knelt beside him, again trying to hide my blush at our sudden closeness as I drenched the rag and began to wipe away the blood.

The cut was shallow, as I knew it would be, but I still wished I hadn't wounded him at all. The location of my blade was less than half an inch off from where I thought it was and this was the result of my miscalculation.

Around the wound, particularly towards his back, were other injuries. Many were relatively fresh and, although they had scabbed over, I estimated they were only a few days old. Others were so pale they almost disappeared into his skin. I turned him into the flickering light as I continued cleaning the wound, but also examining the scars. Some were short lines, while others were nearly a foot long.

I ripped the tunic into strips, laying some over the wound from my sword and using the rest to wrap around his torso to hold the bandage in place. His muscles grew tense under my fingertips and I focused on keeping my fingers steady.

When the gash was bound, Elliot reached for the tunic draped over the rail. "Thank you."

I put a hand on his arm to stop him. I turned his body until his back faced the light of the candles. He pulled against me slightly, a pained look passing over his strong features. Eventually he gritted his teeth, let me turn him, and stayed quiet while I surveyed the topography of his scarred back. The dancing light cast shadows over the ridges of the straight, smooth scars and bounced over wrinkled ones. There were hundreds of them, arrayed like a game of pick-up sticks from nape all the way to the belt. Lashings, I realized.

I washed and added some bandages to the freshest wounds, all the while unable to hide my confusion at why a boy—almost a man—born to a noble family would be covered in such gruesome marks. Then I remembered our first meetings. He had feared the broken eggs would leave him at the end of someone's whip. I had assumed his tunic had been covered in dirt or muck, but had it really been blood? And in the forest, he was so desperate to bring venison home to his family. Was his desperation more fear than care? Fear of punishment? It wasn't right for a person to be treated this way, and by their family no less.

"How could they?" The question escaped my lips like a secret, barely more than a breath. I dared a touch, over some particularly wide and raised scars. He twinged, not from pain, I thought, but from shame. He wasn't used to sharing this part of him. I touched the small marks—the oldest ones, I guessed—they would have been made when he was much smaller, much younger.

He sat silently allowing me to observe the scars, even as the muscles beneath grew hard and he shifted uncomfortably. My fingers caressed them, something personal and intimate, but also beautiful and infinitely more painful than I could understand. They were like a painting in the disappearing light, the artwork of his battles, the courage of his endurance. If only someone had been there to save him, to take him away from whoever had inflicted this atrocity—like I had managed to do with Emily.

How could such evil exist in this world? What had I done to merit a life free of such cruelty? Tears burned my eyes, my guilt returning tenfold. I released Elliot's arm and pulled my hand back from his skin, clasping my palms together tightly.

This was why he needed the knighthood, why he'd agreed

to accompany me at all. He needed an escape from his own life.

They're not my family, he'd said.

"Who did this?" I didn't know if I should ask, but my curiosity got the better of me.

He looked at my face with those stunning, green and gold speckled eyes, and he chewed his bottom lip. Who knew this about him? Did he have an Emily, a best friend, who knew everything? Bruno? Or maybe the drunk old man passed out inside? Or had he been alone in this battle his entire life?

"My family is dead," he said simply. He fell quiet, rolling his next choice of words over and over on his tongue.

"You don't have to tell me anything you don't want to," I said, staring intensely at the scuffed and ripped leather exposing glimpses of my kneecaps, damage caused when I fell off Stell only a day before. The pain was gone, but the holes still remained.

"I know," he said, his words heavy, weighted with stories—horror stories—that maybe he'd never spoken aloud. "I know I don't have to. But I want to. I want you to know why I'm doing this. Why I would risk so much for my knighthood."

I gnawed on the inside of my cheek, shame undulating within me. I felt ill.

"My father died when I was four years old," Elliot said, his voice barely a whisper, "my sister wasn't even born yet. He was a merchant, traveling on business, but was on his way home for the birth when his ship sank, just off shore." He clenched his teeth together, jaw hard. Then he spoke softly, "A few years after my sister was born, my mother remarried, and things weren't so bad. Although I was young, maybe seven or eight,

Silas—my step-father—took me on business trips with him for extra help. I learned much of the Mittelan landscape then. He did not treat me well—ordering me around and such—but it wasn't terrible. I managed. But the year I turned ten, my mother got very sick. Before she died, she asked me to promise to take care of myself and," he held a weighty breath, " . . . of my sister. Millie. She was only five at the time."

I could see how speaking her name affected him. His hand went to something attached to his waist, a small pouch I hadn't previously noticed.

"But once mother was gone," he continued, "my stepfather took all of his anger and hate at the world, and he took it out on me. Then one day, I just couldn't take it anymore. He had asked me to take the last of my father's possessions with me to sell at market and I refused. He gave me a chance to recant, but I didn't. I was so furious with him and I'd finally reached my breaking point. I was able to dodge his anger but I didn't expect him to . . . " he gulped, "Silas grabbed my sister instead and punished her for my insubordination."

He was a child, I thought. *How could anyone be so merciless?*

"If I could," Elliot went on, "I would sell everything I've ever touched to take it back. Because after that, I was so angry, I couldn't stay any longer. I took my sister and we left. But we had nowhere to go. I woke to find her color gone, her skin too hot to touch, barely responsive. I knew I had no choice but to go back home, back to him," his voice broke, "but I couldn't save her. I failed. I failed my mother."

I had to stop myself from reaching out to him. "No, you didn't," I said trying to afford him any ounce of comfort I could give, "you promised to take care of yourself as well."

His fixed stare with the ground lifted and settled instead on me. "After that, I did everything he asked. But he always found an excuse to punish me anyway." He put his palms over his mouth and breathed into them, then wiped at his eyes with the back of his hand. "He had taken the very last living connection to my family. So I set my mind to buying Beauhaven back from him. That's when I began saving my winnings from the arena."

"Beauhaven?"

"Yes. That's my family's estate. Named after the battle for which it was given, the battle of Beaufort. Beauhaven means *beautiful refuge*."

I smiled at the way he perked up when talking about his home, "That's lovely."

"I told Millie once that I would make our home safe again someday. And that day is the only future I see left for myself. My ancestors and my parents are buried there. The only happy memories of my childhood happened within those stone borders." He shrugged, "It's all I have left."

"Is that why you stayed all those years? Why you never tried again to leave?"

"It wouldn't feel like freedom if it meant abdicating Beauhaven to Silas or his son. So I gave every extra ounce of myself to training and to the Games. I had to protect what was left of my family's honor. But yesterday Silas somehow managed to find my money and my sword, and I realized my mistake. Silas was never going to willingly render Beauhaven to me. So when I came upon you yesterday, I saw a different opportunity, a way I could finally keep my promise to Millie and reclaim my birthright. If I could receive my knighthood, if I could explain everything to the queen herself, then I would not only outrank Silas, but I would have the favor of the queen. I'm hoping that she can see to it that Silas leaves me—and Beauhaven—alone."

The sadness ebbed from his voice, replaced with determination and assurance.

"Without you, without the hope you have given me, I would be lost. It feels like a miracle—" He reached out and took my hand from my side. He turned it over to look at my blistered palm. He touched his wounded side and laughed through his words, "—a painful miracle."

I swallowed hard. Pressing my lips together and closing my eyes, I tried to calm the waves of emotion thrashing in my mind. "It's not fair," I said, "that some people have everything and still want more . . . " I thought of the Norrfalt invasion, of the prince, and mostly of the power-hungry duke. Yet even as I said it, I felt the shame of my untouched back and my soft hands that had never labored. " . . . and are perfectly happy to leave everyone else with nothing."

I gulped. I imagined telling him then who I was and the truth I was hiding. "I—" I started, but the truth choked me. What if he refused to come with me once he knew the truth? Or worse, what if he went directly to my mother? His honesty only increased the betrayal of my lies, yet I could not risk telling him the truth. "I—I will be sure my mistress follows through on our agreement," the words *my mistress* ground my gut like a pestle, but I ignored it, "and I'm sure the queen will see your bravery and your persistence and will help you get Beauhaven back. I promise. Monsieur Pentamerone will be lucky to have a savior like you."

His gaze grew honeyed at my words, and I realized the distance between us was steadily closing. My hands were still encapsulated in his and our lips moved closer and closer still.

The clock tolled in the distance. I sat up straight and tossed his hands with a jolt. I counted eleven chimes. I was supposed to meet Emily at midnight. I stood suddenly. "I appreciate your honesty, Sir Cen—" I stopped myself. "Elliot," I corrected. "Now go, get some rest. I am not going to let you sleep past sun up in the morning. I am just going to get some more water for the horses, then I'll be in." He didn't move, save for his eyes which looked me up and down with a tenderness I'd never before witnessed, like he saw something in me that even I never had. "Go to bed," I snipped, keeping any softness far from my tone, but it was impossible to hide the blush that his lingering gaze brought to my cheeks.

He stood, as if stung by my shortness, but I couldn't look at him any longer and hold my resolve. And that's what I needed right now: my resolve. I couldn't let myself—or my guilt—get the best of me. Parren's words rang in my memory, *Whatever happens, you cannot marry the prince.*

I was not deceiving Elliot *just* to avoid an unwanted marriage. Maybe it started that way, but it was bigger than that now. Mittelan could not have a Norrfalter as a king. This was Mittelan's independence on the line. *That's* why I was doing all of this . . . wasn't it?

Maybe someday, Elliot would understand that. I imagined the moment that Elliot discovered who I was, how I'd lied and used him. The thought stung like a whip . . . not that I knew how that felt. Not like Elliot. I shuddered at myself, my shame.

For Mittelan, I reminded myself. I was doing this for my citizens, for my country.

And yet the thought shortly followed that maybe I was getting so practiced at lying that I could even fool myself.

"Thank you, Kiera," Elliot took back my attention as he pulled his tunic over his newly dressed wounds and stepped towards the cottage door. He stopped and looked back at me, hand resting on the doorknob. "I don't know what I would have done if you and your mistress had not chosen me."

❖❖❖

I stormed around the courtyard, furious for prying and for almost giving away my mission. I was angry at myself for lying to him and equally angry for caring. Suddenly I faced a fear that had not been there before: fear of an entire cross country journey with Elliot by my side and nothing but lies between us. And that fear enraged me as well.

I had to stay focused. I couldn't be distracted by my cohort, by his gentleness or his kindness, despite the heartbreak he had endured, and definitely not by his devastating green eyes or the way they crinkled when he smiled. I massaged my temples in frustration. When had everything gotten so complicated?

I knew when. I knew *exactly* when. From the first moment in the arena when I saw his face as he knelt before me, when I knew that I wanted him. Why him? Why had it *had* to be him? I told myself it was his fighting skills, his knowledge of Mittelan's landscape, or his ability to hunt, but it had always been something more. He could have been a bean farmer who'd never seen past his own front gate and I still would have found an excuse to choose him.

It was the truth and I knew it. I suddenly felt very weak.

I snuck onto the front porch and peeked in through the thick window glass. Parren lay fully clothed on top of his blankets in a drunken stupor. That reminded me, why had Parren wanted to speak with Elliot in private after supper? Had the old drunk given away some part of my secret? It didn't seem likely as Elliot had acted completely normal afterwards. Did it have to do with what Parren had told me in the market about being betrayed by the Norrfalt King?

I laughed softly to myself as I watched Elliot pour Parren's liquor down the drain. He left just enough to fool the old geezer and replaced the rest with water. After returning it, Elliot walked over to the window and I ducked just in time. The shadows shifted as he walked away from the window. I dared another glance inside. He had removed his shirt once more and was using it as a pillow beside the fire. He must have been exhausted because the rise and fall of his breathing slowed almost instantly to the steady rhythm of sleep.

I'd been away from the castle for nearly twenty-four hours now. Mother would have the guard out looking for me, but it would still be kept quiet. They wouldn't want to make a scandal out of it just yet. They'd wait until they were sure I was not returning. I hoped by the time the public was bombarded with my portrait and a reward was placed on my head, that I would be halfway to the borderlands.

But we would not be able get there without the additional supplies and weaponry I had planned to retrieve from Emily. She had agreed to meet me at the stables at midnight, and sneaking away was the only way to ensure that Elliot would not insist on coming with me.

I looked back at his sleeping form once more before melting into the shadows.

The streets glimmered like quartz crystals as the window candles shone out onto the wet cobbles. I made it several blocks before a light spring rain began, misting my face in tiny icy droplets. My blouse quickly soaked through but it was too risky to turn back for my cloak. Before moving around each bend, I peeked around the corner, praying that I would continue to find the street ahead abandoned.

I had not expected to spar so late into the evening, and I definitely had not expected to spend so much time with Elliot afterwards. I felt ashamed of my own carelessness. I hurried towards the castle wall, each minute bringing me closer and closer to the midnight toll.

The streets of Swanstone were as silent as the grave. My pulse beat in my throat. The first stretch of roads were relatively empty and I was able to move quickly. However, as I neared the castle, the streets became more active and I had to take my time staying out of sight. I looked down the next block and found two of the queen's guards marching in my direction, looking for me. I glanced back the way I'd come; another set of guards had turned the corner and were walking towards me.

I spotted a barrel hidden in the shadow of the windowsill above it. I crouched into the hiding place, wishing I had my black cape so I could disappear into the darkness. Instead, I hunched as low as possible in the tiny cove between the barrel and the building. My ears piqued, waiting for the clamor of the guards to pass in front of me and leave the street abandoned once more. When the footsteps of the guards disappeared, they were replaced with loud voices coming from beyond the window panes.

"It ain't right what the princess is doing," came a man's low growl. *The princess?* I pushed up towards the window and the wet ground soaked through the already torn knees of my riding pants. "We spent years of our lives killing Norrfalters, she don't get to put a pretty ring on her finger and make us one of them."

The air left my lungs, stinging like knives. They were talking about the engagement. They were talking about me.

A chorus of voices agreed with the man. A dozen, at least, maybe more.

"Mittelan forever!"

"Triumph for Mittelan!"

"Free Mittelan!" The voices chanted, but they did not yell, not wanting to attract the attention of the guards roaming their streets.

When the voices tapered out the man spoke again. "The royals have become nothing more than a joke . . . they don't understand us or our suffering. They are too weak to do what needs to be done." The stranger's words cut like steel. His comrades agreed with him.

"So there is only one way to keep Mittelan free and independent," another voice said. A woman this time. "We must end the royal line."

I stood, the light from the window spilling over me. I had to tell them they were wrong, that my mother was not weak, that she would do anything for her subjects. I caught sight of a single face in the crowd of dissenters. A face and frazzled head of hair that was easily recognized.

Shock left me stammering for my words, when an arm snaked around my waist and a hand smothered my screams as I was dragged into the darkness.

CHAPTER TWENTY-TWO

ELLIOT

"*Ellie, take me home. I wanna go home, Ellie," she whined for the hundredth time that day, using the nickname that only her and my mother had ever called me. The woods were thick and suffocating.*

"The trees are going to eat my memories, Ellie, they've already started." Her voice was growing weak and her bruises more pronounced.

"Millie, the trees do not eat memories," I turned to kneel by my sister's side. I wiped a tear from her dust stained cheek. I knew where we were, how to hunt, how to feed us. But that didn't ease the growing knot in my stomach. We had nowhere to go.

The gash beside my sister's right eye had begun to spew pus. After years of Silas taking out his anger on me, I had somehow convinced myself that he wouldn't stoop so low as to hurt her. But that was before he realized that she *was the best way to punish* me.

"The trees are good," I assured her, "they keep us safe."

"No." Millie stuck out her bottom lip, her gold and green eyes were

wide and determined. "No. I want to go home. They've already started eating my memories, Ellie, I don't even remember what Mommy looked—" she cut herself off with a chest cough that shook me somewhere deep and primal.

Her curls had collected branches and leaves, surrounding her face like a crown of nature and light. She was impossible to say no to, even with the midnight marbling of the bruise that had begun to consume an entire side of her delicate face . . . maybe especially so. Looking at it made me want to retch with anger and guilt.

Why hadn't I kept my mouth closed? Why couldn't I have simply done what the viper asked? I had followed his commands a hundred times, why had I let myself refuse him this time? What was a few more of my father's belongings now that the home had already been stripped practically bare?

"Mommy looked like you, Millie," I tried to mimic the way father used to tell me bedtime stories, soft and full of magic. "She looked like an angel. She had eyes like the forest that sparkled as if fairies lived in them. She had a gentle face and smiled like a princess. Just like you do. The trees can't take her memory away from us. And neither can he," I gently rubbed my thumb over the bruise, "but we can't go back. Not as long as he is there."

Her golden hair shone against the muddy woodland floor, where she laid down, unwilling to take even another step away from home.

I placed the back of my hand across her forehead. The heat that had begun to rise on my sister's skin, despite the chill of the night, made me shiver. A bead of sweat collected on her brow and it cut through the dirt as it rolled down her face and slipped into her nest of ringlets.

"But it's our home, Ellie," her voice cracked, "we've got to go home." Her tears flowed freely and she coughed roughly between each sob. Her lungs rattled as she breathed.

"Shh, shh, shh," I soothed, but deep down, I knew she was right.

We'd been walking all day and had nowhere to go, no one to go to. And I knew, deep in my gut, that something was wrong with her. Something I couldn't make better. "Someday, Millie, I'll make our home safe for us again. I promise. Someday."

We curled up together in the woods with nothing to cover us. I watched as the color drained from her cheeks as we drifted in and out of consciousness.

When I woke, I tried to shake her but she wouldn't wake, wouldn't even move. She couldn't stand. Or walk. Her breathing was labored and slow. Panic surged through me. I stood with her in my arms and began to run back to the viper's den, with the promise in my heart that if he ever hurt her again, I would kill him.

❖❖❖

The nightmare woke me as it always did. But I wasn't on my cot by the fire, I was away from my prison, safely on the floor at Parren's. I could hear his drunken snores in the background, so I closed my eyes tightly and forced the memory from my sleeping mind.

CHAPTER TWENTY-THREE

CHARA

I screamed but no sound escaped. I tried to bite down, but the large fist squeezed my jaw closed. Terror seized me as I struggled against my captor's grasp, dragging me deeper into the dark alley. I dug my fingernails into his flesh as deeply as they would go.

"Dammit, Princess!" the man cried and released me so suddenly that I fell to the ground in a tangle of limbs. I regained my composure quickly, flying to my feet and whipping around to face my assailant. I reached for my sword, but it was not at my hip. *Curses!* I must have left it at Parren's. I raised a fist, poised to swing, before I recognized the man's narrow face.

"Grimm?" There he was in front of me, the same face surrounded by that distinctive red head of hair that I had just seen conversing with those treasonous rebels. But here he was, sucking on his arm where my nails had drawn blood. He looked up at me, his cocked smile barely visible in the shadows.

"What the hell, Grimm?" I looked the stable boy over again, still in disbelief. "I just saw you, in there, with *them*!"

"Hush!" he said, covering my mouth again, gentler this time.

"Let me go!"

He obeyed, but shushed me as he did.

I forced my voice lower, "Fine, but you have to tell me what the hell is going on. Are you one of them? How did you manage to—"

"That's my brother, Jacob," he explained, and I stepped back in disbelief and fear. "You're lucky I got to you before he saw you, Princess. He absolutely hates the royals ever since Marchale fired him from the carriage house when he caught him nicking from the noble trunks he was supposed to be ferrying. He cut Jacob's left pinky clean off. Said he needed to be able to tell us apart, to keep Jacob from sneaking back around. Jacob's never forgiven Her Highness for not hearing his complaint. There's no telling what he would've done to . . ." he tapered off.

That's when I faintly recalled the one time Grimm had mentioned his sibling. We were playing a game of truth or taunt when he revealed to Em and I that Grimm was actually a nickname he took when his brother insisted on twisting his real name—Wilhelm—into the taunt 'Little Willy.' But I would have remembered if he had told us that his brother looked nearly identical to him.

"Then how do I even know you," I gulped, "are you?"

The boy shook his head in agitation before sticking his left pinky in the air, "Well, I've got all ten fingers, for one. And for two, Jacob wouldn't have stopped you from exposing yourself to that group of treacherous gits. But if you need further proof, I can tell you that I had just left that forsaken meeting to go pilfer the key from Marchale and let Emily through the stables to meet *you*. I have never let you down, Princess, I'm not about to start now."

Relief blanketed me and I threw my arms around the boy's neck. "Thank the heavens," I mumbled into his hay scented collar.

When I let him go, I found him scowling. "Well now that you trust me again, want to explain to me exactly what you were thinking?" He hugged his spindly, but surprisingly strong, arms around his middle. "You heard them, good as I. If they found you here, they'd kill you on the spot. Dunno what would have happened had I not stepped out when I did. I recognized you soon as my boot hit the road. You looked like you were about to announce yourself or something. To the rebels. Who just declared their plan to *murder* you," he said it slow and pointedly, as if talking to a child. "Right smart of you, Princess, right smart."

"Rebels." I echoed, my hands moving up to my temples. Shock rolled over me. Rebels. In my kingdom. The enraged guards, the jumpy townsfolk, and the over reaction to the engagement announcement. It all made sense. "Do they have a plan? Are they organized? How long have they been plotting against the throne? How many of them are there?"

I shook Grimm by the shoulders, as if I could rattle the answers out of him. Answers. I needed answers. My hands dropped to my roiling stomach. I clenched them together to keep from trembling. *End the royal line.* Only two people stood between the Perrault dynasty and anarchy. Me and my mother.

Mother.

"I don't know how long they've been unhappy, Your Highness," Grimm said, "or how many there are. My family only really got involved today, after the engagement announcement. But I do know that this isn't all of them," his look darkened, "and their numbers are growing."

Rebellion. First the borderwar, now Norrfalt is trying to overtake the throne. Was civil war next? And would we, my family, be slain as martyrs? What about my plan? If only they knew that I was *trying* to keep Mittelan free, that I would fight by their sides to end the war, to stop the conscriptions, and to put a stop to the engagement that so enraged them. But how could I leave for the war front knowing these people—my own subjects—were plotting to hurt my family?

I couldn't stay, and I couldn't go. All I could do was get to my mother before it was too late.

My plan was falling apart and it was taking Mittelan down with it.

❖❖❖

The whites of Emily's eyes were woven with pink spider webs. She tried to rub them away but no matter how she scrubbed with her fists, they only grew more red. She cried violently, her sobs shaking her frail frame. "Rebellion? In Mittelan? What are we going to do?" she asked.

Grimm had accompanied me through the streets and talked the night guard that Marchale had left in charge into believing that the stable master had sent him to take his place. Emily had been waiting with the accoutrements on the other side of the heavy door.

I finally had everything I needed to leave, but I could no longer go. Would I ever even get out of Swanstone?

"We will find the rebels. And we will fight. Don't worry yourself, Ems," I knelt in front of her and put a comforting hand on her knee. "But for right now, the most important thing is that I warn my mother as quickly as possible."

Emily stood suddenly, throwing the dirty hem of her dress from her hands and wiping her eyes. "What am I thinking, having you waste your time consoling me? Go!"

"I will, but first, quickly, I need your help. Listen closely, Emily." I stood and squared her shoulders to mine, "Master Parren lives on the northwest edge of Swanstone, not far from that little bakery you like. You know? The one with the lemon spritz? I need you to go, find Elliot, and tell him everything. Tell him who I am, about the rebellion. He won't know where I've gone and he needs to."

My heart broke as I remembered the way Elliot's hands had ever-so-softly cleansed the blood from mine. I looked at the still throbbing blisters, running a finger over the peeling skin. I remembered the scars littering his back, the desperation in his gaze when he told me why he'd agreed to my mission. He might never forgive me for my lies, but I would go to him as soon as my mother was safe. I would knight him then and there, and I would beg for his forgiveness.

"Tell him I will find him. Tell him he will have everything I promised. Grimm will go with you." I put my lips to Emily's head, her frizzy hair tickling my lips. "Be safe, Ems."

"You too, Char. Now go!"

I left her there, standing with her fists on her hips on the threshold between my world and my kingdom beyond.

I didn't like sending Emily out into the unsafe world, but only she could fully explain the situation to Elliot. Grimm would keep her safe, I told myself with more confidence than I felt. The eerie story of Jacob's dissent scratched at the back of my mind. *There's no telling what he would have done . . .* What kind of monster was this boy who looked just like my friend? But I didn't have time to think on the matter. Grimm would ensure that Emily was safe.

The courtyard was crawling with the Queen's Guards, searching every square inch of the castle grounds for me as if they would find me hiding beneath a bush or laying amidst rusting tools in a shed. I was inside the castle gates now; it didn't matter if they saw me.

I ran between them, in a full sprint now, to the doors of the castle. I navigated the maze of hallways quickly and effortlessly, like reading a book with the words memorized. When I reached my mother's chamber, I was surprised to find the guards in their seats instead of standing on alert as they always did as she slept. They jumped to their feet at my arrival.

"I need to speak with my mother, it's an emergency!" I shouted, breathless from the run.

"She's not here, Your Highness," said the shorter of the two guards, wrinkling his nose at me. I looked down at myself, still in my riding clothes, covered in filth and grime. I didn't even bother to shrug.

"But it's the middle of the night," I argued, "where else

could she be?"

"She's been waiting in the throne room," he said, refusing to meet my gaze, "waiting for news from her guards."

Maybe she already knew of the rebellion, maybe she was waiting for more news of them. "What news?" I asked.

The guard shifted his weight between his feet, but did not speak.

"What news?" I pressed angrily, almost shouting.

The taller guard spoke, "She's been there all day, Princess. She's been waiting for news of you. She refused to rest until you were found."

My head fell back. Of course. How could I be so foolish? I said nothing else to the guards, but turned and sprinted to the throne room. The paintings hanging on the walls rattled against the stone and the tapestries shuddered as I ran by them. Only a handful of lanterns in the hallways were still lit, but I didn't need them.

I burst through the double doors into the colossal throne room. Every candle on the chandelier was still lit even though it was late into the night. Two familiar guards stood below the marble steps. They wore the uniforms of interior castle guards, no armor, just swords hanging around their waists. My mother sat in her throne atop the dais, her painted face buried in her palm, elbow on the armrest.

"Mother!" I tore across the tiled floors, relief flooding me that she was safe. Skipping the middle step, I fell to my knees by her side.

"Chara, where have you been?" She was still fully dressed in her day gown and heavy bags hung beneath her weary eyes. Tears gathered there when she saw me, tears of relief.

Guilt engulfed me once more.

She cleared her throat, "Sir Daren, please alert the castle and your fellow guards that the princess has returned safely."

I barely heard him acknowledge her and leave the room.

Burying my face in the folds of her skirt, I hadn't realized until that moment how terrified I was of losing her. How could I have abandoned her like I did? The mud from my face and newly opened wounds on my hands tainted her velvet dress, the color of fresh peaches served with cream, now tarnished with my filth and blood.

"I'm sorry to worry you, Mother. I will explain it all." I grabbed her hand, trying to soothe her anxiety. She locked gazes with me. I ran my thumb over her tensed hand. "It's because of the marriage and the duke, but first I have to tell you what I saw in the village."

She glanced up, eyes wide, at the unmistakable sound of a blade being drawn.

I swiveled on my knee and found the second guard standing over us, his rapier raised. Mother screamed and I felt the gold candle holders on the chandelier tremble. The other guard was gone. My sword, gone. We were defenseless. I stood to disarm him but I was too slow. He buried the blade in my mother's chest. She reached up and wrapped her hands around the steel. There was a sickening squelch of flesh as the guard dislodged the blade, destroying her hands. I thought momentarily that I would retch at the sight of the life seeping from my mother's deep copper eyes, when out of the corner of my vision, he drew back his blade once more, this time leading with his hilt.

I swung my legs around and kicked his feet out from under

him. The guard stumbled backwards as I leapt to my feet. I dug my elbow into his gut as he regained his footing. He lunged for me, but I avoided his blade with a sidestep maneuver Parren had taught me only just that day. The steel slid across my arm, cutting through my blouse, leaving a deep slash on my left arm. I fought the desire to cover the wound. Instead, I kneed the guard in the groin, grabbing onto his sword bearing arm as I did. The impact weakened his grip on the hilt and I swiped it with my opposite hand. His foot slipped on the marble steps when he stumbled back from the force of my blow, sending him to the floor at the bottom of the white marble stairs. His head thunked hard against the tile.

Holding the blade between us, I took the three steps as one and held the blade over his chest. He lay unmoving, his eyes open and locked on me. A salty tear flowed down my cheek to rest on my bottom lip. I licked it away. I hadn't even realized I was crying.

He said nothing: no apology, no justification, no final declaration of allegiance to this rebellious cause. Just a set jaw and a faint look of surprise. He hadn't expected me to fight back, or at least, hadn't expected me to win. He hadn't expected to die today at the hand of the royal line he was attempting to end.

I should question him, I thought. *I should offer him mercy. I've never killed a man before . . .*

But all my thoughts disappeared with a glance back at my mother still bleeding on her throne. Without another second of hesitation, I drove the blade directly through his heart. His blood bubbled up from the wound, mingling with hers. I pulled out the sword, as he had done, the sound planting the seeds of a thousand nightmares. I recognized the face of the guard, unable to recall a name but I knew that he had been a member of my father's guard, then Mother's. He was trained by Parren. A guard who'd protected this family my entire life was now a rebel assassin.

My hands began to shake violently. I dropped the blade onto the floor beside him. It clattered to the ground, chipping a tile on the chest of the small boy pictured on the mosaic floor. I turned weakly before sprinting back to my mother's side and taking her hand in mine. I felt the inside of her wrist, praying for a heartbeat, but her flesh stood still. I stroked her palm and buried my face in her skirt again, unable to look at her soft, lifeless face.

The rebellion's plot was less than a day old and they would already celebrate one victory.

Tears tore down my face unbridled. I braved a look at her distorted features, frozen with the worry lines that I had given her. Her auburn hair and her russet eyes, both like mine. Her curved cheeks and delicate nose, not like mine.

She looked strange in death, and I realized for the first time that evening that she was not wearing the necklace my father had given her—the one she always wore. Likely she had forgotten to put it on in her haste and consternation over my disappearance. It was the first time I had seen her without it, the first time she had been without the seal of his protection, and it was my fault.

I turned the ring around my finger and wished that I had my father back. Or that I could go back to just minutes earlier before Mother dismissed Sir Daren and gave this rebel his opening. I wished that I had done something, *anything*, different to save her, but I knew my wishes were empty and that it was my fault I was here alone. I should have accepted the marriage and stayed here at my mother's side. This would never have happened if I hadn't left.

Her eyes stood wide open, full umber moons between eyelash frames. I reached up a hand, gently pushing the long curtains of her eyelashes down over her empty gaze.

This was all my fault.

CHAPTER TWENTY-FOUR

ELLIOT

The smell of vomit woke me. The dream I'd had of Millie's final hours still felt real, the emotions newly fresh and still infinitely painful.

But today things were different. Today, I would begin the quest that would lead me to my redemption, to my knighthood. Beauhaven would be restored and I felt sure the queen would banish the viper to the endless Almoran desert.

Today my life would begin to change. I just knew it.

The fire had grown cold, but the small stone house was stifling nonetheless. Bright sunbeams streamed through every window, heating the place like a greenhouse. Sweat beaded on my skin and my hair stuck to my neck and forehead.

I winced when I sat up, a sting at my side reminding me of the damage done by Kiera's blade. The bandage had not soaked through, which I took as a good sign. I looked around for Kiera or Parren but saw no one. Parren's bed had puke streaking down the side, and I wondered how I could have slept so deeply as to not hear him retching.

The only sound now was that of dew dripping from the eaves and a mouse scampering back to his home.

Pushing to my feet, I stood and rubbed my eyes. Where could Parren and Kiera have gone? Parren was easy, the liquor bottle I'd watered down stood untouched on his dresser. He'd likely gone to Lucifer's to drink away his hangover.

But Kiera had specifically said that she would not allow us to sleep late this morning and judging by the light coming through the east windows—I peered out and found the sun well on its way to high noon—it was already mid-morning. We should have already been to visit Lady Pentamerone and begun our long journey.

However, Kiera had been acting dodgy about me meeting her mistress, perhaps she had gone this morning without me. I grabbed my tunic from the floor where my head had been and pulled it on.

I'd left a blanket on the fainting couch for Kiera and it remained untouched. Had she never returned last night? Her satchels were still spread by the door where she had dropped them when we'd entered. Our swords lay side-by-side as we had tossed them when we finished training yesterday.

I opened the front door and found Gus and Stell happily gorging themselves on the bucket of grain left from the night before. Where would Kiera have gone without her horse? Had she spent the night at her mistress' home? Why wouldn't she have told me if that was her plan? And why would she leave without her bags? Without her sword?

I returned to the cottage, cursing under my breath for not staying up to make sure she got to bed safely. The scars on my back tingled at the memory of her silken touch.

Something felt very wrong. The Kiera I'd met would not have left for anywhere without her blade. My stomach contorted uncomfortably.

I knelt down beside Kiera's satchels, dumping them out to search for any clue of her whereabouts. Maybe Lady Pentamerone's street was listed on something in her bag, or a crest, or something. Anything that would lead me to her. My heart beat wildly and I forced myself to inhale and exhale slowly.

I hardly knew Kiera. I didn't know her habits. I didn't even really know if I could trust her. I felt certain now that Kiera was hiding something, but did that make her untrustworthy? I wasn't sure if it was the tenderness in the way she'd bandaged my side, the concern in her delicate touch of my wounds, or the way she listened to me when I suddenly felt the need to share my history, but I felt as if I'd known Kiera much longer than I had.

Trustworthy or not, she could be in danger. Without her, I had no means of gaining my knighthood and no hope of restoring Beauhaven. I had to find her.

Strewn around me were her things: some hard cheeses and a few more pieces of dried meat, some simple clothes, and a couple bottles of remedies. Nothing of consequence. I reached for my new blade, tucked under hers. Her sword fell to the side exposing a small seal pressed into the leather scabbard. She'd worn it backwards every time I'd seen her, with the seal facing the belt that strapped it to her.

My breathing hitched as I recognized the seal. I'd recognize it anywhere. It was colorless here, but still distinguishable as the image that was emblazoned on every flag flying from every turret and tower on Swanstone castle. It was the crest of Mittelan's capital. On the flags it waved, contrasting red and black daggers crossed over a pure white swan. This was the royal seal.

I pulled the blade from the sheath and found the length of it decorated with the swan insignia. Then it occurred to me that the gemstones on the hilt were the black and red of Mittelan. This blade came from the castle, I had no doubt about it.

But how would Kiera have gotten a royal blade? I racked my brain but came up with only one possible solution. Was Kiera hiding the fact that she was working by order of the royal family?

If so, that meant that whoever Monsieur Pentamerone was, his disappearance was a matter of royal importance. But what reason would Kiera have to lie? I didn't have an answer, but I did have a feeling that Kiera could be in far worse danger than I'd previously imagined.

The sound of fanfare trumpets blared in the distance with a familiar tune, unlike the one they had played yesterday when the prince of Norrfalt rode down the street announcing the engagement. This was the tune of the Perrault Dynasty, the Mittelan royal family.

Two royal announcements in just two days? I strapped the blade Parren had gifted me to my side and left through the front door. I would come back for the horses and Kiera's belongings after I found her, but that task would be easier without worrying about Gus and more things to carry.

First thing, I wanted to hear the announcement from the crier. I stepped out of the gate that enclosed Parren's tiny estate to find the streets as crowded as they had been yesterday. But this time, I saw no parade, no royal horses or carriages, and no Norrfalt prince on his horse.

The fanfare trumpeters marched in all black, with black banners hanging from their long, straight horns. The tune ended and the crier behind the musicians projected his thundering voice over the hubbub of the confused onlookers. "On this day, Her Royal Majesty Queen Cordelia Nataline Violet Basile-Perrault has passed from this earth. May the Creator bless her departed soul and bring her to rest in peace. Her Highness, the Princess Charissa Henrietta Cordelia Basile-Perrault will ascend the throne at the end of this day, following this evening's coronation celebration. Long live the queen!"

I numbly joined the chorus' response, "Long live the queen!"

The trumpets resounded once more as they marched further down the street to make their declaration over and over again.

The queen was dead. The realization rattled my thoughts away from Kiera's absence. From what I knew, Princess Charissa was but a youth, not old enough to lead. In fact, if I remembered correctly, she may be named queen at her coronation but she would have no power to rule until she weds. *Who knows when that could be* . . . I thought, but then I remembered the announcement from the day before, the princess was engaged to the royal prick of Norrfalt.

A Norrfalt king on a Mittelan throne? I could hardly imagine such a thing.

The crowds on the streets were similarly overwhelmed, some weeping over the fallen queen while some did not seem dismayed in the slightest. Many shouted their loud protests of the royal wedding.

I barely made it a stone's throw from the gate when someone tugged on my sleeve. I turned to find a girl, a full foot shorter than me and maybe three or four years younger. Her hair was loose and full of messy yellow curls. Her skin was splotched and puffy, like she had been crying. Her simple dress was tattered and worn, her sleeves pushed up over her elbows. Her forearms were black and blue with bruises that appeared fresh.

Her reddened eyes grew wide when I turned to her and the blood drained entirely from her face. Her eyes rolled back towards her skull for a moment and I reached out in case the girl were to faint.

"Jacob! There she is!" A voice traveled over the crowd and I looked up to see a cluster of villagers looking at us. A crotchety woman was pointing to the girl, a gangly fellow with ginger hair standing beside her. The thin young man, hardly a man but not still a boy, led the group in our direction.

The girl could not tear her eyes from me and did not see the group of villagers approaching. "Elliot?" she asked meekly, "Sir Elliot Cendrilon? I've been sent—"

The girl stopped talking as the villagers approached us, fear flashing through her features. I moved in front of her instinctively, protectively, shielding her from them. I grasped the handle of my sword, but did not draw it. I didn't want to make a scene unless absolutely necessary. The strangers gathered around us, the skinny red-head reached out towards the girl,

"Oh, there you are, *sister*!"

The girl shook her head wildly. "I'm not your sis—"

The boy interrupted her, "I know you don't want to go home, but you have to," he said loudly as he tried to step around me, reaching for her with a hand that had only four fingers.

"No!" she stepped further back.

"What is going on here?" I demanded, shielding her from him and pulling my blade out slightly. The boy noticed the shimmer of my steel and flexed his arms. He looked surprisingly strong for his stature, but did not carry a weapon that I could see.

"This is my sister. We're servants," he explained, still grabbing for the girl as I pushed his hand away. "You misunderstand, sir. She's run away again and I've been sent to retrieve her."

"You are not my brother!" I looked over my shoulder to see the girl's glare flame. "He's not my brother! Please, he's lying Sir Cendrilon, I need to talk to you." She spat out the words quickly, like a dumped bucket of water. Like she was running out of time.

But all I heard was her calling me by my father's name and title. Like Kiera did. I turned to her in surprise.

Somewhere I heard a dull thud and my head splintered in pain. My world went black.

CHAPTER TWENTY-FIVE

CHARA

Emily hadn't yet returned to the castle. My mother's handmaid, Madame Colombe, fuddled around me, pinning my hair, painting my face, and muttering to herself as she prepared me for the coronation, even though it was still hours away. Her eyes were cherry lined from crying nonstop since the news of my mother's death broke. Her fingers trembled slightly.

She looked exactly how I felt.

"Your poor mother . . . her body hadn't even grown cold before that vile man ordered this heinous affair," she said for the hundredth time, "it just isn't proper." She dipped the sponge into more powder and dotted it under my eyes. I had cried myself dry, leaving my face sallow and waxen. It didn't matter how much make-up she used, my grief remained etched into every corner of my being.

"The country can't be without a leader," my voice cracked as I repeated the words the Grand Duke had used as he insisted that the coronation ceremony had to be tonight. Of course he wanted to solidify his regency as quickly as possible. Of course he didn't want to miss out on every moment of power he could get his hands on.

After the wedding, Christopher would be Mittelan's king, and if he decided to return home to Norrfalt, he could assign the title of regent to anyone he so chose, and I knew well enough that he wouldn't be choosing me.

The coronation was a sham. The wedding was a sham. And I would be a sham of a queen. This evening's ceremony would not be naming me Mittelan's new ruler at all; rather it would be christening me as the duke's new puppet until he passed me off to my next puppeteer like the lifeless marionette I was. The duke claimed that the coronation would keep the country content until the marriage alliance was official.

"You should be in mourning, miss," Madame Colombe repeated, braiding a loose section of hair and pinning it with the rest.

"It doesn't matter what color of dress the duke makes me wear," I looked over at the pastel monstrosity hanging from my wardrobe door. It was baby blue, the color of Norrfalt royalty and a disgrace to my country and to my mother's memory, "I am in mourning." I felt naked in the undergarments I was wearing—not because I didn't have my dress on yet, but because I didn't have my sword.

If I had been stronger, faster, more thoughtful, my mother would never have died. If I hadn't left my blade at Parren's, perhaps I'd have been able to save her. The excuse was dull, even in my own mind, because I knew that really I should never have left at all. In fact, had the fates not aligned just so—had I not overheard the rebels and had Grimm not found me, or had I left with the haste Elliot had wanted—I might never have seen her alive again.

It was that thought that had left me fixed to her side. Even though I knew she was gone and there was nothing I could do to bring her back, I had stayed in the throne room, paralyzed. I could have returned to Parren's cottage for my blade. I could have found Elliot and Emily, and together we could have sought out each and every rebel and hung them from the castle walls. I could have punished them for their treason myself. I could have punished them for taking her from me. I could have had vengeance.

She was their queen. She was my queen. My mother.

But I had been too weak to think clearly. I wept with my face buried in her bloodied, velvet skirts for too long. Prince Christopher found me there. "You're in danger," he insisted, pulling me from her lifeless corpse.

He assigned three Norrfalt guards to watch over me at all times, even here in my quarters. He—and the duke—said it was for my safety, but I think it was because they were both scared of me, ever since they saw what I did to the rebel guard who murdered Mother.

I wanted to leave the castle now, to go find the rebels and make them pay. I wanted to find Emily and Elliot and be sure they were safe. Without my sword, I could probably take one Norrfalt guard, maybe even two, but three? Impossible. I'd learned my lesson with that mob of disgruntled soldiers.

Any chance I had of running was gone. Any hope of revenge shriveled up. I'd told the duke of the rebellion and he said he would take care of it. But what good did that serve? I didn't trust the duke any more than I trusted the rebels. I still didn't even know what was really happening at the warfront and there was nothing I could do about any of it.

I was trapped.

I couldn't avoid the marriage. I couldn't avenge my mother. I couldn't avoid being made into a pawn. I wasn't a knight, I wasn't even really a queen. I was nothing but a helpless puppet, waiting to be traded away by forces stronger than I.

The cool silk of the baby-blue dress trapped me as if in irons with Madame Colombe dutifully cinching me into it. It settled like poison against my skin, like fabric woven of treason and treachery. I should be in black. I should be mourning. At least, I should be wearing crimson. I should be crowned in Mittelan's colors if I am to be Mittelan's queen.

The dress was the perfect display of the crown's change of hands, from Mittelan's control to Norrfalt's. The gown was smooth, with ruffled pickups three-quarters of the way down the skirt. It had obnoxious, poofy sleeves lined in silver that sat on the edge of my shoulders. There was nowhere to hide a dagger and nowhere to strap on the ruby and onyx sword my father had given me, even if I did have it.

I glanced at the guards. They were present even though I was getting dressed and I knew that if I did nothing to change it, I would spend my future in the cage of one castle or another. I leaned against the wardrobe for strength, for balance, as Madame Colombe pulled the laces of the dress tighter still. It felt like she would cinch the life out of me, and I would let her. It would be merciful, to stop breathing—to leave this prison behind and join my mother and father.

If only I could reign in my mother's stead, maybe then I could find peace in continuing her legacy. But as a mouthpiece for Norrfalt, I would have nothing left of her. I would probably have to go to Norrfalt with Christopher to produce heirs, leaving whoever he chose—probably the Grand Duke—to rule in my place. Who would have thought that my mother's most trusted advisor would stand to gain the most in her death?

Madame Colombe tied off the laces and turned me around to face her. She steadied me as I stepped into the pair of heeled satin slippers that matched the dress. She cradled my powdered cheek in her warm, round hand, then reached down, pulling something out of the pocket in her apron. "I know it doesn't really match," she said, "but I think you should wear it anyway. For her."

A necklace dropped from her fisted hand. I recognized the gold chain instantly, its tight links fine and perfect. Off the chain hung a diamond shaped medallion, gold, and stamped into it was the royal seal of Mittelan. The opalescent swan had two daggers across its chest, one made of a single cut ruby and the other onyx. Red and black gemstones alternated around the perimeter. It was the necklace my father had gifted my mother on their wedding day. The one she hadn't been wearing when she died.

"I had it yesterday," Colombe said, "I was having it cleaned." She choked back tears.

A small bit of relief settled over me with the pendant in my hands. "Thank you, Madame," I whispered, turning so she could put it over my head and fasten it behind my neck. I ran my finger down the slender gold chain and clasped the seal in my hand. Mittelan's seal. My father's gift, my mother's crown. The edges dug into my palm. I squeezed it harder until the sharp corners drew blood. It was my crown now, my seal.

"She would have wanted you to have it," Madame Colombe bent down, her mouth nearly touching the lobes of my ear. She dropped her voice so low, I inclined my head to hear her, "She would have wanted you to fight."

"I—" I almost argued with her, but then I looked at the prince's guards and bit my tongue. *I can't fight!* I thought, *How can I do anything if I can't even leave my own castle? I don't even know who these rebels are! How can I fight back?*

Yesterday's events scrolled through my head. Elliot: his scars, his touch, his breath. The rebellion: their haunting words, my near capture, Jacob. My mother: her worry, her relief, her death. And then Prince Christopher, when he found me in the throne room, still clinging to my mother's body. Genuine concern had seemed to overwhelm him, his touch had been gentle, yet . . . unsurprised.

The queen lay dead and I knelt by her side, crippled with grief, yet the prince didn't even think to ask how this had happened? How had he even known to come search for me in the throne room in the middle of the night? Why had he not looked entirely surprised to find Mother dead? If the rebellion had decided to kill us off due to the engagement, that would have given them less than one day to persuade a loyal guardsman to turn on the royal family. I'd been too devastated and furious with the rebellion to think clearly before. But now, with Christopher's placid expression chiseled in my mind, I knew.

Who would have thought that my mother's most trusted advisor would stand to gain the most in her death?

There was only one traitor with enough access and time to have planted an assassin in the ranks of the queen's guard. There was only one person who directly benefited from the queen's death and the marriage alliance to his own kin. One person who would have shared his plot with the prince.

This wasn't rebellion. It was treason.

The Grand Duke.

CHAPTER TWENTY-SIX

ELLIOT

The lids of my eyes parted into slits, the world obscured through my lashes. My head pounded at even the smallest sliver of lantern light and I squeezed them closed again. I tried to reach my hand up to touch the throbbing crown of my head, but cords cut into my wrists behind my back. My waist felt light with my sword and sheath gone. My cheek stuck to a brick floor slick with grime, where I was laying on my side. The stench of piss and hops prickled my nostrils. Wiggling my feet, I discovered my ankles bound as well.

Through the curtain of my eyelashes, I surveyed the dim room. The motley group of villagers from the market square were gathered around a large wooden table, a lantern casting all of their faces into a wicked array of light and dark. They hadn't yet noticed me wake.

"When the princess is dead—" the voice was the same as

the one in the village, the young man missing his pinky who'd tried to claim the girl was his sister.

The girl! I hoped she was alright.

I closed my eyes and listened to the man plot with his comrades, "—and the royal line ended, the country will have no one to lead it. The duke cannot remain regent without the princess or ascend the throne without a vote. If she is dead, the Norrfalt prince will have no one to marry and will have no claim to the Mittelan throne. We can vote one of our own onto the throne!"

"We will have a democracy!" A woman shouted. "We can bring our soldiers home! No more conscriptions!"

These villagers were delusional. Only a noble would be able to replace a fallen monarch. It wouldn't be a democracy; it would be a new dynasty. A dynasty that some tyrannical noble would head, whoever could get the most votes. It certainly would not be any of these peasants.

"The troops are already coming home, mother," the young man retorted. "But they're only coming home because the regent ordered them home. He's already bowing to Norrfalt because they believe they've won. With the wedding so close, they think Mittelan is already theirs."

"Well I know that, Jacob," the woman said, "but I mean they can come home and stay home. Our leader has already promised, no chance of conscription for my boys." The lilt of her voice sounded like she was talking to a baby.

Our elector? What was she talking about?

The pang in my head grew suddenly worse and bile rose in my throat. My body sprang to my knees and I heaved dryly until the wave of nausea passed. All of the villagers' heads turned to me. I wiped the saliva from my mouth with my shoulder and sat up. I saw the rebels for the first time through wide open eyes. There weren't as many of them as I had thought: ten, twelve at the most.

"Well, look who decided to wake up," the red-haired man—Jacob, the woman had called him—said. I looked through the lot of them and found many of their faces familiar. They'd watched me in the arena. They'd bet on me. They frequented Lucifer's where Bruno had poured their ales. Three men sat at the table whom I didn't recognize and they were dressed far nicer than the majority of the group. Was one of these men the elector the woman spoke of?

"Traitors," I said, leaning my head against the wall behind me. A knot had risen where I'd been knocked out and the wound stung as it came to rest on the brick. The gash in my side from Kiera's blade still throbbed dully. "It's treason. You think you're saving Mittelan, but you're not. You're betraying it. You killed the queen!"

How they'd done it, I couldn't know, but it was the only thing that made any sense. They had killed the queen and now they were plotting to kill the princess as well.

"No," Jacob took two paces towards me, slowly, deliberately, "we *planned* to kill the queen, but somebody beat us to it. Some malady or assassin, no one knows. But it wasn't us."

He's lying, I thought. He had to be lying. I'd just heard them plotting to end the dynasty and force their precious leader onto the throne. But why admit that they were planning to kill the queen, and not claim it if they had? Why not take the credit?

A shape shifted in the shadows. "But we *are* going to kill the princess," said a man as he took a step forward. I recognized the voice instantly. His thin lipped smile was barely visible but I could hear the malice in his words. I would know that voice anywhere. His hooked nose emerged from the darkness first, followed by his slender, snake-like body. Silas Tremaine. "Actually, child, *you* are going to do it for us."

I tried to stand and protest, to fight the old man, but the pounding in my head grew worse. "No!" I yelled. "I would never. I am loyal to the Perrault family. I am loyal to Mittelan!"

Silas crossed the room and stood above me. He put a skeletal finger under my chin and tipped it up until my gaze met his black eyes. "You will kill the princess, Elliot, or I will let these mongrels—" he pointed a lazy finger back to Jacob and his miscreants, "—have your sister."

The wound on my head. It was making me hear things, making me see things. That was the only explanation. Silas himself is the one who told me that Millie had died in the infirmary, leaving me only a lock of her hair. She'd fallen ill while we were on the run, because of me. She'd died, because of me. He had been the very one who'd told me.

"Millie has been dead for eight years, Silas," I grappled to my knees, trying to stand, trying to get to him, to strike him, to kill him, to do anything to cause him the kind of pain he caused me.

But why had I taken anything this serpent said as truth? He said he had no money for a casket or a funeral, so why then did he not bring her body home in a sack cloth? Or her ashes? I had accepted that it was just another way for him to punish me, that I should be thankful to have anything of her at all—even just a single curl—but was there more to it than just his excessive cruelty?

Silas nodded to a round man with long, scraggly hair who left the room. Stifled screams came from the doorway and moments later he carried in a chair with a girl tied to it. The girl from the street. Her ankles were tied around the legs of the chair and her hands bound behind her back. A gag was stuffed into her mouth and secured there with a cloth tied around the back of the chair. Tear lines ran down her face like a maze and her eyes were overrun with fear, wide and green and shining.

It felt like a fist to my gut when I saw her eyes—really saw them—as my mother's eyes, my eyes, and knew that Silas wasn't lying. Not this time.

"Millie," I whispered through trembling lips. My voice hitched at her name. I fell forward, my forehead on the dirty, cold ground, as a sob shook through me. My eyes squeezed shut in disbelief. All these years . . . she'd been alive? I'd spent so many years away from her. I forced myself to look back up to her. Her gaze had calmed and her eyes were almost . . . almost smiling at me. Where had she been all these years if not dead?

I ripped my eyes from hers like sparks and set my flame on Silas. "What did you do?" I raged but he only grinned. "Where has she been? Why did you tell me she was dead? What have you done to her?" I asked frantically, with so much confusion and loathing, my voice extended past its breaking point.

"Shh, boy," he clicked his tongue with disapproval and stuck a finger into the air, waggling it back and forth. "We wouldn't want to disrupt business."

It flicked through my head that we were in the back room at Lucifer's Den, that's why the smell was so familiar. Parren!

Bruno! I wanted to scream to them, certainly one of them was here and would come to my aid.

But even together they couldn't fight this entire room of rebels, and there was no telling what these bastards would do to Millie if I gave them away.

"What did you do to her?" I asked, as slowly and calmly and forcefully as I could manage.

Silas leaned down, his face so close to mine I could see the deep wrinkles surrounding his cruel eyes. "I saved her. Just like *you* begged me to."

He laughed softly to himself and then stood up again, "Well, I saved her, and then I sold her. I had been considering the option for some time. I thought it would be best for the poor girl as she had started to remind me entirely too much of Eliza. When she recovered from her illness, the doctors informed me that the trauma combined with an incredibly high fever had resulted in severe memory loss. They said she would need some special care for a while. What perfect timing, I thought. So I sold her to a seamstress, best dressmaker in Swanstone, I'm told. We needed the money, not another hassle or another mouth to feed. You never would have let her go otherwise and I still needed your help at home. This way, I got your obedience—maybe even a bit of your loyalty for having tried to save her—and you got a clean break." Silas tossed his hands about as he spoke, like he was telling me a boring, useless story, like when he'd gone to bed or what he'd had for supper. "It was a win-win."

Every word he spoke fanned the flames of my hatred until my anger blistered white hot. "How could you?" I roared, standing up before I realized my ankle straps were tied to the wall. I pulled against my restraints but the knots didn't budge. Two of Silas's lackeys forced me back to my knees. "I'd lost everyone! How could you take her from me too?"

Silas acted as if I'd said nothing as he went on, "When Jacob found his brother sneaking a servant girl out of the castle, he brought her to us immediately, thinking she might have some information we would find useful. I recognized her instantly—she has Eliza's eyes you see," Silas dragged his finger along Millie's chin. She struggled against her bonds to pull away from him.

I watched the tears gather in my sister's eyes and wondered how much of this information was new to her, too.

"As a matter of fact," Silas continued, "Jacob had no idea just how useful she would turn out to be. In fact, even her escape led us directly to you. Which brings me to my plans for you."

His words were melting in the kiln of my rage. I shook my head. *No, no, no, I won't help you,* I wanted to say. But fear choked out my words; what would refusing my step-father cost Millie this time?

But even the shake of my head infuriated him.

He turned his large stoned ring around on his hand and whipped his palm across my face. He dug his needle-like fingers into my cheeks and forced me to look at him. "You will attend the coronation ball tonight. You are nobility so your name will already be on the list. These men," he released my face with a rough shove and pointed at the villagers, "have already informed me of your skills with a blade. Apparently, you've been disobeying my commands for quite a while now, but no more. Tonight you will go to the ball, and you will kill the princess. You will be back here by midnight, or else your sister will meet the fate she escaped all those years ago. Do you understand me?"

I tasted the tang of blood in my mouth. I spat red spittle onto Silas's polished black shoes. *No!* I tried to say it, but I couldn't. I couldn't bear the thought of the havoc that one word could bring, should I say it to Silas a second time. I just got Millie back; I couldn't lose her again.

So I said nothing.

Jacob crossed the room and put his dagger across the bare skin of Millie's throat. A cord of her blood dripped down his blade and it felt as if my heart was being ripped from my chest as it had been the day she'd left for the healers.

"At midnight," Jacob said, "either the princess is dead or your sister will be."

"The rebellion is behind me, son," Silas took his handkerchief from the pocket of his suit coat and wiped my bloody saliva from his shoe, "It has been for weeks. Where do you think I was going on all those trips to Swanstone? I did warn you to stay on my good side."

This had happened right under my nose. I'd been so distracted by the Woodland Games, I hadn't even noticed.

"Albeit, the rebellion had no idea our opportunity was going to come so soon," Silas said, "but now that it has, the solution is simple: I provide you, you provide the head of the last remaining royal, they provide their votes. I am their leader and soon I will be their king. You and your sister could even live with me and your stepbrothers in the castle if you cooperate . . . or she can die and you can go on being absolutely worthless."

Silas. King. The thought was something of nightmares. Then

I looked at Millie, who couldn't speak or move. She was shaking her head from side-to-side as much as she could manage in her bonds. She was bruised and bleeding just as she had been on the night I'd lost her. This was my sister, my baby sister. I could not lose her again. I would not.

"Untie me, sir," I locked eyes with my depraved stepfather, "I need to find something to wear to our new queen's coronation."

He nodded to one of the rebels who brought him a sheathed blade. Silas threw it at my feet and I instantly recognized the tiger's eye hilt. "You'll be needing this then, *boy*."

CHAPTER TWENTY-SEVEN

CHARA

Of course it hadn't been the rebels who'd killed my mother. I overheard their plot less than a few hours before I was standing over my mother's body. I had been blind to not see what the duke was capable of earlier, his betrayal ran much deeper than a forced marriage alliance or deceptions about the war.

I'd been so desperate to escape the marriage that I'd doomed not only my mother but the entire country. My self-loathing was eclipsed only by the fires of vengeance that now raged within me.

When I was dressed and ready for the coronation—my mother's medallion now hanging around my neck—I stood from my dressing table and glanced at the inattentive guards. Even though they knew what I did to the assassin, they still didn't see me as a threat. For once, it could work to my advantage to have my skills underestimated.

I rested my hands on Colombe's shoulders and kissed each of her cheeks. "Thank you, Madame," I said loud enough for the guards to hear, "for everything." I paused before pulling away and dropped my voice low, "You are right. Mother would want me to fight. Now go into the washroom and lock yourself in."

She looked like she may protest so I whispered, "Your queen commands it."

She didn't dare to respond, but I saw her swipe at tears as she scuttled into the washroom as if to fetch something, closing the door behind her.

I crossed my bedroom in three long strides, clasping the pendant around my neck. "I have to see about some last minute arrangements for the ball. Guards, please escort me to the ballroom." The first guard nodded dutifully, turning to open the chamber door while the remaining guards fell into place behind me.

The leading guard stepped into the hallway and I followed, but as I reached the threshold, I yanked open the door all the way, slamming it into one of the guards following me and knocking him off of his feet. The second guard that had been following lunged to stop me, but I sidestepped him, slamming the door as I did and catching his fingers in the jamb. I forced the heavy door to latch, his bones snapping like dead branches. I threw the lock. As he crumpled in pain, I ripped the medallion from my neck and stabbed its sharp corner into his neck.

The guard on the other side of the door shouted and pounded to be let in, but the lock held.

I turned around and found the guard who'd caught the force of the opening door already back on his feet and reaching for his sword. I kicked his hand away from his hilt and sunk my elbow into his jaw. Blood spattered onto the puffed sleeve of my dress. I grabbed the sword from his waist and ran it through his stomach when he attacked. Warm blood trickled down the hilt onto my hand, bathing my grip in scarlet. I pushed the hilt away from me. His body fell onto my bed, and rolled onto the floor, pinned on the blade.

The second guard had pulled his mangled hand from the door and was writhing on the floor. Blood seeped from the wound in his neck. I went to him and took his sword from his belt and threw it out of his reach. I noticed a dagger in his boot and extricated it before kneeling on his chest, my dress nearly engulfing him, and held the dagger to his throat. "Did one of your men kill my mother?"

"I did nothing," he garbled, "I'm innocent, Princess!" He tried to push me off of him with his good arm, but I pinned his injured hand to the ground with my foot and stepped down, the heel of the satin shoe crushing his already broken bones. His blood-curdling scream vanished into the tapestries and the thick castle walls. The pounding on the door to my room increased. Guards from the castle would be flooding the hallway any moment to break the door down.

I should go. But I had to know.

"Do you work for the Grand Duke?"

"Norrfalt!" He screamed, "I work for the Ludwig family of Norrfalt!" Tears rolled down his temples. He stopped wiggling, stopped fighting me. I took my foot off his hand but kept the knife at his throat.

"Do you answer to the duke?" I asked, "Did one of your men kill my mother?" It had been less than a day since my finger rested on my mother's wrist, begging the Creator to bring her heart to beating once more. The memory urged me on, despite the panic in his eyes or the wrinkles in his skin just beginning to show his age. But the stubborn guard betrayed nothing. I put my shoe back on his hand and leaned into it with all my weight. His cries increased. I could feel more bones snapping under my heel.

"Yes!" he burst. "The king told us to take our orders while here from the Grand Duke. We knew the assassin in the Queen's Guard was loyal to Norrfalt. The duke gave the order to kill your mother."

My mouth went dry.

I let the guard go. He hobbled up onto his feet, cradling his injured hand. Blood dripped down his neck. His eyes flew to his fallen comrade, the hole in his torso with the blade still through him. Then he looked at the bloody pendant I still clenched in one fist and the dagger I held in the other.

"Bring me to the duke," I said.

He stood petrified, not moving even as I took the belt that held his scabbard off his waist. He didn't even try to stop me, terror plastered on his face. I buckled the scabbard over my dress, grabbed the rapier from the chest of the dead soldier and put it in the sheath at my waist, and tucked the dagger in the belt beside it.

I hid my mother's medallion in my corset, spattering the white lace of my décolletage with blood as I did so. The horrific blue dress got more stained every time my bloody hands touched it. But I didn't care; in fact, I relished the deep crimson stains on the pastel silk. Now that my hands were free, I pulled the rapier from its sheath on my waist and rested its point in the small of the guard's back. He still cradled his ruined hand. The wound from the necklace soaked the collar of his uniform in blood. "Take me to the duke and I won't skewer you like I did your friend. Tell the other guards to stand down as soon as you open the door."

He nodded, stepping forward to unlock the door with his good hand. "Stand down, men," he said. "The princess wishes to see the duke."

Guards, clothed in blue and white, cleared a path for us in the castle hallway. Many twitched, some reached for their blades. "Make a move," I drove the point closer to the man's skin, enough to cause him to whimper, "and your friend is dead. I just need to speak with the duke."

The men all took a step back from me. All except one.

From the guards stepped the chiseled face of the prince. "Ah, Princess," he fell into step beside me, "I had no idea my betrothed was such a fine swordsman, or I would have requested a spar, first thing." I didn't respond, or turn my head to him, or acknowledge him in any way. Even if he had not been the one who gave the order to kill my mother, the assassin was loyal to Norrfalt. The king, the prince, and the duke had probably been working together for years. The prince had my mother's blood on his hands, too.

We walked, an odd trio, to the office of the Grand Duke. The crippled guard opened the door without knocking and his voice cracked as he announced my arrival, "The princess requests your ear, Master Grand Duke." He stepped away from the blade's point and I let him. He shriveled back into the throngs of his fellow guards as they awaited the duke's orders.

"If you are lucky, Duke, I will start by only taking an ear." Nothing stood between us but the length of my sword, and yet, a half-smile graced his lips.

"Such unflattering words for a lady, Charissa, especially a princess," the duke looked me up and down, tsking as he took in the sight of the blood stained gown. "As is that dress. Now why did you have to go and ruin such a lovely thing?"

I chose to ignore his misogynistic comment, not wanting to give him the satisfaction. Instead I just stated a fact, "You killed my mother." Every muscle in my body was coiled, like a snake poised to attack.

"Well, technically," he inched closer to my blade, every movement like a challenge, "Sir Markus Sinia killed your mother."

"You. Gave. The. Order."

"Well, yes." His fat gut was almost touching the tip of my blade, trying so hard to be brave, but he flinched when I tightened my grip on the hilt. "But I didn't really expect you to get involved. It's a good thing he didn't kill you, though, isn't it? We wouldn't want to risk Mittelan's monarchy falling into the wrong hands, now would we? Unfortunately, the regency has its limitations until you are married to my nephew. Then the Norrfalt king will grant me control of Mittelan, and we can be Norrfalt's closest ally. The bloodshed will end at last and neither country will go hungry. Don't you see why this is best for everyone? After the wedding, the prince can either deal with you in Norrfalt or kill you off himself, it doesn't really matter one way or the other to me."

Out of the corner of my eye, I saw the prince's face flash with bewilderment, but he said nothing.

The Grand Duke was underestimating me even more so than the guards had if he expected me to stand by while he threatened to overtake the kingdom, rationalize his hunger for power, and justify the murder of his queen. He was brave to the point of foolishness if he expected me to be afraid of him when he stood, unarmed, within a swing of my blade and my burning hatred.

I pulled back my sword to strike.

"Ah, ah, ah," he shook a finger. "I wouldn't do that if I were you."

"Then it's a good thing you're not," I took a breath, ready to avenge my mother once and for all.

"Well it will be a pity for your friend to join your mother in the afterlife because you were too hasty."

I paused. He smiled, clearly pleased with himself, and backed up to a red tufted chair and sat down as if he were lowering himself onto a throne.

"What are you talking about?" I immediately regretted the question. Dammit, Chara. I should have said I have no friends, no connections, no one they could use as leverage.

"A little skinny blonde handmaiden, always flitting around, attending to your every whim," he ran a fat finger over his greasy moustache.

Emily.

He was bluffing. He had to be bluffing.

"A friend of mine found her sneaking out of the castle and is detaining her for me. Now if anything should happen to me, or to the prince, he will kill her," he threatened. "I was saving this juicy tidbit to share with you before the ball tonight, just to ensure that you were on your best behavior. But I guess now is as good a time as ever for a lesson in obedience."

I felt my resolve waver. I stumbled backwards a few steps, the fire that had been burning in my cheeks moments ago growing cold. Emily *had* been out of the castle, on orders from me no less. And I was surprised that she had not yet returned. I hoped he was bluffing, but how could I risk it when Emily's life was on the line?

"So I suggest," said the duke, sensing my fear and knowing that he had won, "that you go and get cleaned up. You've ruined the dress you are *supposed* to be wearing, but maybe you can scrounge up something suitable. Something fitting for your coronation. It's *very* important to me that tonight go as planned."

Slick with blood, the handle of the guard's sword slipped from my trembling grip, ringing when it hit the floor. I lost control of my body for just a moment, the thought of Emily bound and gagged somewhere pervaded my mind, and I thought I may faint. Before I could recover long enough to retrieve the sword, the duke nodded to two of his guards, "Take the weapons."

I snatched the knife from my belt and held it out uselessly. They approached me cautiously and it took every ounce of control I had not to lash out at them. They retrieved the sword from the floor, unbuckled the sheath from my waist, and took the dagger from my bloody and shaking hands. *Emily*, I thought, *I can't let them kill Emily. I can't lose her.*

"Go now, Princess," the duke said victoriously as he stroked his white moustache, "we don't want to keep our guests waiting."

The guards escorted me back to my quarters, a half dozen blades poised around me, even as I marched in front of them unarmed and completely useless.

CHAPTER TWENTY-EIGHT

ELLIOT

After the rebels untied me, I knelt at my sister's feet for scarcely moments before they thrust me out into the street. In that time, I managed to pull the leather pouch from my hip and tuck it into her tied hands. "I will not mourn you again," I told her, before three men yanked me to my feet.

She broke into a panicked scream, stifled by the gag. But it wasn't her fear or her silenced cries that haunted me the most. It was the peaceful calm, even joy, in her eyes when Silas told her who I was. That happiness plagued me. I was a stranger, and then, for a fleeting moment, we were a family again. The granule of hope in that moment was like a fine plate teetering on the tip of my blade, and it was only a matter of time before it came crashing to the ground.

All I could do was keep it balanced, just long enough to get

Millie out safely. But there was only one way to do that: kill the princess.

Silas swore before releasing me that if I told anyone what I was doing, he would kill Millie. I needed to find Parren, but I couldn't tell him what I was doing, I couldn't ask for his help. But I could ask for something suitable to wear to the coronation.

As I stumbled out of the back room of Lucifer's Den, I scanned the pub for Parren, expecting to find him at the bar surrounded by empty glasses, but he wasn't there. Bruno was also mysteriously absent from behind the bar.

I left, bleary eyed, trying to clear my clouded mind and focus on getting to Parren's cottage. I made my way through the familiar street in a daze until I finally walked through the gate leading onto Parren's estate. I tripped up the front porch step, the memory of Kiera discovering my scars there suddenly seeming worlds away. She was gone, missing, and I needed to find her—but I couldn't even think about that, not with Millie's life on the line.

Kiera's disappearance would be the perfect cover story for me to give to Parren as to why I needed to go to the ball. "Parren!" I shouted as I entered his home without knocking. "Are you here?"

A gurgling sound came from the fainting couch. Had he come home to drink this evening?

"What is it? Too much commotion at Lucifer's tonight?" I hollered, trying to keep my tone light. But then I noticed a circle of blood growing beneath the fainting couch. My heart beat in my throat. "Master Parren?"

I circled the piece of furniture and found my master, my best friend, my mentor, pinned to the upholstery. Blood bubbled from his mouth, and his own practice blade pierced through his chest and into the couch. His hand limply clutched a dagger with a tigers eye hilt, a perfect match to the sword he'd given me. His long hair had escaped his ponytail and flowed around him like molten silver. *No.* This wasn't happening. *No. No. No.*

"Parren! Parren!" I shook him, and he opened his eyes enough to focus on my face, "Master Parren! What happened? Who did this to you?" Panic ebbed in me, leaving only a desperate hope clinging to the flicker of life in his eyes.

"Your mother—" he struggled, the blood in his mouth made it difficult for him to speak and hard for me to understand him. "Your mother would be so proud of you," he lifted a hand to my cheek. "You deserved better family than me."

I pulled the blade out of him and let it fall to the floor. The only explanation for its use was that whoever he had fought had managed to get his weapon from him in the struggle and used it . . . in the end. Who, in all of Mittelan, could be capable of such a thing?

I picked up the dying man, cradled him like a baby, tears the only response I could summon. He was my friend, my best friend, as close as family.

"That's why I never told you. You had *him* giving you enough trouble as it is . . . you didn't need a drunk like me as an uncle," his gray and gold eyes grew glassy. "So I found you, soon as I could. You were just a lad selling those skins. I knew I couldn't take care of you, but maybe I could help in a different way. All those lessons, they were just so I could be with you. Now you'll have a piece of me always," he struggled to pat the sword at my hip. "The set was a gift, from your mother, before I left."

"What? What tipsy tale are you spinning for me this time?" I reached for his hand. *Please, let this not be happening. Please, don't let him die.*

"No, I'm not drunk. Not this time. I left the country as a spy for the king, he sent me to Norrfalt court. But your mother didn't want me to go." He coughed and blood splattered onto his tunic. "My baby sister, always looking out for me."

Could he really be telling the truth? Why now? Why was he telling me all of this now, after all these years, as I sat watching him die?

"It doesn't matter," I said, squeezing his hand—muscular from gripping a blade but filled with raised veins and age spots—and holding it tight. "Name or title doesn't matter. You were always family to me. You *are* family." I choked over my words, my tears strangling me, hot and fierce. "Who did this?"

"This, this was king's—" he coughed loudly, sending blood spraying from his lips onto my tunic. "This was the Norrfalt king's vengeance. I should have died decades ago, when I lost this leg." He tapped his peg leg absently. "But it doesn't matter now. I don't matter. What matters is you and the princess—" a cough interrupted him once more and his eyes drifted closed.

How could he have known what I was about to do to the princess?

"Kiera," the old man spoke of her with near reverence, "take the carriage, take the sword. Go to her. Keep her s-s-safe . . . she's—"

He stopped mid-sentence.

"No! Please, Master Parren, please don't leave me," my

tears soaked into the faded upholstery of the fainting couch.

His gray glimmering eyes froze open. The sparkle of gold flitting around in them grew stoic, and I realized where I'd seen that glow before. In my mother's eyes. In Millie's. In mine.

His breathing stalled. I reached my hand up and touched my fingers to his cheeks, the soft curve of his chin, his small nose, just like my mother. How could I have not seen her in him over all these years? I thought back to his many kindnesses, of him giving me the practice blade and helping me train for four years. I'd thought it was for the money, but it wasn't. He had sought me out. He had trained me and helped me fight for Beauhaven. For her. For me. Because he loved me, because we shared a bond that was deeper than friendship. We were blood.

A sob rolled through me. A sob for Parren. More sobs, for my mother, for Millie, for the princess, even for Kiera. I wanted to give up, to leave with Parren, to join them in the grave. But my mother's voice called to me. *You're strong, little Elliot. Take care of your family—your sister—and yourself. Promise me, Ellie.*

Millie.

Eight years ago—when Silas had stolen Millie from me—I had failed my mother; but tonight, I would not fail her again.

I wallowed in the pain of it all for just a moment. The pain of losing my parents and then Millie and now Parren. I let the grief enter me and consume me. I mourned for the Parren I knew and the uncle I never did. If I could embrace the pain for just a moment, maybe I could go on to fight the battle that raged at my doorstep. Parren deserved more than a moment but that was all I had. The clocktower tolled in the distance. I counted nine bells. That left me three hours.

I looked down at my clothes; they were the same filthy clothes I'd left home in two days ago. I would never be admitted to a royal coronation in these rags.

Parren had known Kiera would be at the castle, I realized. He'd told me to take his carriage, to go to her. Perhaps I could find her, kill the princess, and get back to Lucifer's by midnight. But that didn't leave any time to waste.

Wiping my tears on the sleeve of my dirty tunic, I forced myself to lay Parren on the couch, close his empty eyes, and stand. I dug through his wardrobe but found only training outfits and guard uniforms. I threw them to the floor in a huff. Behind the uniforms were only his winter furs. I was about to give up when a glimmer of gold caught my eye and, moving aside a thick fur coat, I found the gold to be the fringe of an epaulette on a black and crimson double breasted jacket. Behind it hung matching trousers and a black tunic. I prayed that by some miracle, the set would fit me. Wiggling into the pants, I realized the leg was not hemmed like all of the rest of Parren's pants. This must have been from before he lost his leg. I fastened the pants closed, then the tunic, then the coat. Magically, each gold button aligned perfectly, as if the ensemble had been tailored specifically for me.

Around my waist I buckled the two swords, the one Parren had gifted me and Kiera's, which I had retrieved where I had left it stashed discreetly among her belongings.

I gulped and knelt by Parren's side for one final goodbye. I would come back for him after all this and bury him beside Mother. My chin trembled, and I bit my lip to stop it. I reached for his hand, pulling the dagger from his clenched fingers. I held his empty hand for a long minute before tucking the dagger beneath my jacket. I shuddered thinking of what I needed to use that for. Would Parren approve of me using his dagger or sword—gifts from my mother, if he had been telling the truth—to kill the last true Mittelan monarch?

But I had no other choice.

Outside of Parren's home, Stell and Gus still stood tied to the post. I untied them and led them to the small stable with room for only two horses. There was a horse in each spot, Parren's pure white mare, Faye, and her opposite, a black gelding whose name I couldn't remember. Beside the horses stood Parren's sleek black carriage, by far the most expensive thing he owned. It had been a gift from the king, after Parren completed training of his first round of the king's private guards.

I wanted to go on foot, but any respectable nobility would arrive at the castle in a carriage. I doubt they would let me through the gates otherwise. I thought about taking Stell, but I had no way of knowing if Kiera's mare had ever pulled before. I hooked up Gus and Faye, and put Stell in the open stable spot. I put my forehead against Gus's nose and he nuzzled into me affectionately. "I'm going to need your help tonight, Gus," he flicked his tongue out at me, "when we need to get away, I'm relying on you. Alright, buddy?" He huffed a disproving response.

The gate latch clicked open and the hinges whined as they swung open. I whirled around as the crunch of gravel footsteps approached. A lanky figure stood in the darkness cast by the dwindling sunset behind Parren's home. A man. He stepped out of the shadows.

"Lucas?" I squinted as my stepbrother's form came into shape. He stepped forward into the light of the lantern hanging from the stable wall. Jack ran out from behind him at my voice, yipping and bouncing around my feet. I knelt down and ran my hands along his smooth head, pushing back his floppy ears, and scratching. I smiled for the first time all day. His leg pattered against the ground contentedly. The dog's joy brought a prickle of tears to the crescents of my eyes.

"The damn dog follows me everywhere," Lucas drew my attention from Jack. My stepbrother's boots were muddy and he had no horse. He must've walked. His face was down-turned, bags hanging around sleepless eyes. He had many of his father's features, but on him they were less angular, almost soft. Almost kind. I'd never noticed before.

"Lucas, w-what are you doing here?" I stammered in surprise. "How did you find me?"

"I snuck out and followed you," he said with a shrug of his shoulders, "after you left the pub. Father didn't want you to see me there, kept Ramond and I—and the blasted dog—in another room, but I heard every damn thing he said." He wrung his tunic in his hands, "He's been making us go to these meetings for months now and I've played along because I never thought they'd really amount to much. You don't just overthrow the government, you know? But apparently Father is crazier than I thought. I just . . . I can't let you go through with this. For once, don't listen to him."

"Lucas, I don't have a choice," I patted Jack once more and then stood, locking gazes with my stepbrother.

"My father cannot be king," Lucas raised his voice, and I took a step back. He'd only ever been passive . . . quiet . . . an island of nothing in the tumultuous straits of my life. Now, here he was advocating for me to disobey his father and risk my sister's life.

"He wants—no, he needs—power." Lucas spoke with his hands, passionately, like I'd never heard him speak before. "He craves it. That's why he gets it. And now he has had a sample of the ultimate power and he will do anything to get more of it. You, of all people, should understand how dangerous he is. He destroyed your life; what would he do with an entire country? I can't just sit back. He has leagues of peasants and even a fair share of the cabinet who have agreed to vote for him if he can keep the Norrfalt prince from becoming king."

I thought back to the well dressed men in the pub, the ones I didn't recognize. Could Silas really have garnered this much support?

"If the princess dies," Lucas declared, "then Silas *will* be king."

The thought made me feel sicker than I already felt. "It doesn't matter!" My anger exploded, my mind flooded with the image of Millie tied to the chair, knife at her throat, followed by the memory of her tiny form collapsing after he struck her all those years ago.

"It does, matter, Ell—"

"But he will kill her!" I shouted over him, my voice cracking. I threw my hands up and wrapped them around the back of my neck. I lowered my voice, "I can't lose her again."

Lucas dropped his chin, wrinkles covering his forehead. "There has to be another way . . ."

"If there was, do you think I'd be here? Silas let me believe she was dead for nearly a decade, he will not hesitate to have her killed." I put my hands on Lucas's shoulders and, to my surprise, found that he was shaking, "We can worry about the throne later, once Millie is safe. But for now, I don't have a choice. I have to go. I have to do what I couldn't all those years ago. I have to save my sister."

He put his hand on my arm, the most affection we'd ever shown to one another. The most words we'd ever shared having just passed between us.

"Then I am going with you." Lucas swung himself onto the driver's seat of the carriage and grabbed the reins. Jack hopped through the carriage's small door, tail beating the seats on either side of him, waiting for me to join him. I opened the estate's gate and closed it after Lucas walked the horses through.

Then I joined Jack in the carriage, fixing my eyes on the black satin wall opposite me. Jack curled in my lap. His deep breaths calmed me, and I focused on that. I didn't look out the window. I couldn't. I refused to look ahead at the deadly castle that awaited me or at the crypt I was leaving behind.

❖❖❖

"Cendrilon. Elliot Cendrilon." I didn't exit the carriage, but from the window in the door, I watched as the guard puzzled over the unfamiliar name. Jack growled at the disturbance so I scratched behind his ear and he calmed.

The guard at the front gates, dressed in Mittelan's red and black, scanned down the names on his parchment. The ruby guard towers loomed in front of us like the maw of a demon, and I knew that I may never be the same when—or if—I exited them. My foot tapped uncontrollably until, at last, the guard found my name. He nodded to the man operating the gold gate between the towers and it opened soundlessly on well-oiled hinges, entirely unlike the creaky gates to which I'd become accustomed. Lucas clicked his tongue to get the horses moving again. Gus and Faye trotted forward, towing us through the devil's jaws.

Although I'd been to the city many times, I'd never before been within the walls of Swanstone Castle. The many turrets of the white-washed stone were capped in cones of emerald green. It reminded me of the castles pictured in the storybooks my mother used to read to me, books Silas had long since sold. I swallowed my fear as we passed through the gate. It closed behind us like a great prison door. The shadows of mountains loomed behind the castle, the sunset long gone. The bell tower rang again. I knew the number but I counted anyway. Ten tolls. I had two hours—only two short hours—to find and kill the princess, seek out Kiera, and return for Millie.

Fanfare trumpets and colorful banners displayed empty joyfulness; the celebratory blare of the horn like treason so quickly following the queen's death. And I was about to make it worse, so much worse. I was about to end the Perrault dynasty. Our carriage vibrated over the cobblestones leading to the castle's massive arched door. It was painted a deep crimson—yet another reminder of the blood I was about to shed.

The life of an innocent. I knew next to nothing about the princess, but at scarcely seventeen, how could she be anything but innocent? Still, I prayed desperately that the princess was cruel and corrupt. I'd never seen her except from a great distance, as the royal carriage passed through the city streets. She didn't seem cruel or corrupt. In fact, I'd always imagined that she was somehow trapped in that carriage, trapped in her life the way I was in mine.

How would I even get close enough to her without guards attacking and chaining me? How could I complete this mission and not end up at the end of a noose? I rubbed my hand around my neck and squeezed. Fear speckled the corners of my vision, with the blood red castle door at the center. I could very well die tonight, and if I didn't, I would live out my years with a new burden.

But none of that mattered. Only Millie mattered now. Only getting back the life that was stolen from her. And from me.

The time had come. The click of the horses' shoes ceased, the carriage wheels squealing to a stop.

We had arrived.

CHAPTER TWENTY-NINE

CHARA

My arms grew numb as Prince Christopher spun me across the dance floor, and I thought that perhaps my body was playing tricks on me as was my mind. For a moment, I could have sworn I saw a glimpse of Elliot winding his way through the crowd.

Was I searching so desperately for a way out of the prison of this prince's arms that my mind created a fantastical savior who had come to help me free Emily . . . and free myself?

Where was the princess who didn't need anyone to come save her?

She was gone. Broken. And I was left, weak and bleeding, in her place.

The music shifted to beats of three and Prince Christopher transitioned seamlessly into a perfect waltz. I surveyed the crowd intently, trying not to draw attention to my temporary lapse of sanity, but I couldn't stop searching for a head of silky blond hair among them.

"She's not here," Christopher's lips barely moved when he spoke, the first words he had spoken to me since he saw me covered in the blood of his guards, demanding to see his uncle. My eyes snapped up to his, so stern they caught me by surprise. He kept his face completely calm and unmoving. "If you are looking for your friend, she isn't here."

Emily. He thought I was looking for her here. Of course the duke would not be so stupid as to have Emily within my reach, but it hadn't occurred to me that maybe the prince knew something, and I definitely had not considered that maybe he was willing to part with some of that information. Maybe he knew where she was.

The Grand Duke was transfixed on us from his perch on my father's throne. Could he read our lips? The prince seemed to believe so. When the dance faced my back to him, I blurted quickly and quietly, "Do you know where she is?"

He shook his head so slightly, I nearly missed it. "But I do know some—" he whispered when his back faced his uncle again but stopped abruptly as we completed the turn. I began another question but he shook his head and clenched his teeth. "Too dangerous," he whispered, his lips barely even parting.

The murals surrounding Singer Hall bled together as we turned, Swanstone's signature Swan Knight disappearing into a sea of red. So much blood had been shed: from the war, to my mother, to two men dead at my own hands. And if I did anything wrong before the night was over, Emily could end up dead, too.

For the first time, the prince had shown a glimmer of humanity, and it occurred to me that maybe the marriage alliance wasn't what he wanted either. Maybe he was just playing along, complying as I now was. Maybe we were both just doing what we were told, doing what we must to end the war our parents started.

I needed a moment out of the duke's sight to talk to the prince. The song ended with a sudden strike of bows. I curtsied. Christopher bowed.

"I think I fancy a bite to eat," I said, an idea occurring to me.

I exited the dance floor and walked just past the tables, heaping with food, to the perimeter of the grand hall. Women gathered there, waiting for their turn to dance, and men hovered, nervously preparing to ask.

Among the women was a voluptuous middle aged noble dressed in violet satin and sitting on a plush bench, clapping along to the beat blithely. I perched beside her and smiled grandly when she turned my way.

"Your Majesty," her eyes grew to the size of dinner plates at the sight of me, and she leapt up from her seat to curtsy.

"Oh, do sit down, Madame . . . Madame?" I let the question hang in the air as she lowered herself back down beside me.

"Ca-Ca-Carnell," she stuttered, "Duchess of Carnell."

I smiled politely, "Do sit down Duchess Carnell."

She sat beside me gingerly.

I looked at her through wide, innocent eyes, "I wondered if you had a moment."

"Anything for the future queen, Your Highness." Her bustle nearly knocked me off the bench. She twiddled her round thumbs in her lap nervously. I confirmed that her hand was free of a wedding ring and noticed it hanging by a chain around her neck. A widow.

"Is the Duke of Carnell not present tonight?" I asked.

"He passed away, Your Majesty . . . three years ago," her head dropped along with her gaze, "your mother gave him a lovely funeral though—the likes of which she deserved . . . I'm sorry, Your Highness, that's too bold."

"Not at all," I rested my hands on hers. "I appreciate your sympathies, and you have mine as well. It may lift your spirits to know that the Grand Duke of Swanstone told me that he hoped for nothing more tonight than a dance from the Duchess Carnell. Might I tell him he has your blessing to ask?"

She reached her hand up to her chin and not-so-discreetly forced her mouth closed, nodding profusely. "Of course, Your Highness, please do."

I smiled as warmly as I could manage, "Wonderful! He will be so pleased." I stood up and inclined my head to her before leaving.

I left the woman and wove through my subjects towards the stage, slipping my hand into the pocket I'd had Emily sew into my favorite ballgown. The pocket had been simple enough to to add to the rich velvet dress and hid easily between the scarlet exterior and the patterned black petticoat. The pocket seemed eerily empty without the weight of a blade. I felt exposed without a weapon, although maybe now it was fair to consider the medallion hanging around my neck to be a weapon of its own accord. The weight of it brought me strength and comfort, as did being dressed in the bold red and black of Mittelan.

I would get my hands on a weapon before the night was up,

just in case. I sent a silent prayer of thanks that the blood had made for a good excuse for me to change out of that horrid blue dress that the duke had ordered me to wear, and into this one. The three-quarter length bell sleeves of the luscious red velvet fluttered out at the elbows and were well designed for a broad range of motion. And though the neckline of the black embroidered stomacher curved, it was high enough to keep me well contained in a fight. Although I didn't think I would be engaging in battle tonight, if I had to be crowned into a false seat of power, at least I could do so with the appearance of confidence.

I stepped up onto the platform and sat in the empty throne by the duke's side. Prince Christopher stood regally between the two ornately decorated chairs.

"Done dancing with your betrothed so soon?" the duke asked poignantly.

"I am only resting. I believe it is your turn to engage our subjects with the art of dance. That's more than you can say for some of the members of your cabinet, isn't it? I noticed more than a few missing tonight, haven't you?"

"Indeed," the duke muttered, annoyed that I was pointing out even the slightest upset to his plans for the evening. "I am sure they have an excuse and will be here shortly."

"Well, in the meantime," I said, "the Duchess of Carnell just informed me that she is expecting you to request a dance from her," I gestured subtly to the round woman in purple, "and soon. And as her city supplies practically all of the woven goods to the kingdom, I don't think you should disappoint her. Don't worry, dear Duke, I will stay here, chatting with my betrothed like a good princess."

He sneered at me but stood up nonetheless. "You'd better." He toddled off the landing and into the festivities. Before long, the Duchess Carnell was leading the regent around the dance floor.

I looked up at Prince Christopher who was looking annoyingly dashing at my side. "Tell me what you know," I demanded.

"No need to be feisty, Princess, if you'd have stayed around long enough after our wedding announcement, you might have learned that I don't care for this marriage alliance either. But my uncle and my father have come to this agreement, and together, they are too powerful to disobey. I think you've learned that," he looked down at me through unwavering eyes, "and so have I. I play along because it's better to appear as an ally and know their schemes than to openly oppose them and be surprised."

I nodded, smiling at the onlookers who were watching the prince and I converse.

"My Father sent his assassin to the village," he continued, "to settle an old score. I don't know what exactly her mission was but after it was complete, she was to report to the duke. While out, she witnessed a young woman, small and blonde, being taken captive by a group of peasants. The girl was yelling something about working for the royal family and being friends with the princess. I believe she expected her connections to free her, not to put you or her into worse danger. The assassin felt the information worth reporting to the duke and he saw it as an opportunity."

"Are you telling me that the duke doesn't even have her?" Anger wrenched in my gut. I'd had the chance to kill him and

I'd let it slip through my fingers. I wanted to be relieved that she was not within his grasp, but I wasn't. *Someone* had her, even if it wasn't the duke, and now staying here on my best behavior wasn't protecting her at all. But who would have taken Emily against her will? And why?

I fiddled with the seam on the inside of my empty pocket, another reminder that I was defenseless.

"I'm afraid he does not, Princess," Christopher said, "and I don't know who does. Or where she is being held."

My mind raced. "Thank you for telling me," I said, "I know it puts you at risk." I paused and then decided I needed to know one more thing, "So you don't want to marry me?"

He shook his head, his beautiful high cheekbones and tapered chin bathed in golden chandelier light. "Perhaps for a moment," he teased, "after you nearly left me unconscious following our engagement. I've always admired a woman with a good arm."

I almost laughed. Maybe I had judged Christopher a bit too quickly.

As the duke bowed at the end of the song and began to make his way towards us, the prince held out a hand to me. He maintained the façade of our relationship as he led me to the dance floor and pulled my body into form.

As the music began, I leaned in close and whispered, "Then it sounds like we have ourselves an alliance."

CHAPTER THIRTY

ELLIOT

I'd heard of the renowned beauty of Singer Hall, but never before had I seen such splendor. From high, trellised, mahogany ceilings hung gold quatrefoil chandeliers, each alight with hundreds of candles. The walls were decorated with impossibly detailed murals, all telling the story of the legendary Swan Knight and his adventures, the Mittelan seal stamped upon his breastplate. Tables lined the room, filled with more food than I'd hunted and gathered in my entire life. Huge boars, skinned and glazed with maple and honey, were the centerpieces surrounded by roasted vegetables dripping with herbs and butter. Platters the size of shields were filled with cut fruit, and tiered plates overflowed with tiny cakes with absurdly intricate decorations.

How the Grand Duke ordered such an extravagant coronation in such a short time, I couldn't explain.

At one end of the room was a small stage, surrounded by arches, and ornately painted with the greenery and animals of the forest. On the stage sat two gilded thrones. One was empty and, in the other, sat an old man with a thick white moustache and dark eyes. He must be the Grand Duke. I didn't know much about the politics of the monarchy, but I had heard whisperings of the duke's power and knew that he would be regent once the princess was crowned. He surveyed the dancing with keen observation, eyes darting around the dance floor, locked on a single couple weaving throughout the others.

A small band of stringed instruments played from the side of the stage. Their song was joyful, light and springy, sending the dancing couples whirling around the color-filled room. Once again, I was struck by the abhorrent lack of respect being paid to the queen's passing. But the party-goers either didn't care or hadn't been given the opportunity to pay their respects, so they danced to the spritely tune in the manner which protocol dictated.

The duke seemed concerned only about the dancing couple, from whom his eyes never parted. They twirled down the center of the parted nobles who clapped from their makeshift aisle. I couldn't catch the dancers' faces, but could presume only one couple who would demand such attention from the new regent: the princess and her betrothed.

The girl I assumed to be the princess wore a ruby gown with a full skirt. It twinkled as her betrothed spun her down the floor, and when he stopped, I got a good look at the man I assumed to be the Norrfalt prince. He was clothed in gold and white formal military regalia. He was the kind of handsome that could merit teasing from some and devotion from others, but considering the way his austere smolder stayed fixed on his partner, I personally would hesitate before slinging any insults in his direction.

Even from the back, I could tell that the princess would not indulge me with a wicked countenance. Rather, she moved with a regal grace that reminded me faintly of someone. She danced to this merry tune with some sort of an aching sadness, and I could tell she was mourning her mother, the queen, even if she was neither weeping nor veiled in black.

I took a glass of some unknown amber liquid from the tray of a server. I sipped it, and the harsh bite of brandy warmed me from the inside, reminding me instantly of Parren, and that I had my own mourning to do. I forced the image of his lifeless body from my head. There would be time to mourn tomorrow, when Millie was safe.

I returned my focus to the princess as I sipped reluctantly from the brandy. It helped me blend in and I prayed that it would help me face my fate. From where I stood beside the dance floor, I could see the smooth skin of her delicate neck—exposed by her elaborate nest of woven auburn braids—disappearing into the gold trimmed neckline of her ruby gown. Would my blade really have to be what separates that slender neck from its head?

I could see now that her crimson dress had tiny gemstones stitched into the skirt, adding the shine I'd seen as she moved across the dance floor. *The deep color would hide blood stains.* The thought made me cringe as I imagined digging my knife into her soft waist, through the cross section of the bones of her corset and her ribs. Bile burned my throat and I considered once more abandoning this mission altogether.

For Millie, I reminded myself. *For Millie*. I needed to bring Millie a lifetime of the joy that had flickered in her eyes when she saw me in Lucifer's Den, when she realized who I was. If stabbing that damned red dress through was all it took to give my sister her life back, then so be it.

I needed to get a closer look at the princess. On the side of the dance floor, a line of exquisitely dressed women stood, brimming with anticipation. I picked one at random, a petite woman with strawberry hair and a rose colored gown, and offered her my hand. Her cheeks tinged pink and she accepted. I spun her onto the dance floor with relative ease, only to trip as I tried to remember the steps my mother had taught me when I was just a boy. I counted in my head and focused on the music. The woman grimaced, taking the lead as I fumbled through the steps.

The moves came back after a moment, as natural as riding a horse. I shifted my attention back to looking for the white and red couple. I didn't look at my partner as much as propriety dictated; instead, I scanned the room for the ruby dress and chestnut hair. The room swirled in a flourish of reds and pinks and blues. Some wore Mittelan seals and others wore blue and white, the colors of Norrfalt. There. I spotted a tiara of intricately entwined threads of gold and studded with red and black stones. Rubies and onyxes.

An image blazed through my memory. The armored man's blade—Kiera's blade—the tip hovering over my heart, and later my neck. Her fingers gripped the hilt of her sword . . . a hilt embedded with rubies and onyxes. The sword that hung around my waist that very moment. Did that mean that the *princess* was really Kiera's mistress? And, if she was, would she ever forgive me for her murder?

I knew the answer. But the better question was why I was even worrying about such a thing at all? Killing the princess may mean living a life without Kiera in it, so why did that seem like such an impossible thing to imagine?

I moved my dancing partner and I in the tiara's direction. We were mere paces away when the handsome man in gold and white spun his partner away from him, towards me. The princess looked away from her partner for no longer than a moment. A moment in which my world stopped turning in a flash of loose auburn tendrils hugging curved cheeks, terrific midnight eyes, and kind features distorted by fear and grief. All displayed beneath a red, black, and gold tiara.

The princess.

Kiera.

CHAPTER THIRTY-ONE

CHARA

For one moment, a glimmer of gold flickered across his gaze. His jaw tightened. He was garbed in black and red with two swords hanging from his waist, and one of them was mine. There was no mistaking him. Not again.

Elliot. He was here.

I looked back at Prince Christopher, as the dance bid me to do. His hands held me tightly against the rows of buttons down the front of his torso. Together we swirled amongst my subjects, and I knew now that I had not imagined Elliot. What was he doing here? He was in so much danger here, and I could not protect him.

I swallowed hard, realizing he may not have even received the message from Emily. But if he hadn't, how would he have known to come find me at the coronation?

I surveyed the couples dancing around us, trying not to

draw attention to myself as I searched for Elliot among them. Every time a man with blond hair or wearing black whirled past me, the beats of my heart quickened, but the faces were never his.

Then, a voice interrupted the music. "Am I permitted a dance with the princess?" A man asked Christopher, bowing low and offering up his hand to me. My breath hitched at the head of silky blond hair in front of me, the strong and callused hand of manual labor outstretched.

Christopher looked at me hesitantly, and I nodded.

"Certainly," he said with a faint smile as he tilted his head in farewell. Wide eyes lingered on me, concern flitting across them, as he exited the dance floor to stand by his uncle.

Elliot took my hand and pulled me with a firm jerk into his body. The strings began, a song slower than any before, and he fumbled through the first few steps. He seemed to remember them quickly though, and soon we were swaying in perfect sync. Many couples stopped dancing, stepping to the side of the floor to watch the stranger who dared ask the princess to dance.

"What are you doing here?" I asked through tight lips, hiding my words from as many prying eyes as possible, particularly the duke's.

"Dancing with the princess."

I shuddered. I could feel his breath on my bare shoulders, taking me back to the night before, when we'd been together on Parren's porch—had it been only yesterday that Mother was alive and I was free to run away, before everything had gone from bad to so much worse? The edge in his voice cut me open, exposing the pain I'd buried all night. What was he doing here? Had Emily told him the truth about me, or was he just now finding out?

"I should have told you . . . I tried to tell you," I struggled to keep the ache from my voice, "I sent—"

"How royal of you," he interrupted. "You *sent* someone to tell me that you were a fraud? To tell me the truth after I told . . . " he fell quiet. I looked up at him. He was biting his lip and I could finish his thought on my own accord: *after I told you everything.*

I recalled the scars covering his back and the truth he'd shared with me.

"Even after your deception in the arena, I believed you," he said. "I was willing to leave everything behind to help you. Against my better judgement, I trusted you."

"You don't understand, I had to come home—"

"—to the castle," he interjected.

"Yes, to the castle. I found out that my mother was in danger and I had to get to her. But . . . but I was too late." I looked down, unable to meet his eyes. He was dressed beautifully, wearing the most wonderful black suit coat with red embroidery and gold epaulettes. He must have borrowed it from Parren, or Bruno maybe.

I glanced back up. His jaw loosened, his glare dissolving into something molten and confusing. He pulled me closer to him, his hand on my waist sending prickles of elation and terror down my back. My hand rested on his shoulder, only a couple layers of fabric separating it from his thick skin, scattered with whipping lines.

"We need to talk," he glanced purposefully at the doors leading to the Upper Hall, "in private."

"I can't," I tilted my head towards the duke, "I'm being

watched."

"We have to find a way." The musicians faded into the song's ending. We released one another and I curtsied, dipping my chin to my chest, and the crowd clapped politely. When I looked up, Elliot had evaporated into the throng of guests.

I returned to the thrones to collect the prince. I needed his help.

Elliot had disappeared like an expert hunter; he could see what he wanted to see, but remained hidden.

"What was that display?" the duke muttered when I sat beside him on my throne.

"I was only dancing with one of my subjects," I said innocently. "As you have done as well, my lord. Perhaps you should introduce your nephew to the Duchess Carnell."

The eager woman was waddling her way back towards the dais. I gave Prince Christopher a knowing look and he caught on quickly, speaking before the duke could protest. "Yes, Uncle, I've heard much about her, and I would appreciate an introduction."

The duke narrowed his eyes at the pair of us, but as I relaxed deeper into the seat of my throne, he relented. "If you insist," he muttered and began taking large strides towards the duchess.

I caught Christopher's arm as he stepped off the stage and whispered hurriedly, "I've found someone who might be able to help us. Can you keep the duke busy long enough for me to find out?"

A striking smile quirked the side of his mouth. "I can try," he said, following after his uncle.

The clock tower struck eleven tolls. It was tradition to have the coronation at midnight, to symbolize the start of a new era. Only one hour remained until the coronation ceremony, when my tiara would be replaced with the weight of my mother's crown.

❖❖❖

I entered the chamber and let the door behind me fall closed, separating me from the song and dance. I could still hear the instruments, but only barely. The roaring fires of Singer Hall did not radiate this far and gooseflesh rose on my bare arms. The cold stone stole my breath and I held it in the silence.

The Upper Hall was a grandiose passageway connecting the ballroom to the rest of the palace and also the place that I hoped Elliot had planned to meet me. His hazel eyes had rested on the set of doors with distinct intentionality before parting . . . hadn't they? Hopefully I was not reading too much into a distracted glance.

The faint sound of movement startled me, a brush of clothing, a step.

Elliot appeared from behind one of the arched columns that lined the large corridor. Darkness slipped away from him, revealing a faint bruise beneath one eye. I hadn't noticed it in the thrill and surprise of his arrival; but here, in the candelabra light, I wondered if he'd seen his stepfather in the day we'd spent apart.

My chest constricted thinking of his cruel stepfather adding to the plethora of scars Elliot already bore.

I guess I carried new wounds since I'd seen him last, too, though mine were of a different sort.

He walked towards me slowly, and I fought the desire to run to him, imagining him sweeping me up and holding me as I wept for my mother, for the welt on my heart that her murder left that I feared may never stop aching. I imagined him comforting me, and I wasn't sure why. I wanted to be in his arms, to feel his callused hands smooth my hair.

Emily, I reminded myself, pulling my mind away from my imagination. My focus had to remain on saving Emily. And that meant putting mourning for my mother aside for now, and telling Elliot the truth. And though I had no right to ask for it, I needed his help.

I didn't know where to begin, so I started at the beginning. "I lied to you." I took a step forward, "My name is not Kiera, but Princess Charissa . . . or just . . . Chara, if you'd like. I fought in the arena because I needed a companion to take me to the borderlands. That part was true. I needed someone to confirm my false identity to anyone who might recognize me. I needed someone who knew the landscape and would help me travel and hunt and survive until I could get to the battlefield. And then I needed someone who could fight . . . "

Elliot's face did not react to my confession.

"You don't understand, I *had* to go. I overheard the duke scheming behind my mother's back. There was—*is* something happening at the warfront that he didn't want her to know. I had to go. I thought that finding out the truth could somehow put an end to the war. That it would put an end to the wedding. I thought I would, for once, for however short a time, be free," I admitted. It stung to hear the truth of my intentions out loud, but it was the truth, and Elliot deserved to hear it.

"I told myself I was going to discover the depth of the duke's betrayal. I told myself I was going to keep Mittelan free. But the truth is, Elliot, I've been running from my responsibilities for so long, I'm just not sure I am capable of anything different. I was running away but I . . . I just didn't expect to run into you." My voice cracked.

He took a step closer to me and reached out a hand only to withdraw it.

"There is no Monsieur Pentamerone," I continued, "and I have no mistress. I left Parren's last night to meet my handmaiden who was supposed to retrieve armor and supplies for our trip. I couldn't risk you asking to come with me and discovering the truth."

I noticed that Elliot recoiled slightly at the mention of his mentor's name.

"But then I overheard plans of a rebellion," I shuddered at the memory, "a dangerous and violent rebellion. The rebels wanted to end the royal line, so I came home to warn my mother," a lump rose in my throat, "but I couldn't save her." I swallowed the tears.

He took another step towards me, his body so close I could hear his uneven breathing.

"I thought—" I said, but he put his finger to my lips, quieting me.

"Enough," he whispered, his fingertip brushing over my lips as he pulled it away. He cradled the side of my face in his palm. Instinctually, I leaned into his comforting touch.

The faraway music from Singer Hall faded until I could hear only my own heartbeat. Elliot moved his hand from my face, to my neck, over my bare collarbone, onto my shoulder, and down my back. When he reached my waist, he pulled me into him sharply.

I could feel the hammering of his heart against mine. Two hearts drawing closer together, both hurting in their own ways. He tilted his head towards mine. I closed the distance between us, my lips almost touching his. Before they could meet, I had to ask, "Do you forgive me?"

He made a noise, almost like a sob, as he brought his other hand between us, and I felt something baring down through the bones of my corset. I looked down at the knife he held. The stones on the hilt matched those on his sword. The tension morphed and I gasped, confusion blanketing me.

"Do *I* forgive *you*?" He laughed an empty laugh, one that was riddled with unshed tears. "The real question, Princess, is could *you* ever forgive *me*?" The question was more of a plea as he pushed the knife deeper until I felt it prick the skin of my abdomen. His white knuckles gripped the tiger's eye handle and began to tremble.

Without hesitation, I grabbed my rapier from its sheath on his belt and pushed him away before he could react. As trained as he might be, I was still faster. He had hesitated.

He hung his head, shaking it, as he tucked the dagger back into his belt. "So this is what it will come to?" He pulled out his own sword and held it between us. "A match that you know you will win?"

I didn't respond. I couldn't even understand what was happening. All I could do was not die. *I* was the only chance Emily had. I needed to find her and save her. And then I needed to avenge my mother. Whatever happened, I could not die.

Elliot came at me sooner than I'd expected, but I matched his swings pace for pace. He thrust his blade into the empty air where I'd just been standing. I was too surprised at the turn of events to process what was happening.

Was he really so bitter about my lie that he'd resort to murder? Had he been recruited by the duke? Or maybe the rebels?

"Well, I can't lose this time, princess," he advanced again, our blades met two more times before I kicked him away, "my sister's life depends on it."

"Ah-ha!" I yelled, swinging my blade at his neck. He ducked. "I'm not the only one who lies! You said your sister was dead." At the word, he stopped cold. I took the momentary distraction as a chance to disarm him with a well-practiced twist of my blade. He reached for his dagger, but I was faster, a swift kick sending him to the ground, the knife skittering from his grasp. I pinned him, a knee on each of his arms and the edge of my blade across his neck.

His face was almost empty as I crouched over him, his death moments away, should I choose. Only his wide eyes and parted lips gave away his surprise.

"No," he said honestly, "I didn't lie. I truly thought my sister was dead. For eight years I've thought her dead. But my stepfather lied to me. He sold Millie as a servant to some dressmaker and now he is leading a group of rebels and has her held prisoner in the village. He's deranged. He said he is going to kill her if I don't bring him your head before midnight."

"What?" I fell off of him, my blade clanging to the stone of the castle floor. *My head?* I was almost less distracted by the fact that Elliot had been sent to kill me than I was by the plight of his sister. The situation sounded eerily familiar. I'd just heard from Christopher that villagers had been detaining Emily against her will. And now Elliot's sister was being held as well. And had he really just said that she had been sold to a dressmaker? Could it really be?

"Elliot, who is your sister, exactly?" I asked.

He wrinkled his brows. "What do you mean?"

I slugged him across his shoulder, "Her name, you idiot!"

He sat up beside me, rubbing his bruised arm. He didn't bother to reach for his sword or his dagger. He swiped his hand over his sweaty brow, pasting his white blond hair to it. His familiar glittering gold gaze fixed on me with a surprising amount of trust for two people who had, moments before, been preparing to kill one another.

"Her full name is Emily Eliza Cendrilon," he said, "but I've only ever called her Millie. And you must understand, Princess, I will do whatever it takes to see her happy once more."

My breathing grew shallow as the pieces fell together. I knew something had seemed familiar about him from the very beginning. Emily was Elliot's sister. Emily *was* Millie. Looking at him now, I saw her gaze reflected in his eyes. How had I not seen it before?

Emily had told me many times of the horrors that the dressmaker had inflicted on her, including how the woman refused to fill in any of Emily's missing memories from her childhood and punishing her when she asked. Had this been why Emily had reacted so strongly when discovering Elliot's name? Elliot said he hadn't seen her in eight years and she had been in the castle nearly seven. The pieces all fit. Emily was Elliot's sister, daughter of a knight. My best friend, my family.

I explained the situation to him as quickly as I could, and

understanding—and horror—flickered in his eyes.

I sat on the cold stone floor of the castle, my dress fluttering around me like an open rose in a most un-princess-like way. My hand felt around my waist, my finger finding the tiny hole in the abdomen of my gown, carved through the layers of my dress and corset and skin, by Elliot's dagger. Even though the wound was not deep, my finger came out bloodied.

"You tried to kill me!" I punched him again.

"Stop doing that!" he yelped, rubbing his arm. "And you tried to *kiss* me, so we're even."

"Ah, ah, ah," I wiggled my bloody finger, then wiped it on my dress, "*you* tried to kiss me first. And as a distraction so you could stab me, no less. You should be ashamed of yourself."

He leaned, propped up on his elbows, and turned to meet my eyes, "Wouldn't you have done it for Millie, as well?"

He was right. Emily had been my best friend for years; I'd only known him for days. If the roles had been reversed, *I* would not have hesitated. He'd be dead. I didn't say it out loud, but I didn't have to. He knew.

"In another life, I'd let you take off my head right now. I'd let you take it to the rebels who sent you and retrieve your sister. You could live happily ever after."

"It wouldn't be happily ever after." He pushed himself to his feet and offered me a hand up.

I blushed at his insinuation.

"How could I be happy when I know you'd spend the rest of your ghostly existence haunting me?"

"Ha! Probably accurate," I smirked, my blush fading fast as I let him pull me to my feet. "But my mother is gone. If I die, who will rule?"

"Someone a hell of a lot worse than you," he said, peering out the window at the glowing clock tower. "Now we only have until midnight, which is less than an hour away. So unless you are reconsidering death, we need to come up with a pl—"

Before he could finish, my head whipped around as the door from Singer Hall squealed open. I threw my hand over his mouth and pulled him back into the shadows, but it didn't matter. The Grand Duke had already seen me. And behind him marched a very frazzled looking Prince Christopher, four members of the cabinet, and more than a dozen Norrfalt soldiers.

CHAPTER THIRTY-TWO

ELLIOT

She had actually thought we could go to war—a princess and a servant boy—to expose the duke and defeat Norrfalt on our own. Yet here we hid, in the shadows of her own castle, being marched on by a dozen Norrfalt soldiers.

I had a more realistic view of our capabilities. I knew that, even together, against the duke, the prince, and a dozen soldiers, we'd be hard-pressed not to lose at least my life or that of the princess. Maybe both. But they wouldn't kill her, they couldn't kill her. They needed her. Right? To marry the prince?

She had her sword, but I was weaponless. My dagger lay in the middle of the passageway, clearly visible in the lantern's light. There was no way to get to it. Why did she have to be such an expert in disarming me? Had I really almost killed her? Should I have just done it? She had expected an embrace, and instead, I tried to stab her. But I didn't when I could have, and that moment of hesitation, that was my choice.

Now, where had she kicked my sword? I surveyed the hallway for it, the guards closing in on us, the duke's face boiling red with rage. I spotted the rapier, its stone studded hilt poking out from behind an archway, just down from me. I moved in the shadows as quietly as possible, then stuck my foot into the candle light of the passageway, nudging the blade until it was in the shadows with us. I snatched it up. It didn't matter, though. We still couldn't take them without endangering one or maybe both of us. Who would rescue Millie then?

I had a feeling that if one of us was going to die, it wasn't going to be the princess. She was of value to them, for the regency and the marriage alliance. The thought of my own impending death and the princess's imminent survival gave me a dangerous idea.

"Follow my lead," I whispered into her ear. She shrieked as I pushed her out into the open and onto her hands and knees. Her sword slipped from her grasp, clattering to the floor out of reach. She jumped up and lunged away from me, but I caught her skirt with my foot and sent her back to the ground. I grabbed her by the arm and yanked her up so her back was against my chest, circling my left arm firmly around her.

She was pinned against me, arms locked at her sides. Her muscles grew taut at first, surprise locking her joints and muscles stick straight. But then she began squirming frantically beneath my arm, struggling against my grip. Perfect. She could beat me in a fair sword fight, but I bested her now with sheer force. The guards drew their blades.

I lifted my sword, the perfectly sharpened edge hovering

over the untouched hollow of her neck.

She gasped, "Elliot, don't!" Her voice was like a whimper, a plea. She fiddled with her dress and then her pulse slowed and writhing ebbed as her hand disappeared into a fold of her skirt.

"Tell your dogs to put their weapons down or I kill the princess," I snarled at the duke, like Jack when Silas came too close. The guards didn't react to my threat. Had I misjudged her worth to them? I pushed the blade closer to cutting. I could feel her every breath, see the beads of sweat rising along her hairline, causing the little hairs there to curl.

The duke shifted uncomfortably, indecisively. The seconds ticked by, each one brought me closer and closer to losing my sister. Again. For real this time. *Millie.* I didn't have time for this. I didn't have to see the clock or hear its tick to feel the sand slipping through the hourglass.

I was running out of time.

"Go ahead." The duke waved his hand, "Save me a chore and take care of her yourself."

He was bluffing. I drove the edge of my sword into her neck as deep as I dare. I drew blood, Kiera's—no—Chara's blood, for the second time that night.

"Uncle . . . " the handsome man in white stepped forward, putting a hand on the duke's upper arm. His voice was calm, tempered, like he was recommending a wine pairing for dinner instead of navigating a hostage situation. "We have no claim to Mittelan without the marriage. The regency—"

"Shut up, boy!" the man roared, pulling his arm from the prince's grasp and pushing him away from him at the same time. The prince stood tall but backed away from the angry duke whose lip had begun to twitch beneath the white curtain of his moustache. He weighed the boy's words, still angry at him for confirming my suspicions.

I could tell that the young prince was right, but the duke was still reluctant to admit his dependence on the life of a girl.

This was my chance. My only chance. Chara wriggled in my grasp. What could possibly be going through her head? She probably thought that I had decided to kill her after all and save Millie. Save myself. She thought I would do it. Maybe she thought I should. Maybe I should.

In one swift move, I pulled the blade across her throat and threw her to the ground.

"No!" the duke ran to the princess's body, which lay in a crumpled heap, surrounded by pools of her crimson skirt. It encircled her like leaching blood. Much of her hair had come loose from its pins and now haloed her head in a craze of auburn curls. Her tiara remained perched, fastened there excruciatingly well.

Chara's lifeless form lay on the castle's smooth stone, her face down, buried in the crook of her arm. I shuddered. I envisioned my sister the same way, this very night, if I didn't get the princess to the rebels in time. I imagined Millie, her blonde ringlets frantic, no tiara among them. She wouldn't be in an extravagant palace, her cheek on polished stone, but on the cold, muddy ground of a piss and ale reeking pub. She wouldn't be surrounded by crimson velvet, only bloodied beige rags, stained with her own blood. Cendrilon blood.

I would be too late. I would turn her over and find her throat slit. The hope of learning of her family and being reunited with me would be gone. There would be no gleam in her eyes, only the empty stare of death that Parren had left me with. The soft chin of my mother would go slack on Millie's youthful features and she would be pale and frozen on the basement floor of Lucifer's Den. I would lose her again, just as I lost father, then mother, and Parren.

I would be completely and totally alone.

I'd run out of options.

The duke turned the princess over.

CHAPTER THIRTY-THREE

CHARA

I lay as still as I could, not even reaching up to wipe the blood which dripped in heavy droplets from my neck. I had gotten my wish: I was at war. No, I never made it to the border-lands, never won a battle, never discovered the duke's secret. Yet here I was, a knife wound in my gut and a slice across my throat. My mother was dead, and I was wounded—battle wounds inflicted in my own home, my own castle.

I'd landed intentionally when Elliot had feigned slicing my throat, falling dramatically from his arms and landing on top of where my sword had been launched from my grasp. My hand found the gem studded hilt, attracted like a great magnet to its mate, and I clenched it tightly. My breathing was labored, but I was breathing. I hid the breaths as well as I could.

Had Elliot meant to take off my head, or even to mortally wound me, he'd have done so. He wanted me here, appearing dead, lying on the ground. Was it meant to buy us time? *Follow my lead,* his breath had been hot and hurried in my ear. I had trusted him and not used the knife in my pocket to free myself of his grasp. Had I made the right choice?

"No!" the duke yelled. A whoosh of air and he was by side, his filthy hands running over the velvet of my dress, over my back, shoulders, and waist. These hands bore the blood of my mother. *He* betrayed her. After years of trusting him, of practically ruling as king by her side, he was ultimately responsible for her death. His fingers dug into my collar, making the scrape from Elliot's blade across my neck scream, as he forced me over.

I fell lifelessly to my back, not releasing my grip on my sword. He pinched my face in his fingers and forced it towards him. The curtains of my eyelids flashed open. Shock flitted through his gaze, and then relief. I tightened my grasp on the hilt and drove him through with my sword, a gift from my father, from the man he'd tried again and again to replace. His pupils doubled in size as he clutched the blade, body sliding down the steel until my fist was slick against his bloody flesh.

I watched the life drain from his face exactly as it had my mother's. His round cheeks faded from blush to pale. His moustache turned down and his hard glare went flat. He had not been worried about me for a second, only what power he would lose through my untimely death. His full weight fell on me. I could feel the eyes of the soldiers and Prince Christopher and Elliot all on me as I hoisted us up off the ground. I yanked my blade from the duke's body, and he fell unceremoniously to the palace floor with a smack.

For the second time this evening, my dress was covered in

blood. Some of it my own, but most was the duke's. Unlike the soldier's blood stains on my blue gown, here the crimson marbled in with the scarlet velvet, disappearing into one solid color: the color of Mittelan.

I stood over the dead duke.

It didn't feel like victory, it didn't feel like betrayal, and it hardly felt like vengeance. It felt necessary.

For Mother. For Emily. For Mittelan.

I wiped the blood from my neck, and Elliot gave a slight nod of his head. If this had been his plan, he'd navigated it expertly; otherwise, we were just plain lucky.

It occurred to me briefly that the members of the cabinet who had just seen me kill the duke must be complicit in his treason. The duke must have promised them powerful roles when he was the new leader of Mittelan. I looked for them among the guards, to call them out for their crimes, but they were already gone.

A Norrfalt soldier in the front line drew his weapon. His comrades followed. They began to advance. Then Elliot was beside me, two warriors facing off against more than a dozen soldiers. Our blades were at the ready.

Prince Christopher stood in the soldier's midst, his handsome face shocked at seeing his conniving uncle dead on the ground, his blood on my hands. One of the soldiers unsheathed his sword and yelled, "Advance!" They rushed forward.

"Stop!" Prince Christopher commanded, rushing forward to put himself between the Norrfalt soldiers and us. "Stand down. I order you, as your Crown Prince, to stand down." He put his hand up in front of the guards and they froze. He turned to me even as he continued addressing his men. "For the good of Norrfalt—and Mittelan—my men will forget what they witnessed here tonight. Or they will answer to me."

"What?" I strained my neck towards the prince, pain sizzling along my newest wound. I knew he struggled against his uncle and father's will, but his father would never forgive him for letting us go tonight. "What about your father?"

"I will tell him the truth. That the duke is dead, at the hands of a cunning pair of assassins. These men will confirm," he said as his shaking fingers stroked his chin. He was obviously nervous, but thinking quickly. "I will tell him you escaped from your coronation. And I will tell him that I sent every Norrfalt guard out to drag my bride back to the castle."

I swallowed hard.

"In return," he said, "you will make sure that when you are coronated, the marriage alliance will no longer be an option." His eyes fell to rest on Elliot.

What was he alluding to?

Christopher's shoulders shrugged heavily as he took several paces towards me and dropped his voice so his soldiers could not hear. "Norrfalt is *losing* the war, Princess," he admitted, "my uncle did everything he could to convince your mother that Mittelan's only hope for victory was the marriage alliance. But truthfully, Norrfalt is desperate for a way out."

This! This was the duke's deception. Had I made it to the warfront, I would have found Mittelan on the brink of victory and Norrfalt looking for any solution besides surrender.

"Please," the prince begged, "this heinous scheme is evidence of my father's desperation. Without the opportunities our union would allow, and without my uncle as candidate for regent, I am certain that—with your cooperation—we can come up with an alternative peace agreement. I will help you escape tonight. Go to your friend, free her. And then, when you are queen, you can help me. We can help each other. We can do better than our parents. We can establish mutually beneficial trade, we can create a lasting alliance."

The depth of the Grand Duke's deceit, the way he had been lying to and manipulating my mother for years, made my blood boil. I reveled in his death and even considered spitting on his corpse, but there wasn't time for my pettiness. He was dead. That was enough.

And here was his nephew, risking the wrath of his father for a chance at peace between our nations. His troops could easily turn on him at any moment, and yet he trusted them to obey his command. He even risked trusting me.

I let my sword bearing arm relax to my side.

He reached out his hand to me, "Now, please, don't punch me this time."

I couldn't help but laugh as I put my free hand in his and squeezed it gratefully, "Thank you, Christopher, thank you for everything."

He placed his lips, warm and soft, on my knuckles. Out of the corner of my eye, I spotted Elliot's jaw harden, his knuckles white on his hilt.

"How am I supposed to make the alliance not an option?" I asked quietly, so Elliot could not hear.

"I think you'll figure that out yourself, Charissa Henrietta Cordelia Basile-Perrault, Princess of the Great Country of Mittelan." He winked at me, and I felt heat flood my cheeks. "Now, go. Save your friend."

Overcome with gratitude, I threw my blood covered arms

around his neck, my sword hanging down his back from my fist.

He pushed me away, gently, "For now, we are still at war, and I will have to send my guards after you," he said, "but I think I can give you a bit of a head start." A glittering smile twitched at his perfect lips.

I turned from the prince to Elliot, "We have to go." I hiked up my gown with both hands and took off down the hallway in a full sprint. "Run!"

I glanced back to see Elliot desperately looking around for something before shrugging his shoulders and tipping an invisible hat to the prince. Then he barreled down the hallway after me, leaving whatever he had been looking for behind.

CHAPTER THIRTY-FOUR

ELLIOT

I had to leave Parren's dagger behind. The matching tiger's eye rapier swung now in its scabbard at my hip, but the dagger lay abandoned somewhere on the castle floor. The missing knife was a passing thought in my desperate attempt to make a plan to save Millie without getting Chara killed, or worse, killing her myself.

The new memory of the princess's body up against mine, my blade across her throat, tormented me as we ran. Chara expertly navigated us through the back hallways of the castle. Servants bowed their heads and let us pass as soon as they recognized who she was. Some tried to stop her, but she pushed them aside. We ran past a grandfather clock and I refused to believe that less than forty minutes stood between my sister's life and her death.

"Where are they keeping her?" Chara asked as she ran.

"Lucifer's Den, in the pub district."

"We don't have time to run there," she said as we passed through the castle's exit into the open air.

I let out a long whistle that reverberated around the courtyard. Several footmen glanced up at us but then back to their boots. "Good thing I came prepared for a getaway." A moment later, Faye and Gus came into sight, pulling Lucas high atop the black carriage.

"But I can't go out the front gates, not dressed like this, they'll recognize me," Chara held out the skirt of her dress, as if she'd forgotten about the more obvious tiara on her head. "I'm sure the guards are already on high alert. They know I'm a flight risk."

"Well—"

"But I have another way out," she said, cutting me off.

The carriage slowed to a stop in front of us. Chara swung up into it gracefully, and I followed her in. I had forgotten about Jack, who jumped up onto our laps, and wagged his tail adoringly.

"Over there," she said out the window to Lucas, pointing in the direction of a carriage house beside a long line of stables up against the far wall of the castle's courtyard. "To the royal stables."

"Elliot . . . " he said hesitantly. I knew what he was thinking. *She's supposed to be dead, Elliot.*

"Go, ahead, Lucas. Trust me," I said to my stepbrother. He clicked at the horses, pulling the reins to direct them towards the stables, deeper into the castle compound, closer to danger. We pulled into the stables when a boy—a familiar boy—blocked our path. He was lanky and plain with a grey cap and dirty, well-worn clothes. The boy's crooked smile fixed on the princess as she hopped lightly out of the carriage. She threw her arms around his neck. Once again, my stomach flipped obnoxiously at seeing her so friendly with yet another man.

"Grimm!" she exclaimed, holding him tightly in the embrace. "Thank heavens you're here. You have to open the gate."

Before she released the boy, he locked eyes with me over her shoulder, and I realized instantly where I recognized the boy from, all the way from his narrow form to the shaggy red hair peeking out from his hat.

I pulled my blade and ran at him without hesitation. He pulled Chara's sword from her sheath and she stumbled backwards into a pile of hay.

"Whoever you think he is, Princess," I yelled as the boy the rebels called Jacob and I held our blades at the ready. "I can assure you he is not a friend. This man is a rebel, and a bloodthirsty one at that. They captured me. They took Millie. He and his family are the reason I'm here."

"Don't listen to him, Your Highness!" The boy begged Chara, but I took his plea as permission and struck out at him with full force. He yelled between blows, "You know me, Princess!" He struck at me clumsily. "Princess, it's me," he whined as he backed up against the stable wall. "It's *his* father that's leading the rebellion, that man wants the monarchy for himself."

I jabbed again, and the boy hopped out of the way, the tip of my rapier narrowly missing his shoulder. "He is not my father!" I roared, slicing the blade at him again. My anger overwhelmed me, every scar alight with loathing.

Chara leapt up and I nearly took off her hand. "Enough!

We don't have time for this!"

She was right; we didn't have time for any of this. Why didn't she believe me that this boy was a threat?

"Elliot this is—" she began but her words fell off instantly as her eyes came to rest on the boy's white-knuckled fists clutching her blade with two trembling hands, the left of which was one finger short. Understanding flickered in her eyes.

Seeing his opportunity gone, the boy looked at me, and I watched his features shift from innocent to malicious in one moment. He smiled a nasty grin, "Somebody had to come and make sure you finished what you started."

"Jacob?" Chara asked, panic rising in her voice. "What have you done with Grimm?"

I didn't know who or what she was talking about, but Jacob used our momentary confusion to lunge at me. I managed to dodge his sword, but he reacted by sinking his elbow hard into my jaw, and I fell to the stone floor in pain.

Chara didn't hesitate one moment longer before leaping into action, pulling a dagger from her skirt. *How long had that been hiding there?* I wondered briefly.

Blood splattered on the stable walls as she managed a deep slice along the boy's forearm. I forced myself to stand but my vision spun, barely able to focus on the two of them fighting.

The sound of marching feet caused all of our heads to turn. The Norrfalt guards would soon be closing in and we were trapped. We had to go.

Jacob moved to strike against Chara with her own sword but she was faster, ducking beneath his swing and popping back up to land a sharp blow with the hilt of the dagger to his jaw. She grabbed his arm in her free hand and bent it at an unnatural angle until he dropped the blade. She threw him to the ground at her feet and snatched the sword from his side. She stood over him, blade poised above his heart. "Now, where is Grimm?"

Jacob spat a mouthful of blood on the ground beside him, but said nothing. She drove her blade down just far enough to break the skin. "For his sake, I've spared you but my patience is not limitless. Now is not the time to test me."

He narrowed his eyes at her, as if trying to decipher if she was really capable of following through on such a threat. He must have found the same intensity in her severe gaze that I had witnessed many times already because he relinquished, nodding his head towards a seemingly empty stall.

She moved her blade aside and drove the heel of her shoe into his face, knocking him unconscious. Reaching down, Chara patted the legs of the boy's trousers, looking for something.

As she did, I rushed to the stall Jacob had gestured to and opened it to find a nearly identical boy bound and gagged, sitting beside the lifeless body of a middle aged man.

"Ah! We will be needing this," Chara said behind me and I turned to see her pull a large iron key from Jacob's pocket.

"Grimm!" she exclaimed, rushing to his side and pulling the gag from his mouth. "Your brother—"

"Your Highness, I'm so sorry," he interrupted her but kept his eyes downcast. Chara cut the ropes binding him while he moped. "It's all my fault. He caught me with Emily, he recognized her. He *knew* what she meant to you, knew they could use her. I'm so sorry I couldn't keep her safe from him. He took her to the rebels and he forced me to bring him here. He murdered Marchale, m'lady. These people, they're deadly. We have to get to Emily before it's too late."

"We're on our way now, but I need you to stay here. Take care of your brother," she tossed the ropes aside. I grabbed one and tucked it away, just in case.

Chara helped her friend stand. "Yes, ma'am," the stable boy nodded fervently, "anything."

Chara reached for the key she'd taken off Jacob and handed it to Grimm. He led us down the main aisle to the stable's end. Only when he put the key in a large iron lock, almost invisible behind stacks of hay, did I realize that the wall was really a gate.

The clank and clatter of the soldiers was growing closer, and I knew the midnight hour was nearly upon us. "No time for goodbyes," I ordered, and Chara nodded as we both jumped into the carriage. Lucas swung up to the driver's perch and whipped the reins, leading us down the aisle of horse stalls, over the threshold, and out into the open night.

"Lock it, Grimm!" Chara yelled out the window behind us, before pulling her corseted bodice back into the carriage. Jack hopped onto the seat beside her, warming to her instantly.

"A murderous rebel's twin brother has keys to a gate that leads directly into the castle?" I asked as the carriage bumped down the cobblestones, "And now you've left him to guard said murderous rebel brother? And that's all fine?"

She didn't respond immediately. I watched the moonlight dance on her trembling bottom lip, her eyes fixed on picking the drying blood out from under her fingernails. Silence stretched between us.

"Emily," her voice caught in the middle of my sister's name. "We have to focus on saving Emily." She looked up, out the window into the city of Swanstone, its highlights and shadows bouncing off the gabled roofs and delving into the black alleys.

I should have told her about Parren, about the assassin from Norrfalt that was roaming the streets, maybe even the castle. But what I wanted to do was cross the gap between us, which felt suddenly as deep and cavernous as Walter Ravine. I wanted to kneel in front of her and offer my allegiance to her, to place my hand on hers, to touch a finger to still her quivering lip. I wanted to offer her any comfort I could, to kiss her, to hold her. I wanted to apologize for all the pain I'd caused, for the searing stripe across her neck. I needed to kiss her so she'd know why I did it—so she'd know why I couldn't kill her, even if I should have.

But I couldn't do any of those things, not when she may still have to die. So I looked out the window too, finding the bell tower which glowed from a flickering lantern shining through frosted glass. I watched the minute hand tick past the ten, only nine ticks remaining until midnight.

Nine minutes divided my present from my future. I would be with Millie one way or the other. She would live, or I would die trying to save her. I wouldn't be the only Cendrilon anymore, not now, not ever again.

Nine minutes until Silas held up his end of the bargain.

Silas? Bargain? What was I thinking? Silas was a liar.

I realized with heart-shattering clarity, Millie could already be dead.

CHAPTER THIRTY-FIVE

CHARA

"Where did you get that dagger?" Elliot asked as the carriage barreled down the street towards Lucifer's Den. Our semblance of a plan wasn't much to go on, but it hinged around one key element: the rebels—much like everyone my entire life—underestimating me.

I pulled out the knife that I'd stashed back in my pocket after our fight with Jacob. The polished, brown stones had quickly taken on the chill of night. "You mean, this dagger?"

Elliot laughed at the sight of the knife in my hands, a perfect match to the sword he bore. "How did you . . ."

"I managed to snag it from the castle floor," I explained, "When you threw me to the floor a *second* time."

His face fell. "That's what you were reaching for? In your dress? As I held you," he gulped, "captive?"

I nodded, noticing the horses slow as we approached the

shadowy stairwell, the black cat sign dangling over the ominous pit.

"You had it hidden in your skirt . . ." he put his hand on mine where it rested on the seat beside me, "but you didn't use it. You could have disarmed me. But you didn't."

I nodded again. "Against my better judgement," I ran a finger over the slice across my neck, "I've come to trust you."

Elliot took the blade from my hand and then reached across the carriage's width to run the pad of his thumb over my cheek, down my neck, and across my exposed collar bone. He barely touched the scrape at my throat, yet I knew that's what he was apologizing for. He wrapped his hand around the back of my neck, his palm cool against the rising heat on my skin. He pulled my face towards his.

The wheels of the carriage stopped in front of the pub. "There's not much time," Elliot's stepbrother interrupted. "Whatever happens, you have to stop him, Elliot. Whatever the consequences."

I released my breath as Elliot moved away from me.

"I think you'll be needing this," he said, handing the dagger back to me.

I tucked it back into the safety of the weapon pocket of my skirt, making sure he saw where I put it. Then I unbuckled the belt at my waist, "Since I can't have a visible weapon, you should wear this until I need it." I handed him the sheathed rapier, surprised at the fear that settled in my gut without it.

Elliot nodded and then swung open the small, satin covered door. After stepping out, he buckled the second sword around his waist.

The night wind passed over the exposed skin of my neck

and collar as I joined him on the cobbles.

"I will do my best," he said to his stepbrother with a certain finality, "thank you for your help . . . and not just today."

The boy merely nodded.

Elliot redirected his attention to me. "I apologize in advance, Your Highness—"

"Don't," I cut him off, "don't call me that. Chara is fine. And you have nothing to apologize for." The clanks and shouts of soldiers rushed the street, focused on their mission to bring me back, and each clattering step brought them closer. "Go, Lucas, the carriage will lead them right to us."

Lucas nodded again and clicked to the horses. Jack jumped out of the carriage window at the last minute. I scooped up the yipping dog, but Lucas was already out of earshot. I set the dog back down and he sat loyally at Elliot's feet. I turned away from him and put my wrists together behind my back. He grabbed them gently and pulled me towards him. He bound them together with the rope that had recently held Grimm and placed the loose end in my palm. He turned my head gently and kissed my cheek softly, "I really am sorry, Princess."

My pulse quickened at his sincere touch. "It will be fine. We will all be fine. Emily will be fine. Now, how many are there?" I asked. I wanted to have some idea of how many angry rebels we were about to face.

"I don't know," he whispered as we started down into the stairwell.

"It doesn't matter." My mother's pendant beat on my sternum with each step down and I touched the brass ring from my father. Having them both with me brought a small comfort. I could feel the weight of Elliot's knife in my pocket, bouncing against my leg as we walked down the steps. The stench washed over me in a wave as the bar—eerily empty for the night of a royal coronation—came into view under the light of a half dozen lanterns. An ugly man with a long nose and a proper suit coat appeared from a door behind the bar. Elliot pulled me against him roughly. My heart leapt to my throat.

"Ah, hello, son," the man set a bloodied knife on the bar in front of him, "and who is this you've brought with you?" His voice roiled with menace, "Looks like someone had a little trouble following directions, doesn't it, *boy*?"

The midnight toll struck.

CHAPTER THIRTY-SIX

ELLIOT

Silas. His thin lips pulled into a lazy smirk at the sight of my hostage: the Crown Princess, her tiara still pinned tightly to her head. I pushed Chara across the room as she, quite convincingly, acted as if she was trying desperately to pull her limbs from my grasp. I genuinely struggled to keep my hold on her.

"I've brought her to you, Sir." I threw her down in front of him, trying to control my recoil at the sound of her knees coming down hard on the muddied floor. Unspoken apologies repeated in my head.

Silas picked up a stubby knife from the counter in front of him before coming around to my side. He dragged the blade's tip along my jawline. I could feel the warm stick of wet blood left by the knife. It was not my blood. I shuddered.

He leaned his face close to mine, the knife still poised

against my skin, "You and I both know that's not what I asked you to do."

My teeth ached from clenching them together, hardening my jaw against the knife's edge. But the knife's caress was almost gentle, a threat, not meant to wound.

His arms fell to his sides, "Bring her to the back." He turned and led us through the door, glancing behind to make sure we listened to his order.

I pulled Chara roughly up to her feet, careful to dig my fingers hard into her arm in case Silas looked back again. I hated myself for the display of cruelty, but it was her only chance at survival. Millie's only chance of survival.

The door swung closed behind us and the rebels looked up from the table over which they were all hunched. Many flinched at the sight of their princess—body still attached to head—standing in front of their traitor selves.

Three impeccably dressed men shifted uncomfortably in their seats. I remembered seeing them in the rebel meeting earlier, and I found myself wondering again, what wealthy nobles were doing amongst peasant traitors? Chara's brows furrowed at the sight of them and she pursed her lips. She recognized them, which meant they must be important.

Jacob's mother nearly fell from her seat into a curtsy until one of her fellow rebels yanked her back up. She had their ginger hair and narrow face, but otherwise looked nothing like her twin boys.

Jack had snuck into the room behind me and now cowered silently in the shadows. I prayed he stayed put.

No gagged screams came from any corner of the dark room, and as my eyes adjusted to the darkness, I realized with a jolt of insidious fear that Millie was not here.

"Where is she?" I spat at my stepfather, who walked circles leisurely around his group of followers—there were fifteen, maybe twenty—my other stepbrother, Raymond, among them. Many of the other faces were either strangers or cast into shadows.

How many more rebels—rebels that were not trusted by Silas to have been invited here tonight, followers, not leaders—were there? What was Chara and her monarchy up against?

"I will tell you where your sister is as soon as you've finished your task," Silas goaded me, strutting around the table, the knife still limp at his side, "which, considering it's already past midnight, I'd say I'm being quite lenient."

"How do I know you will uphold your end of the bargain? How do I even know she is safe?"

"She's safe, I give you my word," came a gruff voice, a familiar voice, as a brawny man stood from the dark side of the table. I recognized the voice instantly. My heart sank as the man's kindly face came into light.

"Bruno," Chara breathed his name as my friend circled the table of rebels.

Silas lied about Millie. Chara lied about her identity. My own stepfather was blackmailing me. Parren hid our kinship from me for years, and yet this betrayal cut the deepest. As bartender, it made sense that Bruno arranged for the rebels to use this space, which begged the question, how long had he been tied to them? Tied to my step-father? Even when he *knew* what Silas had put me through. How long had he been lying directly to my face?

And then I remembered how Silas knew *exactly* where to

look for my sword and winnings—right after I'd lost so much at the opening tournament and so had Bruno. He had known every facet of my plan, right down to where I stashed my blade. He'd come to every tournament and listened to me converse with Parren countless times, sometimes even joining our training sessions. He'd taught me to handle a throwing knife, how to track a deer and even how to gut it. We'd laughed countless days away sharing a booth at the market. He was my only childhood friend and now he'd betrayed me to my worst enemy.

"I thought you were my friend. You turned me over to *him*," I said through a set jaw and barely moving lips, "how could you?"

"I . . ." Bruno began but, in the end, had no excuse. Some part of me had hoped he would deny my accusation, give me a reason to think my assumption was wrong. But he did no such thing. Instead he shifted weight from foot to foot as his face contorted from guilt to anger, "What about you?" he accused. "You told me this girl was some handmaiden, not the princess. Was that all some kind of trick?"

"No. In fact, I only just found out myself. But her deceit stings considerably less than *some*." I threw the implication with precision, hoping it would land where it would wound.

"I swear, I didn't know a thing about your sister. Not until tonight," Bruno's pitiful excuse for an explanation fell flat, even while his beard twitched and eyes glazed with genuine apology, "Elliot, you have to understand, I lost so much on your fight. My family has nothing. I gambled our future away, betting it all on *you*. And now, I've been conscripted. If *she*," he points a stout finger at Chara, "is allowed to marry that prince then I would have to serve at the mercy of a Norrfalt king. I wish there was another way, but there's just not. This rebellion is my only hope. So I stand for a free Mittelan. We stand with Tremaine."

The group chorused back at him, "We stand with Tremaine."

I looked at my stepfather, the unknighted money counter, Silas Tremaine. He held his chin high, thin lips in a proud sneer, and I could see that—in his mind—he had already ascended the throne.

Bruno stepped closer to where I still held Chara in mock submission. He reached down and tore the tiara from her head. He winced as she cried out in pain, the pins pulling chunks of her hair from her head. He bent the delicately woven gold in half, repeating until it snapped, and threw the sparkling pieces onto the ground of the dirty tavern.

❖❖❖

Her golden hair shone against the muddy woodland floor, where she laid down, unwilling to take even another step away from home.

I placed the back of my hand across her forehead. The heat that had begun to rise on my sister's skin, despite the chill of the night, made me shiver. A bead of sweat collected on her brow and it cut through the dirt as it rolled down her face and slipped into her nest of ringlets.

"But it's our home, Ellie," her voice cracked, "we've got to go home." Her tears flowed freely and she coughed roughly between each sob. Her lungs rattled as she breathed.

"Shh, shh, shh," I soothed, but deep down, I knew she was right. We'd been walking all day and had nowhere to go. No one to go to. And I knew, deep in my gut, that something was wrong with her. Something I couldn't make better. "Someday, Millie, I'll make our home safe for us again. I promise. Someday."

We curled up together in the woods with nothing to cover us. I watched as the color drained from her cheeks as we drifted in and out of consciousness.

When I woke, I tried to shake her but she wouldn't wake, wouldn't even move. She couldn't stand. Or walk. Her breathing was labored and slow. Panic surged through me. I stood with her in my arms and began to run back to the viper's den, with the promise in my heart that if he ever hurt her again, I would kill him.

CHAPTER THIRTY-SEVEN

CHARA

Everything burned as I fell forward, catching my chin so hard on the ground that the pain seemed to reverberate up to my ears. Blood seeped from my face, leaching towards the shattered pieces of my tiara. It was my mother's before she was crowned queen. Would I ever get the chance to be half the leader that she had been?

"No," I said through threatening tears, but I wasn't loud enough to be heard over the commotion in the room. I used all my strength to force myself to my knees, not yet ready to reveal my loosened bonds.

"No, you don't understand!" I said, more loudly this time. I didn't fully comprehend the intentions of these rebels, but I knew that Bruno had seemed kind when I'd met him. I also knew that the three nobles sitting at the table were members of the cabinet. If they had not sided with the duke and were here instead, perhaps they could be swayed.

I had wanted to go to war, I thought I could negotiate my way to peace. This was my chance to prove it.

"Bruno, Count Xavier, Duke Chapelle, Count . . ." I struggled to remember the last cabinet member's name, cursing myself for not paying closer attention at the meetings that Mother had forced me to attend. "Count Baudin," I remembered, "please, hear my plea. The Grand Duke of Swanstone has slain your queen. I watched as the traitor *he* planted in her guard assassinated her as she sat unarmed on her throne. I have heard the duke's confession from his own lips. He wished to rule as a Norrfalt regent upon the completion of the marriage alliance. But please—"

The man they called Tremaine crossed the room, fist raised, but Duke Chapelle stood and put up a hand to stop him. "Let her finish, Silas."

I had already crouched to cushion the blow and my eyes flew wildly from Tremaine to Duke Chapelle. I swallowed, knowing I would only have one chance to say the right thing, to stave off this rebellion once and for all. "Please, the Grand Duke is dead," I said as assertively as I could manage. "This is his blood on my hands, my dress. He died for his treason, for choosing Norrfalt over his home country. Now, I have spoken with the Norrfalt prince and he—"

The room erupted in angry whispers. "Don't believe her!" shouted a sniveling young man who had not left Silas's heels since we arrived.

"You *must* believe me," I raised my voice above the ruckus. This was getting out of hand, I was losing them. "Please, I have done everything in my power to avoid the marriage alliance—I would die to avoid Norrfalt rule!" And for the first time, I knew that it was true. I had tried to run away to gain my own freedom and I had killed the duke to avenge my mother, when all this time I should have been focused on these people. They were my subjects; I should be serving them, not the other way around.

Determination choked my words. "I've spoken with the prince and he does not want this marriage any more than we do. He believes that with the duke gone he can persuade his father to make a peace agreement. He even admitted to me that Norrfalt is *losing* the war! Don't you see? This has all been in an act of desperation, a farce, a way to manipulate an advantage that they do not even have."

I swallowed my fear, "I know that you are afraid. You are afraid to trust me, afraid that I will lead in the same way that my mother did. She was a great ruler, but didn't listen to the needs of her people. But I am here. I see your plight. And I vow that, when I am queen, I will continue to do so. Please, please release the girl. Call off your assassin . . ." I gestured towards where Elliot towered over me. My lips trembled but I stopped them. They needed to see that I was confident, that I was powerful, that I would be the leader they needed. "Release me and I will be *your* queen, I will *serve* you. You are good Mittelan subjects, you do not want this blood on your hands."

Silas's eyes grew wide with rage as I spoke. The air in the room shifted, as if the angry shadows urging the rebels forward were beginning to fade. They were actually considering what I'd had to say.

"Enough of this nonsense!" Silas fumed, fear and madness overtaking him. He pushed past Chapelle to get to me. "This wicked, deceitful girl dares appeal to your good nature with empty promises and outright lies. She would send each and every one of you off to die in some bloody war if it helped her gain wealth and power. She will force you to fight and die in her name, just like her mother did. She does not even know the law of her own land. She cannot be your queen without a king. As soon as we release her, she will run into the prince's arms. She *needs* the marriage alliance. She wants the power of two countries!"

"No!" I cried.

Silas's fist released like the strike of a snake as it whipped across my cheek and sent me to the ground. "Bring out the girl," I heard him order the rebels.

"No," I sobbed, "no, no, no."

He spun, arms wide and triumphant, "It's time I make good on my word."

CHAPTER THIRTY-EIGHT
ELLIOT

My heart broke seeing Chara in shambles on the pub floor. I rushed to her, torn between continuing my disguise as her warden and validating her claims. What would save Millie? What would save Chara? What could I possibly do to fix this?

I felt like a cornered dog, rabid with anger and fear, with no way out. Should I play along and wait for the perfect moment to attack, or lash out now before it's too late?

"Get up," I snarled at Chara, deciding it was safest to continue the act as long as possible. I could tell there were rebels in the room questioning their allegiances. We just needed to give them a chance to speak unafraid. I pulled Chara to her feet roughly. They needed to believe I would kill her when I saw my sister in danger. They could not suspect that I had befriended the princess.

Raymond and a man I did not recognize shuffled Millie in roughly, each gripping one of her arms tightly. I sent a seething look to Bruno so that he would know what he had done. The chair she had been tied to was gone, but her hands remained bound and a gag was still lodged in her mouth. Small cuts ran up and down her arms, and bruises were developing from the men's callous handling of her. Rage boiled within me, a volcano waiting to erupt and destroy everything within its reach.

If he ever touched Millie again, I would kill him.

Her glittering eyes were swollen from crying and they grew wide when they saw me, and wider still when they saw the way I held Chara hostage.

My sister's face contorted with disgust at the sight of me. I felt sick.

Chara's hopes for diplomacy evaporated apparently at the sight of her friend bound and gagged. Unable to put off her wrath for a moment more, Chara reacted instantly, pulling the loose string on her bond, grabbing the dagger from her pocket, and yanking herself from my grip. She whirled in a flurry of wrath and blades, pulling her sword from my waist before I'd even unsheathed my own.

Jacob's mother screamed out in terror as the men around her leapt to their feet and began fighting the princess. The man I didn't recognize dropped his hold on Millie and Chara felled him with ease. Three more were dead before the rest had even pushed their chairs out from under the table. The cabinet members huddled in a corner of the room to avoid the firestorm that was their princess, beautiful and terrifying.

Two men came at me and I cut them down quickly, they were untrained and wielding unfamiliar weapons. I tried not to cause any mortal damage.

With the room engulfed in chaos, Millie began thrashing, violently trying to escape Raymond's hold on her. She threw her head backwards catching him in the nose. He released her, both hands flying to his face, and she fell to the ground. She crawled away from him as well as she could with her hands still bound.

Snarls erupted from the corner as Jack attacked Silas who had lunged for Millie. Of course Silas didn't want to lose his leverage. That's all she was to him, all she'd ever been. It was all either of us were to him, things to be used.

Silas fought off the growling and biting dog, eventually swiping him clear across the room. Jack landed hard against the wall, sliding down to the floor, unmoving. Silas's face was covered in puncture wounds from the dog's teeth and there were deep gashes in his clothing from his sharp nails. Blood dripped from his temple to his cheek.

I tried to reach Millie but the rebels attacked me without pause, perhaps seeing me as a more surmountable opponent than the princess. Raymond had recovered enough to grab Millie by the ankles, dragging her back to him. Chara leapt towards them, Raymond dropping his hold on Millie to engage the princess.

I searched among my assailants for Bruno but he was nowhere to be found. By the time I noticed Silas within reach of Millie, it was too late.

"Enough!" he bellowed, yanking Millie from the floor by her hair. "Everyone stop!" He held my sister tightly in front of him, a fist full of golden curls, his knife at her neck. He had never looked more terrifying than he did now, his maniacal features further distorted by rage and terror and oozing blood.

Chara froze, as did I. The room went dead silent.

Silas's demented stare fell on me. "You know this is all your fault, right?"

He pulled her hair harder, dug the knife deeper. Millie cried out, but Silas's grip did not loosen. "You never accepted me as your father, you never loved my sons as your brothers! I lost my first wife, and then your mother, too! I lost everything. And on Eliza's death bed she had you swear your protection to your sister . . . " he said, agony turned to fiery loathing. "Protect her from what? From *me*? And what about me and my sons, did she pay no thought to us? Well it is time that you make good on your promise to your precious mother. If you want to save your sister," his quiet voice rose to a maniacal scream, "then kill the princess!"

He'd heard me make that promise on her deathbed? *You're strong, little Elliot. Take care of your family—your sister—and yourself. Promise me, Ellie.*

Had mother meant to include these devils in her command? My focus had always been on *your sister*, but for the first time it occurred to me that maybe that had not been her intention.

Silas pressed the blade harder against Millie's skin and lowered his voice, "Kill the princess or I will do what I should have done all those years ago. The princess or your sister? Choose, *boy*. A stranger? Or your family?"

Shock at his words washed over me. "My mother . . . " I stuttered for the right words, "I was a child. She wanted us to be a family but you could never let that happen. You always treated us like we were less, less than family, less than *human*. This isn't what she would have wanted. Don't you *dare* blame your own wickedness on her." Any reasoning with him vanished in the chasm of hurt, rage, and hate that separated us.

His glare darkened. Blood welled up from Millie's neck onto the short silver of the blade. "The princess or your sister?" he asked with such finality that I knew any sliver of the man my mother had wed had died with her.

Only the viper remained.

CHAPTER THIRTY-NINE

CHARA

A clattering of metal echoed around the room as my sword slipped from my fingers. Some of these rebels may have been convinced by my speech, but Silas had sown enough doubt in them that I had had no option but to fight.

But if I was going to save the people I loved, I couldn't fight anymore.

I had run out of options.

I turned from the rebel I'd been battling, leaving him frozen with his sword at the ready. I crossed the room and stopped in front of Elliot. The room was still, but any action out of turn and I could see in Silas's crazed expression that he would plunge that dagger deep into Emily's throat and she would be gone.

Then Elliot would be next.

I was their only hope.

Elliot stood in front of me with more pain etched into his features than I thought possible for one human to bear. "Nothing I say will convince them, Elliot," I said, reaching up to brush a stray lock of blond from his soft eyes. "You must do as he commands. For your sake and for your sister." I dropped my voice to a whisper, "For your mother." Even I was surprised by the lack of regret in my voice. I had no doubt that this was what had to be done.

I turned to the rebel leader, "Tremaine. Swear in front of these people, your future subjects, that after my death no harm will come to Emily or Elliot. Swear that you will return their parents' land to them and that you will leave them in peace."

His brows furrowed together, his indignation momentarily cut with delight that this evening was finally going according to his plan. He may not like agreeing to give up Beauhaven, but it was worth it to gain a castle. "I swear," he said with an evil grin that twisted my insides into knots.

I turned my focus back to Elliot. "He will go to Swanstone and Beauhaven will be yours at last. You will have your family back. Take care of her, Elliot. She's my best friend," I said through barely concealed tears. "Take care of yourself."

I was not afraid of death, only afraid of the life I would leave behind: no more laughs or troubles shared with Emily, no more spars with Elliot. I would never be able to help them heal from the injuries of their pasts.

For the first time, I mourned that I would never be queen, that I could never hear the plight of my subjects and make actual, real change, *for them*. Avoiding the crown had once been my greatest wish, but now that it was coming to fruition, the weight of it felt like a millstone around my neck. I felt guilty for ever hoping to avoid my future.

Running my hand down Elliot's arm, I found his empty fist and raised it until it was between us. I took Parren's dagger and placed it in his grip. His hands trembled, but I kept my touch gentle.

Reaching up, I cupped Elliot's cheeks in my hands and drew his face to mine. The brush of my lips over his would be my last selfish act in this world and, despite how they quivered, I felt love, peace, and reassurance in that kiss.

Pulling back, I met his glittering green eyes for a final time, and gave him a slight nod. I wrapped my hands around his fist and nestled the dagger into the hole he'd already carved in my corset.

A tear slipped from my face onto our entwined hands.

I hardened my jaw and gave him one order: "Finish this."

CHAPTER FORTY

ELLIOT

She'd kissed me. Her lips left a tingling imprint on mine, her tear wet on our knotted hands.

My sister's muffled screams faded to the background as Chara forced our bodies closer, pushing the knife deeper. Just like the moment I'd surrendered to her in the arena—even though I didn't know who she was or how that armored stranger would change my life—the world seemed to fade and only we remained. Time seemed to slow.

And yet, I couldn't completely block out thoughts of Millie. She would never forgive me for killing her best friend.

When I looked down at Chara, her eyes were soft, almost peaceful. Her face had blood splatters across it, but her skin was smooth—not a single scratch, save for one deep gash on her chin. Despite that, her jaw was set with strength and determination. She was willing to sacrifice her life for her friend and for me, and letting her do that was the most selfish thing I would ever do. But it had to be done.

You're strong, little Elliot. Take care of your family—your sister—and yourself. Promise me, Ellie. My mother's voice.

I wasn't as strong as I should be, not strong enough to do what needed to be done. Not like Chara. I didn't want to prolong Chara's suffering, but I had no willpower left to plunge the knife in.

If he ever touched Millie again, I would kill him.

I'd sworn that to my twelve-year-old self. Yet, here Millie was, covered in wounds, his knife drawing blood from her neck. I pushed the dagger further in and felt it resist as the knife widened against the corset's boning. A little wiggle and the blade broke through to flesh. I slowed, almost stopped.

But she felt me hesitate, so she pressed me forward. My hands were trembling around the hilt of the dagger, but her hands encompassing mine were steady as stone.

I looked over at Silas, hoping the sight of Millie's blood would give me the final burst of fortitude I needed, when I noticed Bruno lurking silently behind them. Silas still held my sister firmly, completely unaware of the man behind him.

Bruno raised his shoulders, taking an exaggerated breath.

"Focus." He mouthed the single word and the phrase he'd said to me a thousand times came flooding back: *focus your mind and take a deep breath.*

With that, I understood. I knew what I had to do, and I trusted Bruno to clear my path.

I dropped my head in the slightest of nods and mimicked his motion with a rise and fall of my shoulders in a deep, cleansing breath.

Silas leaned forward in anticipation, ready for my knife to plunge and for the princess to crumple. His hand loosened from her neck, not much, but just enough.

Bruno and I acted simultaneously. He lunged forward, his strong arms yanking Millie from the clutches of my stepfather who released her in surprise. They fell to the ground in a heap at his feet. At the same time, I whipped my fist out from between Chara and me, slashing across the bodice of her dress. With a step forward, I sent the knife whirring through the air. Chara collapsed, blood leaking from her abdomen.

My blade hit its mark, lodging itself deep in Silas's right eye. He fell over backwards without another word.

"No!" Raymond screamed, running to his father and falling to his knees at his side. He shook him desperately, but the snake didn't move.

I had slain the viper.

❖❖❖

Bruno helped Millie stand and cut her bonds. As soon as her hands were free, she tore the strip of cloth that had been gagging her out of her mouth.

I knelt at Chara's side, feeling for a pulse. Faintly, as if far in the distance, I felt the steady beat.

"Chara!" The first word from my sister's lips since the reveal of Silas's deception was the name of the princess. Millie flew across the room to where her friend lay motionless on the ground. "Chara! Wake up! Please, Chara, please, wake up!

You swore to me you wouldn't get hurt!"

The princess's eyes fluttered open, a hand reaching to the freshest of her wounds. "Ouch." Her finger found the hole we'd dug together through the corset, but the slash only went as deep as her bodice. The corset boning had protected her from the slash of the blade as it whipped across her abdomen. I released a relieved breath.

"You're alive, Chara! You're alive!" Millie cried and laughed over her friend, pushing her chestnut tendrils from her face and bending over to hug her again and again. She helped Chara up to sitting. "Are you alright?"

"It's just another scratch," the princess shot a sideways glance at me, "way better than it could have been . . . than it *should* have been." Millie helped her to her feet and then wrapped her arms around Chara's neck in a tear filled embrace.

The girls hugged until, suddenly, Millie forced them apart and slapped the back of Chara's head.

"Ow!" Chara said, reaching up to rub her skull. "What was that for?"

"You stupid girl! What were you thinking, Char? You can't just up and *die* for me. You have a kingdom to think about!" Millie scolded and Chara blushed. Then my sister's hard glare softened, "I'm furious with you, don't get me wrong, but still . . . thank you." She hugged her again.

I watched the scene unfold as if I was a stranger, and it suddenly felt as if I knew neither of them at all.

Until Millie moved her emerald eyes to me. Her hair was everywhere, just like it had been as a little girl, a nest of curls and light. Her jaw quivered and there was so much life in her.

How could Silas have ever made me believe that she was dead? A tear escaped down a freckled cheek, and she looked like a token of my mother, embodying all of her sadness and beauty.

She put a hand out to me. "Ellie?"

I nodded, taking her hand in mine. It held the small leather pouch which I took and tossed aside. I didn't need a relic anymore. I had the real thing.

I swallowed nervously, "Do you remember me?"

"I'm not sure," she admitted, "but I think so. I am not sure what is memory and what is dream, but we have each other now. You can tell me what is real."

I smiled. The chance to show her Beauhaven and to reclaim the childhoods that were stolen from us gave me more hope than I could ever remember experiencing.

Jack stirred in the corner and then stood up. I'd almost forgotten about the poor pup, about what he'd done for me. He shook his head, his long ears whapping against one another loudly. He looked around the room, confused. Then—without ever having met her—he ran across the room, jumped into Millie's arms, and attacked her with his long tongue.

CHAPTER FORTY-ONE

CHARA

I wasn't dead. My wounds wept all over the grimy pub floor and yet, I wasn't dead. And neither was Emily. And neither was Elliot. We had somehow managed to survive. The rebels were fleeing at the sight of their conquered leader, but I could barely even think about the rebellion. Aside from my joy, I could think of only one thing: the marriage.

It wasn't just at Prince Christopher's request that I needed to put an end to the marriage alliance. I had survived near death at the rebels' hands, thus bringing my country back from the edge of civil war. I had taken vengeance on the duke and kept him from gaining total control of Mittelan. However, the fact still remained: without a king, I could not be queen.

I stroked Emily's blonde hair and took in the resemblances to her brother that I had somehow missed. I wanted to sit with them, to join in their celebration, but the spinning gears in my head held me back. *What do I do now?*

The entire country knew of the marriage alliance, it had been the queen's final order before her death. Now I needed some way to make it completely unexecutable.

To do that, I could see only one solution: marry someone else.

I was the only heir to the Mittelan throne, yet I had no power to change a single law until I was married. It was an old, outdated tradition, but a completely unavoidable fact.

Perhaps if I were already in power, I could repeal it, but until then, there was nothing else I could do. My mind raced over my predicament while I clutched at my seeping wounds.

Elliot sat beside his sister, the shiny brown and black dog on his back between them, wiggling as if completely unaware that he had been unconscious mere minutes before. They finally had their life back. Elliot could claim Beauhaven and return home to live the life that he'd fought so hard for. He could finally be whoever he wanted to be. He had the freedom of choice over his future that I had always craved.

Who was I to take that away from him?

Duke Chapelle and the two Counts fell at my feet. Their village counterparts had shrunk away at the sight of their slain leader, hoping that I would not remember their faces, that I would not enact my vengeance upon them.

But the noblemen could not just disappear. I knew exactly who they were and if they were convicted of treason, they would not only lose their lands, holdings, and titles, but likely their lives. They were obviously terrified to confront me, but even more afraid to leave.

"Your Majesty," Duke Chapelle begged, "we are your humble servants. We were only trying to do what was best for *your* country, madam."

"The Grand Duke, he threatened us," Baudin said defensively. "We knew we could not trust him, although there were some of the cabinet who did."

"Please, spare us. With the queen dead, we simply—"

"Hush." I interrupted Xavier before he could add his excuse to the pile. I was struck by their sudden willingness to serve me. Perhaps, Silas had given me three new allies.

"You are all guilty of treason," I declared, putting on the most regal voice I could muster, "however, Duke Chapelle, you did make an effort to stop Silas, to give me a chance to explain the changed circumstances. I will not forget that. And you two," I gestured to Baudin and Xavier, "are lucky that he did. There will come a time when I demand your recompense, and you will not hesitate to remember the mercy that I've shown you today."

Standing in front of the cowering men, I felt—for the first time—like a leader.

The men nodded frantically, not daring to say anything else, and scampered from my presence like rats disappearing into their holes.

I ran my hand over the slash in my bodice, the hole in my corset, and touched the scrape across my neck. The wounds were both relatively shallow and, even though they throbbed with pain, I knew I was lucky to be alive.

Thunder sounded as footfalls cascaded down the stairs and barged through the door in the back of the pub. Norrfalt guards surrounded us, with all their swords pointing at me.

"Hello, gentlemen," I said confidently, "I am ready to return to the castle for my coronation now. And these two will be my honored guests," I nodded to Emily and Elliot. "I believe the prince will be expecting me."

❖❖❖

A yawn stretched over Emily's lips as we reached the castle. I peeked into the Throne Room as the guards escorted me to my chamber to be attended to.

Usually, the coronation began at midnight, but that hour had come and gone, and much of the court had retired. The Mittelan guards remained, as did the Norrfalt guards, several of whom were keeping their eyes locked on me.

In the large hall, the Duchess Carnell sat in the corner amongst a small handful of nobility who'd decided to stay. Her eyes darted around the room, undoubtedly looking for the Grand Duke. She would soon be sorely disappointed.

Chapelle and his friends had already made it back from the pub and were attempting to blend in with the other members of the cabinet. I was sure they were hoping it would appear as if they had been there all night. They all sat on brocade chairs near the dais, each sipping a different color of liquor.

Madame Colombe arrived in her nightdress at my quarters. She diligently scrubbed the blood off of me yet again, keeping her questions to a minimum after my initial answers had been short and cryptic. Emily washed in the tub after me, while the castle nurse came and bound the wound in my torso. I slipped into my underclothes as Emily dried herself and put on her undergarments as well. Her nimble fingers took to braiding her own wet ringlets as Colombe brushed and plaited my hair.

Emily picked up the stained dress and apron she'd been wearing from off the floor.

"No," I said and she looked up at me. "You're not my handmaiden anymore, Ems."

"What?" Her eyes grew wide with hurt, "Chara, I'm sorry about what happened, but please, don't—"

I put my hand on her shoulder and she stopped talking. "You're not getting sacked, more like promoted," I smiled. "You are the daughter of a knight, a lady, and are still—as you have always been—my best friend. You can borrow one of my dresses tonight as you will be attending the coronation as my guest."

Her cheeks warmed and she threw her arms around my neck. "Thank you, Chara. For everything," she whispered. "No matter what happens, you will always be my family."

I squeezed her as tightly as my wounds would allow, breathing in the smell of lavender soap that lingered on her skin and imagining her returning to Beauhaven with Elliot. I imagined them cleaning the small house and tending the land. They would no doubt make it the most beautiful country estate in all of Mittelan.

If, of course, I didn't marry him.

I had no doubt that I cared deeply about Elliot, but was I ready to marry him? I knew that his future would be quite different as king. Is that what he wanted? Is he what I wanted?

I pulled away from Emily's embrace and walked to my wardrobe. I ran my fingers over the line of tender flesh on my neck where Elliot's blade had opened my skin. I glanced over at my mother's pendant where it lay on my vanity. I touched the crossed daggers. They reminded me of Elliot and I. No matter how many times he and I crossed blades, I knew that he would never hurt me. Not really.

I pulled out a dark silver and gray dress for Emily, with white floral appliques on the sleeves. She'd always had a soft spot for that one.

"I couldn't . . ." she said, even as she put her hands up and let me slide it over her head. A small gasp of ecstasy came from her parted lips when the beautiful fabric slipped over her underclothes. She ran her fingers over the silk embroidery as I laced her into it. It was the first time I'd ever done such a task, but it felt right that I do so for Emily. I didn't mind one bit.

I couldn't hide the smile tugging at my lips. Her world had turned over, from rags to riches, and no one deserved it more than her.

My life had changed as well, but in a completely different way. I was still the only heir Mittelan had, but now I wasn't afraid of my future. I no longer felt bound by it. Instead, I felt fulfilled. Now I knew that *I* was the queen that Mittelan needed and that I needed to fight for her. Not with my blade, not at the warfront, but here: in Swanstone, at court. I needed to fight to become the queen that she deserved.

Since I'd met Elliot, my view of honor and duty had shifted. He'd challenged every fiber of my being, creating growth without changing *me* at all. He'd helped me become the person I was destined to be.

I cared for him. Maybe I even loved him. Was that really enough?

"Wear this one," Emily said, pulling me from my thoughts. She'd pulled a dress from my wardrobe. I crossed my arms and shook my head violently when I saw which one she'd selected. My mother had had it made years ago, but I'd never had occasion to wear it before. I had never *wanted* to wear it before. It always seemed like too much. It was jet black silk satin, with red and champagne gold details delicately stitched over almost every inch. It sparkled with rubies and diamonds around the draped sleeves and bold neckline. The black honored the mourning season of my mother, but it was also regal and extravagant. And, even if I didn't want to admit it, it was perfect.

"Fine . . ." I gave in to Emily's excitement. "But only if you promise not to stand anywhere close to me. I wouldn't want you to outshine me," I joked.

She laughed and brushed the compliment off, but it held an element of truth. Despite the cuts and bruises the last day had inflicted on her, she glowed with a joy that I had never seen on her before—a wholeness—and it made her even more lovely.

As Madame Colombe helped me into my dress, my heart constricted as memories of my mother flooded me. I missed her more than I had ever missed anyone in my entire life.

When the dress was on, Colombe took the medallion off my vanity and handed it to me. "Not for a weapon this time, alright, m'lady?"

She hooked the clasp behind my neck, letting the heavy charm fall between my exposed collar bones. My heart ached for my mother, with a pain deeper than any gash. But with the crest near my heart, I suddenly knew what I should do, what mother would have done.

She always put Mittelan first. She had never doubted the loyalty of her subjects, even when maybe she should have. I recalled the duke and the cabinet members who had followed him into the Upper Hall, claiming their allegiance to him by doing so. They had known of his deception, they had known that he killed my mother, and they saw me strike him down because of it.

I wondered, briefly, where *they* were now. They had probably woken their families in the middle of the night and fled to seek sanctuary in Norrfalt, or maybe Almora.

The cabinet members who had sided with the rebellion would be far better off, despite their own betrayal. They had not had the opportunity to flee, and they were probably grateful for that now that they were sipping their drinks by their cohorts' sides in Singer Hall.

Unlike the power grappling of those who sided with the duke, I understood the motivation of the rebels and sympathized with their desperation. They had not wanted to see Mittelan under Norrfalt rule. Neither did I. Could I really blame them for that?

Chapelle and his friends may have started the night as my enemy, but now I hoped that they would bring in the new day as my most adamant supporters.

The time had come for me to lead Mittelan into a new future, an independent future.

I knew what I had to do.

Grabbing my sword in its scabbard, I buckled it around my waist. I took one last look in the mirror and found there the woman that my mother had always believed I would someday become.

The time was here and I was ready to claim my mother's crown.

CHAPTER FORTY-TWO

ELLIOT

The black of night had begun to release its grip, and soon daybreak would be here. I knew that when dawn broke it would be on a new world, one where I was free from Silas.

My joints ached as I stood amongst those whom I assumed were the country's most loyal nobles. Although, I did notice that the well-dressed men from the rebellion were there, standing amongst their peers as if they had not just tried and failed to commit treason. Chara had pardoned them much faster than perhaps I would have, but I understood why she did it. With a new regent to be assigned, it would serve her well to have some of the nobles in her debt.

There were no more than fifty people gathered in the throne room, a stark contrast to the hundreds who'd danced in Singer Hall hours before. The Norrfalt Prince had stayed, surrounded by a small charge of a half dozen guards. His presence made me nervous, but I don't know what else I had expected.

The girls went to the princess' quarters and Chara had insisted I stay in the throne room with the other guests and wait. I had managed to track down a wash room and had cleaned most of the blood and pub grime off of me, but the nice clothes I had borrowed from Parren were now dirty and ripped, and I had been unable to find a comb to try to tame my hair.

I shifted my weight awkwardly. I had given up trying to avoid the curious eyes of everyone in the room as they studied me. *Who is this outsider?* I could practically hear their thoughts in their confused, disgruntled, and exhausted expressions.

I should be exhausted as well, but I wasn't. My mind still circled around the life changes that the last twenty-four hours had brought. The recent memories, both good and bad, played like dreams inside my head: my childhood name, *Ellie,* spoken by my little sister; my sister, no longer dead, but alive and safe; Parren speared to his chaise; and, of course, the tiger's eye studded dagger protruding from Silas's right eye and the clunk of him falling to the floor.

Silas was dead. But so was Parren: my uncle, my mentor, my friend. The last four years he'd been a piece of my mother in my life and I hadn't even known it. Now he was gone.

And Chara . . . she was still Kiera in my mind: the foolishly confident handmaiden who cared so deeply. Now she was someone else. A princess. A queen.

She had kissed me. I still felt the prickling imprint her lips had left in their wake.

Was Chara still going to marry the prince?

On our return trip to the castle, I had told the princess of

Parren's murder at the hands of the Norrfalt assassin. She'd seemed shocked, and burdened with even more sadness, but had insisted that Prince Christopher was different from the rest of the corrupt Norrfalt royalty.

Was she really willing to align Mittelan with the country whose king sent Parren's killer? She couldn't ascend the throne without him, or some other bridegroom, so maybe the rebels had been right. Maybe she had no other choice.

Millie entered the throne room first, wearing a lovely ash-colored dress, showing her regards for the queen mother, I expected. Yet, she didn't look like she was in mourning. She looked happier than I could ever remember her, and in that joy, she looked exactly like the little girl I recalled. Chara entered behind her and they linked arms. It was an honor that said to the entire crowd of witnesses: *This girl is no handmaiden. She is a friend to the queen. She is whomever the queen says she is.*

Then my eyes fell to Chara. How could I have been looking at my sister with this woman by her side? She held her chin high and promenaded into the room with every ounce of a queen's beauty and grace, but also with the strength and bravery of a knight. She looked like a queen, but with her sword tethered around the bodice of her dress, she looked more like a warrior.

The black satin of her dress hugged her waist and the sleeves rolled off her shoulders. She looked intoxicating—as though one kiss from her would make any man fall in love so deeply they'd be incapable of falling out.

My finger reached to my lips subconsciously, to the shadow of her kiss that lingered there. It had already happened. I was already in love with her. I was in love with the woman who I'd hated for besting me in the Games. It felt like an eternity ago. I was in love with the fool who took on six rowdy soldiers. I was in love with a knight who thought she alone could expose the duke, void the marriage alliance, and win a war. And, it turns out, she wasn't wrong. In the end, she had managed to execute the traitorous duke, befriend an enemy prince, and squash the rebellion that threatened her nation.

Along the way she had made me fall in love with her, and now she was going to marry the enemy prince.

The panic must have been evident on my face because when Millie parted from Chara's side and came to stand beside me, she placed her hand gently on my arm and said, "It will be fine, Ellie. I promise."

Her voice, which had haunted my dreams for so many years, took me aback, like I was looking at a ghost.

"You can trust her," Millie said.

All I could do was nod.

The small crowd divided, and Chara ascended the marble steps to where her throne sat on the dais. She hesitated, running her hand along the queen's golden seat. She finally turned, and I found her brown eyes so stormy, they looked almost black, and her bottom lip red from where she'd been biting it.

She was about to replace her mother and it was anguish.

Two men ascended the dais. I recognized one, a tall man with a large hat and black robes, as the high reverend. The other robed man carried a large golden crown in gloved hands. I assumed he was a subordinate religious or political leader. The pair stood between Chara and the throne. She knelt before the high reverend and repeated the vows of the monarchy back to him, including that she would be subject to the regent established by the cabinet until the day of her wedding. Following a prayer, the reverend turned to his comrade and took the crown from him, blessed it, and placed it on Chara's head.

She stood and faced her subjects, who dropped in a sea of bows and curtsies.

The reverend announced, "I present to you, Charissa Henrietta Cordelia Basile-Perrault, Queen of the Great Country of Mittelan. Long live the queen!"

"Long live the queen!" the crowd echoed.

Instead of turning to take her seat on her mother's throne, she remained standing and reached out to the crowd with open hands. Their dutiful clapping slowed.

She cleared her throat, and silence fell like a heavy sheet upon the room. "May my first official act as queen be to alert you, my country's most loyal lords and ladies, that a traitor has lived and flourished in your midst for many years."

The room lit with whispered gossip. Chara ignored it and continued, "Not only did this traitor serve his own selfish desires above the needs of the monarchy and the country, he took his orders from the enemy. He is responsible for the late queen's—my mother's—death. But take comfort. For from the lowest ranks has risen a hero who has avenged the queen, and in doing so, saved my life."

My cheeks burned and it wasn't that Chara's hand was resting on her bosom, it was that her other hand was gesturing to me. Every eye in the throne room—from the servants, to the barons and counts, to the dukes and duchesses—had come to rest on me.

"This evening," Chara continued, "the Grand Duke of

Swanstone made an attempt on my life."

Her subjects gasped.

No, that was me, I thought frantically. *I tried to kill you. Twice.*

"But thanks to Monsieur Cendrilon I stand before you tonight."

Thanks to me? I wanted to shout. *You killed the duke!*

"Elliot Cendrilon, please, come. Kneel before your queen."

I froze. I willed myself to walk to her, but the shock from her lie left me frozen in place.

"Go!" Millie urged, pushing me away from her towards the front of the throne room.

I stumbled, but regained my footing and walked to Chara. Dropping to one knee, I placed an arm across my chest.

"Much like your ancestors before you," Chara declared, pulling her sword from its sheath, "you have served your country and its leaders with bravery and courage. Therefore, as Queen of Mittelan, I wish for all to recognize Sir Elliot Cendrilon as a trusted Knight of Swanstone." She placed her blade on my shoulder, resting it there for a moment before returning it to its home at her waist.

The crowd clapped dutifully.

"Rise, Sir Cendrilon," she said. I did as she asked, looking up at her stern and unwavering face. "Since the Grand Duke died without a Mittelan heir," she declared, "I grant his lands and title fall to the man who saved this kingdom from corruption. Sir Elliot Cendrilon, newly titled Grand Duke of Swanstone, will fulfill the duties that had previously fallen to the duke, including serving as head of my cabinet and regent until my wedding day."

No, no, this was too much. She can't do this for me. My eyes flew to the cabinet, many of whom I was sure would be vying for the recently vacated position. The brows among them furrowed and angry whispers were drowned out by the crowd's applause.

One voice rose among them, the crowd quieting. "I, as representative of the cabinet, support the actions of the new queen." It was the man Chara had addressed at the pub as Duke Chapelle. He had spoken against Silas at the pub. Chara had pardoned him several hours before.

"And I," said another of the three men.

"And I," said the last.

The rest of the cabinet whispered amongst themselves. It seemed only four members, aside from the three rebels, remained. Where were the others? Then, one by one, the remaining members of the cabinet granted their acceptance of the queen's proclamation.

Then I realized, Chara wasn't doing this for me. She had found a way out. She was using the debt these cabinet members owed her and the upset to their hierarchy to get out of the marriage and gain control of her country. She was doing this for Mittelan, to give her a partner who would allow her to lead her people. She was not going to wait for the cabinet to organize and determine a new regent. She was going to make their decision for them.

"Thank you for your support," she said, nodding to the cabinet, some of whom still looked flummoxed at the turn of events. With three of their members already supporting the queen and some apparently missing, it seemed the rest did not dare embarrass themselves by quarreling or challenging the new queen's declaration in front of their peers.

Once the reverend bestowed the title upon me, there would

be no changing it.

Chara reached out a gloved hand to me, and when I took it, she pulled me up the gleaming steps to stand by her side. She whispered, "As head of cabinet, and regent, *you* will have the power to change the law requiring my marriage. I can rule alone. I *will* rule alone."

She was brilliant. She had evaded the marriage and won the loyalty of the cabinet in one swift move.

And I . . . I was finally a knight and, at least for now, Mittelan's regent. Chara was putting her ultimate trust in me.

"After the law is changed," she whispered hurriedly, "then you are free to do as you choose. You can resign, go home, go wherever you'd like. Or you can stay here, with me. But, most importantly, you will be free. And I will be free to marry . . . " her breathing hitched as her brown eyes locked on mine, "or not marry, when and *if* I choose. The king of Norrfalt won't want his son to marry a queen whose power is equal to his own. The alliance will no longer be an option for him."

"You want me to give up the regency?" I laughed. She rolled her eyes.

Even in front of all these people, I wanted to kiss her again.

"Yes! Although, someday," she began, "maybe—"

I was so distracted by the slow fall of her eyelashes, that I didn't see the knife as it whirred through the air towards us.

CHAPTER FORTY-THREE

CHARA

A flash of steel. A clumsy throw. I leapt in front of Elliot and knocked the blade from the air with ease. I recognized it instantly as Elliot's dagger, the one he tried to kill me with—twice—and whose stone hilt was tarnished with Silas's dried blood. It skittered across the tiled floor, coming to rest on the mosaic face of the conquered giant.

"Liar!" A furious bellow erupted from someone in the crowd and it echoed in the otherwise stillness of the vast hall. Everyone turned towards the intruder, a frazzled looking boy with a slightly hooked nose emerging from their midst.

I recognized him as Elliot's stepbrother, the one who had held Emily captive and rushed to Silas's side at his death.

"Don't listen to her!" he said, marching towards us, eyes wild. "This man is not the hero she claims. He's a killer!"

"Don't, brother," Lucas stepped from the crowd, grabbing at his brother's arms as he lunged towards us. The crowd gasped.

"Guards!" I yelled, "Guards!" Instantly, two of my guards were on either side of the angry stepbrother, locking his arms in their iron grip. They had not hesitated to react to their new queen's order. "This boy is part of a lethal and treasonous rebellion. He is a traitor to this country! Put him in the dungeon to await his fate."

"No."

I spun around in shock at Elliot's voice, my jaw slack, brows knit. *What was he doing?*

He couldn't sow doubt in the people now, or they would never allow him to be named regent and I would never ascend the throne alone. We were so close. I was so close. I looked up at Elliot's calm and resolved features with open confusion. He looked at peace, as if he hadn't just almost been murdered.

"I am what this man claims," he said.

The crowd released an audible gasp.

Elliot, no. Don't do this, I thought. But there was nothing I could do to stop him.

"I did kill today," he said, stepping down from the dais and entering the crowd. The room was completely silent. Not even his assailant made a sound. "I killed a man who extorted my mother, abused me and my sister for years, and lied to me about her death for nearly a decade, but none of those things made him deserving of death. What sealed the viper's fate was when he formed a rebellion with the intention of usurping the throne and murdering your beloved monarch. Earlier this very night, he held my sister hostage in an attempt to force me to kill the princess." He paused, letting the people feel the weight and earnestness of his words.

"But, as you can see, I did not follow through with his command," he said. "I could not. For his treason, Silas Tremaine had to die. However, this boy should not be punished for his father's misdeeds. He was complicit, without doubt, but I believe that he deserves an opportunity to seek and manifest his own character, apart from that of his traitorous father. In fact, from this day forward, he will work in the castle so that I, the queen, and *all* of her guards can keep a close eye on him."

He crossed the floor to his stepbrother, put a hand on his shoulder, and dropped his voice so low I could barely make out what he said. "And now, brother, you owe me your life. This grace is for my mother, it's what she would have wanted. But don't make the mistake of thinking I will show you such mercy twice."

Holding his step-brother tightly, Elliot only released him after a nod brought one of my guards back to him. The guard checked Raymond for weapons and then stood at attention by the boy's side. Elliot clasped Lucas's hand and gave him an appreciative smile.

He returned to my side, "Was that alright? To grant him pardon? You are my Queen, after all, of course you get the final say." The gold in his eyes shone bright in the honeysuckle comb of dawn that peeked through the stained glass windows of the throne room. He held out his arm to me, and I hooked mine through it.

"*My Queen . . .*" I felt my lips curve into a smile and nodded, "I guess I could get used to hearing you say it like that."

"You'd better," Elliot murmured into my ear and I felt it,

the responsibility that I had feared for so long, settling over me like an embrace.

Elliot stood in front of the reverend with me at his side as he accepted the title and duties of the Grand Duke of Swanstone. His eyes remained fixed on the royal crest that hung around the reverend's neck, glancing my way for only a brief moment. We locked eyes, and the crowd of my subjects faded away until I saw him again as I had in the arena, full of potential and ready to fight by my side—even if he didn't fully understand the scope of it quite yet.

Sunrise broke, the light of a new day cascading over Mittelan. I peered down at my mother's pendant, my father's ring, and my sword resting against the inky black of my skirt. It was like I was seeing myself for the first time. I was no longer a pawn waiting for a wedding to grant me the honor of my birthright. I wasn't the dutiful princess my parents had hoped for or the glory-seeking warrior, running away from the castle in search of a quest. No, I was the leader—the ruler, the diplomat, *and* the warchief—that my people needed.

I stepped down from the dais and addressed my people. "Throughout the last few days, I have entered into your midst. I have seen your pain, your trials, and your fears in a way that someone who sits on either of those thrones," I gestured to the pair of gilded seats behind me, "rarely gets to witness. I have seen people previously held in the highest esteem betray their friends and family grappling for power."

I looked upon my people—both those standing before me and those spread among Mittelan's fields and mountains and woodlands beyond.

"When power is the goal of a leader, the people will suffer.

My mother died at the hands of someone close to her who sought nothing but his own glory. Now, I stand in her place and vow to lead you in the way she always wished to: with the empathy and compassion that those around her always endeavored to thwart. I come before you not to reign but to serve. To listen. To fight for you. To fight for Mittelan."

I lowered myself slowly to a knee, "As your new queen, I pledge to give you—the people of the great, free country of Mittelan—my hand in service and my unyielding loyalty." I dropped my chin to my chest.

Who wants a knight for a queen? Emily had asked me this question while I stood at the precipice of an adventure I had so desperately craved. But it took until this moment, as I knelt to serve Mittelan with Elliot at my back, to realize that the answer was important and very simple.

I do.

I wanted a knight for a queen, and I wanted that knight to be *me*. A knight's duty is to serve the needs of the people, to fight for their freedom, to advocate for them, and to give them hope.

And that was the kind of queen I wanted to be.

I stood and set my gaze on the rising sun, bathing my country in new light.

THE END.

EPILOGUE

EMILY

FOUR YEARS LATER . . .

"Are we not done yet?" Elliot whined. I peeked over the top of the book I was trying to read to find Elliot massaging his temples as Chara shoved yet another invitation response in front of his face.

Apparently, my big brother could handle being a knight, he could handle being the Grand Duke of Swanstone, and he could even handle being regent turned head of cabinet. But planning a wedding turned out to exceed the boundaries of his limitations.

"Oh, come on, Elliot, only a couple more," she said from her seat beside him at the small table in the study. The bookcase lined room was Elliot's favorite in the whole castle, and it had become mine too, as Elliot and I often used it as a quiet place to sit beside its quaint fireside and talk. He told me many stories of our mother, father, and Beauhaven and had patiently answered all the questions I still had about our childhood. It took a long time for me to share the painful memories of my time with the dressmaker and for Elliot to tell the particulars of his years with Silas. Slowly our friendship developed, tethering us together through our shared experiences and interests and beyond the bond of our blood.

We visited Beauhaven often, slowly restoring it to match the image in my head of *home* that I had long since dismissed as dream or fantasy. Lucas, our step-brother, resided there as caretaker.

Chara had named me her first advisor—a position I had functionally served for many years, but now I served in title as well—after the marriage requirement had been removed from law and she disbanded the regency that bound her. I knew Chara well enough to know that she brought Elliot here today to try to raise his spirits despite the overwhelming task of sorting through the wedding response cards. He looked at her sideways, not even trying to hide his annoyance with an exaggerated frown.

She scrunched up her face at him and put her fingers on either side of his mouth, forcing his scowl into a makeshift grin and planting a playful kiss upon it. Instead of pulling away laughing, he leaned into the kiss, wrapping his hands around her neck and drawing her into an intimate embrace.

"Um," I cleared my throat loudly from the plush chair where I sat not five feet from them, "I'm still here, you know."

Chara let out a deep breath as Elliot held her face near his. "I will look at as many stupid response cards as you command me to, my Queen," he said adoringly, ignoring me entirely.

She laughed and kissed his nose.

"Disgusting," I teased, "I really thought these gross displays of affection might die off after you announced your engagement."

"You want disgusting?" Elliot challenged, "I'll show you disgusting." He pulled Chara into an exaggerated embrace, planting big sloppy kisses all over her face. She struggled away from him, laughing the entire time.

I huffed in mock revulsion and held the herbology book up in front of my face, "Can you two just get married, already? Although, with my luck, you'll get even worse."

Chara wrinkled her nose at me. "Soon enough," she said as she opened the next card from the stack in front of her and tossed it into the pile to her left before picking up another envelope.

I still didn't understand why Chara insisted they had to read each response personally, but Chara was unrelenting in her attempts to keep herself grounded amongst her subjects. She wanted to be a queen of the people, which is why all of Mittelan was invited to the wedding and the nobility's exemption to conscription had been dismantled. Not that we had any need for the conscriptions anymore, Mittelan had been at peace for almost half a decade.

"Elliot," Chara's voice dropped from lighthearted to concerned.

"Oh no, who can't make it now?" he asked sarcastically.

"It's about Christopher," she put the letter she was reading down onto the table between them, "something is wrong."

"Wait," I asked, my heart jumping to my throat as it often

did at the mention of the youngest Norrfalt royal, "do you mean *Prince* Christopher?"

Chara nodded.

I stood and crossed the room to peek at the letter over her shoulder. It was written in beautiful calligraphy on smooth ivory stationary, with the king of Norrfalt's crest blazoned in blue and embossed silver across the top.

To my dearest ally, Queen Charissa Basile-Perrault,

I write to you on the advent of your wedding only out of sheer desperation. My country and I are already in mourning upon the sudden passing of our Queen Margueritte. To add to our grief, Norrfalt's only heir, Prince Christopher, has vanished. Tensions between Almora and Norrfalt have been tenuous of late and I am deeply fearful for my son's well-being.

As we both owe to him the present peace between our great nations, I implore you to help in any manner you can spare. I have exhausted my resources searching the tundras of our land, as well as every valley and mountain, for our prince. I beg of you to extend the search within your borders and possibly even inquire upon your allies to the south.

I shudder to think of the consequences Norrfalt may face without a clear heir. It is with the utmost humility that I call upon Mittelan for aid.

Sincerely yours, and eternally in your debt,
King Johann Everett Charles Ludwig II

The Prince of Norrfalt? Missing? I paced nervously, running one hand along the book spines and absentmindedly chewing the fingernails of the other. Chara had told me of my Uncle Parren's time serving the Norrfalt King and his warnings that he was not to be trusted. What was the king hiding behind this call to arms?

"Pretty bold of him to ask for our help, if you ask me," Elliot said with a scoff, tossing the letter back onto the table carelessly. "You discovered that the duke had been lying about the status of the war the entire time, that we were on the verge of conquering the king and his country, and still you agreed to a treaty. You gave him the food his country needed in exchange for—let's be honest—a modest, at best, amount of their goods. And now he expects us to fund a search party? That's ludicrous."

"I don't care about the king," Chara chewed her bottom lip as she thought, "but we have to care about Prince Christopher. We owe him much."

She was right, of course. I would be dead without the prince's help, a fact I thought of quite regularly and without fail every time the prince had visited the court in the last several years. Chara's reign, Beauhaven, my own position at court, all of it could have been taken from us had he not given his trust and his aid when he did.

I faced my brother, still taken very much aback at seeing my own hardened gaze staring back at me. "Chara is right, Ellie. Without the prince, we wouldn't even be here arguing this. We need to do whatever we can to help him."

❖❖❖

ACKNOWLEDGMENTS

Before I get started on naming all the members of the village that helped make this book a reality, I want to start by thanking you for picking it up. Whatever led you to this book, thank you for helping me fulfill my dream of putting a story I've written into the hands of readers. I hope it transports you somewhere that is simultaneously new and familiar, while inspiring you to always ask, "*What if?*"

Now, I have to start by thanking all my family and friends for sludging through my early drafts, for bearing with my constant monologue about my fictional friends, and for giving honest feedback, even when I didn't like it. *Especially* when I didn't like it. To my husband, my parents, and my in-laws, who read version after version and didn't give up on me or my story. And an extra helping of gratitude to my husband, Zachary Olsen, who stayed with me every step of the way and never hesitated to take well beyond his fair share of house and kid-work to enable me to chase my dreams.

Thank you to my friends—specifically my early-draft readers Mollie VanCamp and Meg Pressley—for reading, encouraging, and giving your input. I would never have kept going without you! Thank you to my costuming friends Whitney, Julia, and Laura for bearing with me as I asked a ridiculous amount of questions about dresses, fabric, and the logistics of swords and corsets. And to my forever friend, Laura Snead, for staying with me through all of life's ups and downs.

Thank you to the editors of #RevPit for pointing me in a direction of real growth—specifically Sione Aeschliman, for being my first real editor and challenging me to turn my story into a novel; and Jeni Chapelle, for being the first person in the industry to really give me the confidence I needed to believe that my writing was worth pursuing.

A massive thank-you to my editor, Aimee Robinson, who read my book and saw in it the potential that I'd dreamt it held from the moment it first appeared to me as a precocious little seedling of an idea, hell-bent on becoming something exciting. Aimee, I can't thank you enough for all the time and effort you have put into me and my book since we were first introduced. I know that you have already, and will continue to make me into a better writer. Thank you to the rest of my team at Big Small Town Books, including Dustin Street, my copyeditor Krista Billings, and Sierra Palmer, who is responsible for the beautiful artwork on the cover of this book. Thank you all for having faith in me and giving my story a platform.

Thank you, my little monsters, Sylvie Ann and Tobias, for inspiring me daily to never stop working towards my dream.

Even though you make the practicalities of being a writer a hundred times more difficult, you also help me realize why it's worth it. I hope when you are old enough to read this that you enjoy it and know that Mommy thought often about telling you a story where all people can be strong, caring, and brave. May you always strive to be all three.

And lastly, thank you God for giving me a passion for words and leading me to a vocation that allows me to be home with my children, the greatest blessings you have ever given me. Thank you for the opportunity to tell an old story in a new (and what I hope is inspiring) way.

ABOUT THE AUTHOR

A Colorado native, **HANNAH B. OLSEN** has swapped the Rockies for the Appalachians where she now resides with her husband and two children in Eastern Tennessee. After studying Creative Writing at Valparaiso University, she went on to write for magazines, websites, and blogs, taking pretty much any writing gig she could get her hands on. But her true love of writing has always been that of telling stories. As a fiction writer and full-time mother, Hannah rarely manages to find time that she isn't reading, writing, or kid-wrangling; however, when she does, Hannah enjoys photography, graphic design, traveling, and doing pretty much anything in the kitchen besides cleaning it.

CPSIA information can be obtained
at www.ICGtesting.com
Printed in the USA
LVHW040357020321
680337LV00019B/148/J

9 781734 166040